WHEN WE
SPEAK OF
NOTHING

By Olumide Popoola

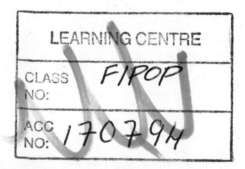

CASSAVA REPUBLIC

Abuja London

First published in 2017 by Cassava Republic Press

Abuja – London

A CIP catalogue record for this book is available from the National Library of Nigeria and the British Library.

ISBN (Nig) 97897855177-1-2

ISBN (UK) 978-1-911115-45-8
eISBN 978-1-911115-46-5

Printed and bound by Bell & Bain Ltd., Glasgow.

By the same author

this is not about sadness
Also by Mail
breach (with Annie Holmes)

For Tamu

People talk about me, Esu Elegbara, the snail-shell dancer who scrambles all messages, who can speak in any tongue, take on any voice. They talk about me in hushed tones, afraid, confused. How I came one day and walked in-between two friends' fields. One was on my left, one on the right. I was wearing one of my favourite hats. Two-tone, you could call it. Multifaceted is another expression that springs to mind. It all depends on your position. Either way, I talked to both of them, exchanged pleasantries, cracked a few jokes. They were easy, ready to take a break, they didn't even wonder who I was or why I was there. I stayed almost a whole hour before they returned to work, waving goodbye. In the evening I heard them arguing, right in the village square. They were calling each other names, accusing each other of lying. Their friends and neighbours tried to understand what the problem was, why they were so angry with each other.

One was shouting about the man, me, with the black hat. The other was shouting back that he was blind, ignorant in fact. The hat had been red. I laughed at first, then I waited for a long time. I waited for them to see.

But they didn't stop. They shouted and shouted until their faces were burning from the inside. They couldn't see what they were missing.

Not everything is the same everywhere. They couldn't see it at all.

They shouted all night. In the morning, I showed them the hat.

1

**It is easy to be outnumbered
when you are lost in your tracks.
Keep close to the source.**

If not for Abu flicking his head back every so often, waiting
a split sec, full-on profile, to make sure Karl was keeping
track, it would've been impossible to tell them apart. Those
two? Like twins. The funny thing? Abu's parents already
had twins and they were a sweet-but-annoying seven years
old. Was almost as if Abu had needed to find his own match,
so he had someone to leave the house with. Even funnier?
His mother, and later the dad, accepted Karl as the brother
from another mother. Meaning Karl was in and out of their
house like trains out of St Pancras station. More in than out
actually. And to bring that funny *haha what a coincidence*
thing home, they even looked alike. Karl's face a tad longer,
shoulders narrower, hair cropped, eyes much more dreamy.
Both their lips full – in a different way, but still. If you'd
thought about it you'd say: *the works*. You'd say: *dang, those
are some alike-looking teenagers*. Their friendship must've
rubbed on to their bodies, accepting that they were a pair,
in tandem. Teamwork.
    That day, the way that white stuff poured from the sky had
made them go out – not that that was rare or anything –
and they slid and slipped across the streets, trying to chase
each other, snowballs buzzing. The way it drizzled down?
Now that was movie classic. It was all very *haha, so much
fun, yeah, defo but too cold, wha gwaan wit this season? Get
this one bruv* and bang! A whole load straight into the face.
    Then, out of nowhere, three wannabe guys they knew
from sixth form jumping them, right at the corner to Leigh
Street. Like real jump. Two of them at Abu calling him

Abu-ka-ha-ba-ha-ha-ha-r-pussy and other things that shouldn't
be said in front of anyone, twisting his arm back in its socket
like they just got their GCSEs in bullying.

It was crunching. Abu whined.

Abu with his skinny self. Eyes busy, always moving, checking
here, there, everywhere and missing lots by being all that
hectic. His ears pointed forward slightly, like he was some
digital receiving device (you'd really have to look for it but
then you'd never not notice it again, it was like, *whoa how did
I miss that?*). That same Abu who was so messy at home yet
jeans ironed and all – that Abu got his jewels kicked. Very
neatly. Karl? My boy was being dismantled by the leader of
the threesome, his hands on Karl's wrists, banging him into
a corner between a wall and a fence. He hovered there, the
metal slowly digging into his good jeans.

> **representation/** rerɪˈzɛnteɪʃən /
> noun
> > 1. Not just the state of being represented but of
> >   adding to, connecting.
> > 2. The description or portrayal of someone in a
> >   particular way.

Karl. That one. So immaculate. It was troubling. Abu even had
a little fit earlier that evening because Karl had been doing
his usual, *must look pretty* thing. Without words, obviously.
Ironed denim wasn't enough. It all had to be prepped properly
and colour-coded until it was just so. Spending a lot of time
in the bathroom, blocking it for the rest of the family. Then
a very light grey pair of jeans, which had made no sense
unless he wanted to match the weather – they were bound
to get dirty in the snow.

When the boy slammed Karl into the fence, the black paint
peeled off the metal straight on to the nice, nicely ironed,
not-good-for-the season denim. It was really shit.

And hopefully Karl was thinking of the stain rather than
staying in the moment, breath and all. Hopefully, instead,
he was lamenting this unnecessary affront against his style
(and you know that type is serious, for real), because the
guy, the one holding him, went straight for the soft parts.

Karl didn't say a word; no sound left his lips. His upper body folded over as much as it could, as much as the guy would let him.

Abu wasn't as quiet. When is he ever? He was talking away, cursing and shouting and *fucking this* and *fucking that*, but the snow swallowed it all as if it had been planned.

This country is not equipped? Ha! The one time everything is out of action and the snow makes everyone feel all Christmassy and you know that spells giddy and means silly, effing miracles can happen. Imagine.

Abu cursing louder and more. His voice always over the top because he wants to make up for something. Someone said that. That he wants to show the world something but actually the world couldn't give anything at all about what Abu has to prove. And of course that doesn't stop him. It's not about someone hearing him, it's about him expressing, saying, or shouting.

Like now. Shouting because he's scared.

For Karl.

That one is so sensitive, it's ridiculous. But still he's so, so, so together. Basically so quiet. No crying or cursing or anything. Just taking in scenes, waiting them out, all behind the miniature curtain that drapes from his eyes in that longing kind of way. The curve of his lashes keeping everything out, preventing anything from entering his pretty head, where the real feelings are. But still it reflects, the way his eyes close so that Abu wants to shout even louder. *Man, your denim. Yourself. You get what they're doing?*

It's easier to focus on someone else's hurt when you are down. That magician's trick: deflection. I have used it many times.

A siren blared and the blue lights bounced off the snowy street. The guy who was kicking Karl commanded *'Run!'*, and all of a sudden the two holding Abu ricocheted off him, using his weight to get a good start as if the siren was a shot at the beginning of a race. They bounced, jumped and ran. From Marchmont to Tavistock Place and that's the last Karl and Abu saw of them. For that day.

Abu fell over, of course, from the push they used to get themselves into proper gear, and from all that tension right around his private bits, his face plunging into the snow. And Karl? Just kneeled into the white stuff, quiet, very quiet, in

slow motion, all graceful. It was almost as if he had rehearsed
this, alternative swan-like dance moves. Ridiculous. He said
nothing. Just pretty and defeated, in communion with that
white wetness.

The police sped by in totally the opposite direction. Abu
kissed his teeth. 'Cowards. Wasn't even for them.' He pulled
Karl up. 'Let's get home. Get warmed up.'

Karl all speechless, whole self sunk into the gut, squeezed
tight by that blow and probably stuck somewhere between
the rib and the intestines. Abu all high on release endorphins,
but also because he just can't keep quiet. Still babbling away.

'Three of them? Can't believe they didn't even bother to
cover up. Like they own the street. But we ain't that stupid.
Can get our own people to straighten them out. I got options,
you get me. Could go to the police. They're finished. They
are. I know some guys. They can really take care of this shit,
once and for all, show them who's boss—'

'Shut up,' Karl said. 'Just stop it. Keep it to yourself for a
minute.'

Abu not even offended. It's that sensitive thing. He was
not only pretty, he was the whole shebang, all of it together.
They're not changing the rules of their neighbourhood any
time soon. Abu just needed to mouth off, feel like he could
make things be different.

Abu pulled Karl by the sleeve. 'Come on now. Let's go
home. It's OK.'

Karl kept staring. Eyes in sync with his mouth, lips showing
all that was going on inside. *I'm not down with this shit no
more.* When he stood again his hips were uneven, one lanky
knee bent. But at least he walked now. At least. He had a
delaying mental thing going on. Deep and thoughtful but at
least he also moved his arse now.

He followed Abu's lead around the corner, dusted off snow
mechanically, looking at his pants and not seeing the black
stain the metal left. How not is incredible. Where are we,
you'd think, right? Some alternate universe?

Abu looked at it, then to his friend.

It did upset him. Nothing wrong with a sense of pride in
one's appearance and a little colour coordination. Nothing
wrong at all. But nobody knew where Karl's mind was at
that precise moment and that was enough fighting for Abu
for an hour.

He looked up at Karl. Tried to send some telepathic sense into him: *Look man, they're your good trousers. You know how you love your stuff clean and correct. You need to get angry, like proper vex.*

But he suddenly noticed how his bony shoulders were aching. Throbbing away, rubber bands released after all that tense contraction, all stretched to no more good use, and the cold crept into the wet clothes, creeping him out 'cause now he was trembling and it wasn't fun any more. Nothing was. Not here. No one'd bailed them out. As if.

When they arrived at the gate, some other youngsters were still out throwing snowballs here and there. Very half-heartedly. Lazy they were, inside of the gate, didn't even bother to take to the streets. *The youth of today, always staying close to the next power outlet. Might have to recharge the gadgets.* They looked suspiciously at the pair, not for any other reason than both were acting suspicious. Abu all authoritative, rushing through.

What was the point? He was hurting, Karl was out dreaming life away and both of them were colder than they should be, so he kept at Karl's sleeve, dragging him all the way to the fifth floor, no waiting for the lift.

Abu's mum opened for them. Abu stormed in but Karl was softer. Abu had got used to him and his mother smiling in silent understanding, the hallway light burning away in its bare bulb. There'd be a whole *hello, how are you* and *how can I be of use, help, disappear without being a burden, make myself useful?* thing going on. And his mother would be just like, *all is OK and good. Do nothing at all.* Perfect bonding heaven for the two. Abu didn't stop for it any more. Karl could do no wrong. Ever.

The twins ran around in the living room, the TV on, cartoons playing while they laughed and hit each other with the plastic toys they'd outgrown a while ago. How it came to be girl and boy was beyond Abu, just seemed too perfect, too well divided, equally distributed. Azizah, the girl, first and slightly taller, taking after Abu in terms of yakking. Aazad, the boy, smaller, with his brows almost fused, always looking serious but was 'cheekiness in the making', as Karl liked to say.

'Don't trust his face. Most likely he hid all your good things and will try to bribe you to get them back, one by one, while you are still checking out his grown-up eyes.'

'You should know,' Abu had answered.

'All that jealousy will still not make you more handsome,' Karl had laughed.

'Very funny. I'm almost pissing myself!'

The twins ran to Karl, who smiled again but was doing his *will be with you just now, give me a sec* thing. When he came out of the bathroom, his face was washed and he was no longer camping on Moon Fourteen, successfully avoiding the here and now. He had finally seen the stain on the trousers and it was not that big a deal. Either way it was just a device. Deflection, remember. For Abu. All would be back to normal once the washing machine handled it.

Karl plopped on to the couch and grabbed the remote. 'Excuse me please, my good people. This is not acceptable. Not acceptable at all,' he said, lowering the volume. 'There are OAPs present. Seniors. You get me? I have to urge you to refrain from loud noises.'

The twins rolled over, first on the floor before jumping up on him from both sides. They chuckled, hoping for a play-fight; Azizah pulling at Karl's ears, only slightly, scared they'd start waving like her older brother's. But Karl indulged them only for a minute, the remote rotating through the air, diving here and there, still firm in his hand. He was distracted and out to help Mama Abu, or at least exchange another smiling agreement. He needed her calm.

She didn't look the mama type, more the slender version of Abu and the twins, a young face, eyes that saw everything, like proper. A slightly amused mouth that kept track, together with the eyes, of any stories that were not close to the truth. She had a detector for that. It could cover the whole neighbourhood, beeping when any rubbish story was put forward as a sorry-arse excuse.

Karl had asked Abu once how he could ever lie to her. 'That face breaks your heart.'

'You make sure your story is tight. Otherwise ...'

'...otherwise you have to deal with her secret weapon.'

And Abu had laughed. His mother didn't use many words but she had a lot of silent communication. Like that time he had tried to make fun of some kid down the road when he was much younger. Tried. Wanted to see how it felt, that power thing. Using something against someone just because you could. When you knew right then, right there they couldn't use yours. For some reason his mother had come back from the shops just at the moment he was starting to load off on Brian from a year down about why his school uniform was so old. Her eyes had opened and pierced his. Surprised. Then she had said all that needed saying without words. Abu had apologised on the spot, with understanding and all, shown proper empathy, and stayed out the rest of the afternoon to avoid more of her disbelieving stare.

Abu thought he had some of that telepathic-ness himself but Karl never seemed to quite get it with him. Only with his mum.

Abu had rushed straight through to his room, where he started listening to music on his bed. No more babbling. The endorphins crashed like a jet fighter abandoning plane. Pain in his shoulders, in his muscles. All that pain now.

'He called again.'

'He did?' Karl was standing by the washing machine, playing with the door. He looked up at Abu's mother. His eyelashes were long and thick; they looked fake. As they fluttered open and closed again, there was a gap. Like on some Tube platforms, those really dodgy Central Line stations when you really have to hop over the void. And for that particularly dangerous one on every stop throughout the whole bloody system they tell you to mind it. The gap. For Karl this was just a split second, not enough to catch his breath.

'You have to call him back, Karl. You know that all of us like to have you here. But you have to call him.'

Her eyes. If you could see it. Too much. He looked away.

More of that gap was revealing itself, rapidly. Whole dips, slopes and descents.

Karl stared at the wall. These kinds of decisions were hard for him. When to call, stay here in the present. He wanted to do a runner, chat some stuff. Knowing Abu he'd be all *whatever* now. *You want to be cute all of a sudden, dish me some deep story 'cause you got shit on your mind?* He needed the chatting before, like really needed it.

'When did he call?'

'Just after you left. Karl,' she said, very soft now. 'You'll call him tomorrow. Or better, go and see him.'

He nodded. He could feel his lashes scissoring in, neatly closing. The hairs touching each other sideways, the tiniest bit of friction.

> **form** /fɔːm/
> noun
>> 1. The visible shape or configuration of something.
>> 2. A particular way of appearance.
> verb
>> 1. Bring together parts, all sorts, internal, external.
>> 2. To create the whole, or the intention.

The twins came running, circling around him, holding him by the hand, pulling him back into the lounge, giggling.

'It's too loud again. Come, Karl. It's too loud. It's unacceptable.'

2

**So much stuff ...
piling up like the ghosts
you chase away at midnight.**

Karl was on what was his bed in Abu's box room: a fold-up mattress next to Abu's single bed. His eyes were now in the complete opposite mode to earlier when he had been with Abu's mum. His lashes open as if legging it over some big puddle and then frozen in time.

Sleep? No chance. The who to call and what to say. And more than anything, the how to act. Godfrey, his social worker, would be all understanding but doing his authoritative thing. *You need to check in, man. It doesn't work like this. I know where you're staying but it's your responsibility to let me know. That's the deal.*

The estate on the other side of the street seemed to get into gear. Lights flickering on. One right across switched on, then off, came on again, stayed bright while shadows crept up along the yellow-lit window, turned off for good. Maybe the person was looking for something.

Like Karl. Like everyone.

Abu did his sweetest *I'm rushing you now* thing while stomping from bathroom to kitchen. That banging, he had it down for real. Wasn't the first time. Karl just couldn't make it out of bed.

'Karl. Bruv! It's time. Mr. Brendan, first thing. Not gonna be late man, you know how he gets.'

Karl was busy. World War II bombers and heavy fighter planes were hitting London; he was running to get somewhere safe. All courtesy of Mr. Brendan's history class. A voice cut through the hissing. *Move, you have to move, otherwise* ... And Abu's mum at the door, her soft voice mingling in.

'... before you leave. Come, Karl.'

Karl's eyes all gluey. His body hugging the blanket tight. The dream crashing into him, like the day ahead. Like college. Past the wannabes, keep a good face to everything.

Abu had made his bed already. Karl let him in on a thing or two about tidiness, mainly to show off to Mama Abu, earning his keep you could say, but it helped keeping the tiny room liveable for the two of them.

He rolled off the mattress. Standing. Facing the Monday. After the weekend with shit weather.

Sixth form was just up the road. Not even fifteen minutes. The larger estates were already behind them, as they walked by the small houses lining one side of Regent Square. Town houses. Pretty. It wasn't particularly busy on the small road that led to much busier streets. Most people were already on their way to work. The odd black cab sped by. Some mums on their way to nurseries with prams. Those that were on the street had a reason. A morning reason. This was not random strolling time. The majority of youngsters catching up after the snowy weekend as they started bumping into each other close to college – *I mean end of April, for real?* – came from the blocks that towered between the beautiful of Bloomsbury. Unassuming, blending in. Beautiful outside as well. Sometimes. Not so small, not so private all of the time.

'I thought they'd give us today off.'

'Yeah, remember last year? Lots of snowdays. Bare fun.'

'Dunno. All we do is sit in some room that has no space for anyone, or freeze outside. Also, how they give us a snow day when it's supposed to be warm already? Can't wait for spring.'

'You a baby or something?'

'It's cold. That's all.'

A sulky face stomped off. There was a general pushing and shoving, friendly bantz popping like champagne, then landing all over the place to be taken up by the next hopeful contestant. There were those who always talked and usually also won, others who gave their 5p.

Karl's skinny body in dark jeans now. His face blushing; it was freezing. Was easy with his light-skinned self. Abu was always amazed how much embarrassment could be shown on a single face. *Never ever drag me into something you have to lie your way out of*, he said to Karl on more than one occasion. *Nobody is going to believe you when you blush like some fire alarm.*

'Hey, you two.'

A pretty girl caught up with them, her breath steaming the air around her lips a little.

'Good weekend? OMG the weather, it's like, so pretty but really cold, right?'

Both Abu and Karl flashed their white teeth. Coordinated, on cue: approach, recognition, reaction. Nalini's make-up brought life into this grey-white morning. Her friendliness jumped their way like a net swung out for fishes. Both of them bagged.

Her friend Afsana tore loose from a couple of other girls who were on their way somewhere else. Other school, or other plans; who could tell? She joined the little group. She had the same purple lips as Nalini, lips that leapt off her flustered brown skin. Their lashes, both dunked in blue mascara, blinked into space, sending messages. A couple of construction workers in hi-vis vests passed them, takeaway cups in hand. They were already on their way back from a break. The building in the area was just not easing up. The cranes had shifted back from the main junction but you could still see them. Otherwise it was still the same: scaffolding and blocked-off paths. The area taken over by dusty men with yellow security vests. You couldn't escape them, even here where it was quieter, away from King's Cross construction mayhem, although you could still hear drilling sometimes when they were on a real mission. Abu thought the ground would give then, some days it was so much. A crack might open and make the whole area disappear, swallow it whole. No more major traffic knot. No more endless congestion just to make it around the corner or down the street at King's Cross station. It would be amazing. A hole of nothing and underneath major chaos piled up on each other, invisible from the world above. He felt like that sometimes. Nothing. Invisible. All the chaos of him hidden underneath.

'How was the weekend?' Karl asked, giving Abu a look. Where was the chattiness? Acting all shy just because it was girls. Why these double standards in his *can't stop chatting even if I tried to*? Any time they appeared Abu stayed for two minutes max then made a disappearing act. When was he getting over that? It was getting tired. And embarrassing.

'Oh really nice. My cousin was over, we, like, all had a really good time. Taking the young ones out, you get me.'

Abu and Karl got that, for sure, had done almost the same themselves with the twins, but then things had sort of just become the two of them. Like, less hassle.

'And you?' Nalini stopped for a moment, waved at someone.

'Same old, same old. Not much really.'

'A lot of snow though.' She laughed.

Abu looked at Karl to see whether any of yesterday's attack was creeping into his doe eyes. But Karl seemed not at all concerned with the previous day's encounter. He had some speedy processing mechanism after first stalling when things happened.

'But so beautiful, isn't it? It makes everything so quiet. Like a blanket, absorbing all the noise. Maybe to give us all a rest. Almost feels like we're somewhere else, you know, protected from all the harshness that comes from city life. 'Specially here in King's Cross, innit.'

He was on a roll. Karl.

Nalini and Afsana did some nodding, still blinking bright blue streaks into the atmosphere. Yes, the harshness, the city, they were all very in agreement. So intense, everything. Snow helped, sometimes, it did.

They had arrived at the gate to the college. It was hectic here. Traffic piling up, pushing impatiently against the thumping city, inevitably getting stuck courtesy of too big, too busy, too small a junction. And no swallowing hole in sight. Their little group was growing.

'You coming Camden later?'

'Can't be making that journey blud. Oyster card anaemic.'

'Where's your Zip one? Going by that shop with the discount trainers. They have some new stuff.'

'What's the point? Shopkeeper is just going to follow us around anyway. Can't take the hassle of being called a thief just 'cause I want to look at some clothes. Not today. Too cold. Anyways, lost my Oyster, so using my mum's. And it ain't got no credit anyways.'

A lot of *haha wazz going on* buzzed like swarms of bees meeting for a family reunion. Karl was talking about something or other. This was his department. The way things were out of control. Always being followed around, given lip about this or the other. Being wrong. Etc., etc.

Abu was tired of it all. To him, it was simple: coppers and sorts didn't like brown or black people. Avoid or find a way around. No need for all that deep shit and how it all sat in the whole history of mankind. Not on Monday when he was still sore from the fucking jump the day before.

And either way, it was only because Karl had some proper issues: mixed kid with white mum and all. No dad. Ever.

Although Rebecca, which she made him call her, was like really on point and better than any other mother Abu knew (minus his own, obviously). She wanted you to be her equal, talk to her with opinions and everything. But she was not around much. Meaning available. Mentally. Always worn out, always in pain. Often down, but proper. So Karl was missing some of that processing talk you were supposed to do with your parents. Abu wasn't sure if it was really that, but he had heard someone say it once. Not enough family cohesion. Whatever that meant. Rebecca would know how to do that, the cohesion stuff, so the whole point was a bit rubbish anyway.

Nalini's fuchsia-framed smile spilled across her whole face, then she started laughing, her little shoulders and upper body trembling. Happy and shit. Afsana held on to her fake leather bag. They all fell into a rhythm, had obviously hung out outside school together before. Karl and the girls, or as he lately said, women.

Abu lost interest. How Karl always went from having to be dragged out of the house to then getting all deep at the college gate. All within half an hour? And of course his pale self was spotless, a *just throwing something on* outfit. Whatever. Looked more like fashion scientists had assembled a careful combination after some intense research.

The previous day's wannabes were coming up on the far end of the street. It was their inner circle: Leicester, Connor and Sammy. They were walking amongst the other immaculate soon-men, towards the gate. Connor was wearing a trendy sweater he would have had to borrow from his mates. Everybody knew it. Still, he pretended to be all on top of fashion. As if there was money for anything like that at his home. The other two almost drowned in their classy, as in totally now season, down jackets they must have quickly bought in the middle of the fancy ice-cold. It wouldn't last, but when else would you get to show off proper winter gear?

These three? The gang. Abu. What to do?

The laughing had put some tears in Karl's eyes, and his dimples were indented to the max, achieved max effect, with no effort whatsoever. Abu watched the trying-hard-to-be-gangsters stroll closer. They wouldn't do anything to them. They wouldn't even say a word. Not now, not here. No acknowledgment, nothing. It would all be very casual, very *yu'aright?* and straight to the gate.

What is worse? Getting jumped or not existing at all?

And what to do with both when, at any time, anything could change like the weather mid-season, unexpected, unannounced and with no sense of logic?

Abu turned back and looked over his shoulder.

'See you inside.'

Karl didn't see the wannabes. He was now carrying someone's bag while the owner was showing him something that required stepping forward and hopping. Was lost to Abu, who'd missed that train half a block earlier. Whatever.

'We're coming now anyway.'

No one moved but Abu. Nothing unusual here. Your typical Monday. Except for Abu's throbbing shoulders and aching neck. And even that wasn't new.

In the afternoon the snow started melting and the greyish day turned completely rubbish. Abu's mum opened the door for them with tired eyes in her heart-shaped face. Her lids looked like someone was pulling with both hands. Aazad had been sent home when he fell on the icy school ground. Nothing much to worry about, just a twisted ankle and crankiness in front of the TV. But you know that can be a whole lot, especially when you didn't expect it. She had just returned home, after the long wait at A&E, twins on the couch: one in pain, one sulking.

And there was the call Karl had to make, hanging in the air, waiting for credit. But when Karl came into the kitchen, Godfrey was already sitting there.

'Hello, stranger.'

3

Junctions.
There is always too much choice.

Karl nodded, his whole face shutting down.

'It's nothing new,' Godfrey said. 'Come on. We agreed. I don't even get what the big deal is.'

He waited. No answer. Nothing that could be swung like *blah blah because of this, you get me, blah*. No reason whatsoever other than Karl liked to run. At night. Away. Not to disappear, just to run. And to not call any-bloody-fucking-one. Not Godfrey, not Rebecca. No one but Abu.

Usually in the middle of the night, underneath Abu's grand mansion of an estate around the corner from the big old new St Pancras. Posh and all. Prostitutes and druggies moved somewhere else. All cleaned up and shiny. You could use it as a mirror if you were so inclined. Watch yourself disappear. Soon to be pricing them all out, council flat or not.

Abu would walk to the front door, asleep, and buzz Karl in, often his mother awake also, by the time Karl slowly climbed up the stairs. She would be standing in the hallway in her nightie and the gown that was really a bit too big for her. And sometimes when Abu's dad had come home from the night shift, he would come to the hallway from the living room. Nodding at Karl. Karl would go to shake his hand. That sort of respect thing between them. Abu's dad treated him like an esteemed extension of the family. Even if Abu's dad seldom had a lot of words. It was different to Mama Abu's silent reasoning. He had them for no one. Night shift can do that to you.

'Will you come to the hospital, at least?'

Karl's hands in the pockets of his jeans.

'She doesn't have an infection this time. It's a relapse. She'll be home day after tomorrow.'

'How does she look? Pale again?'

Rebecca had looked as if she had got mouldy last time. Pale wasn't even the bloody word.

'She looks good, Karl. Her cheeks are almost as rosy as yours.'

The corners of Godfrey's lips twitched. Supposed to be a smile. If the youngster would finally let him. What the eff was it all the time? This *can't make a phone call am too sensitive yet wanna act all grown up* thing? But he knew better than to let any of that seep from his lips. He got up from the kitchen chair and put his hands on Karl's shoulders.

'I think it will be good for you.'

Oh, the social workers of this world. Knowing everything that was well good. Godfrey was all cute like that.

When they got to the hospital Rebecca was sleeping. Her face was rosy. Healthy. The doctor said she didn't really need to stay; they'd release her the following day. She was smiling in her sleep. Karl said he would go by later so they went to Rebecca and Karl's flat, where he lived when he wasn't running away. And although everyone knew where he was, running was running and the point was still the same: to be away. Because his mum, Rebecca, wasn't there, couldn't be there. Couldn't really be there for him like proper because she was in hospital. This time. If not that, then seriously unwell. Again. Godfrey was taking care of him, Abu was, Abu's mum was and the dad, all of them were having Karl's back, in some real, big-time way. And the girls on their way to school and their other friends. The ones they really had. Not the wannabes, not them, of course not them. But it wasn't enough.

Karl had helped his mum pack the bag he had got her for Christmas. The one that was super busy with the intense flower pattern. Cute though, if that was your thing. He hadn't been sure if it was a good present. It was something she would use those rare times it really was too bad and she needed the hospital ASAP. Just in case. Just to get back to the right level. Where one could manage this MS. Multiple Sclerosis. It was major. But also it reminded them that she wasn't all that well a lot of the time.

Last time Karl had scrambled out of the house when he heard the ambulance pulling up the road. Put the pre-packed bag by the door, left her on the chair, ran down the stairs, opened the door to the building for them, and said: 'Second floor, first door on the right. Her keys are in her coat, the bag is by the door, she's ready to go. Please close the door. Make sure it's shut.'

And dashed. Split. Nothing could hold him and he ran and ran until the cold air almost cut into his face. Fingers throbbing, temples wanting to burst. His breath was broken and fast and spitting air with all that other stuff that was tight inside his stomach. Inside. Outside. If there were better ways to handle the difference, he would. We all bloody would.

The flat had been left mid-action. It was almost tidy if you discounted the mess around the gas cooker, the unwashed dishes, the crusty plates – two for the both of them – and the cups he had started soaping when his mother thought it would be better to call the ambulance. Better because for two days her balance had been way out and her legs were cramping and shaking. My friend, you couldn't look at it. It was heartbreak proper. Karl had helped her move from kitchen to living room, to bedroom and back. Her face scrunched up like McD wrappers thrown in the wet dirt just outside the estate. Grim. So slow that Karl thought they wouldn't make it. She didn't want to call the doctor but then she said, 'just in case'. Last time she'd gone in, she'd caught an infection that had knocked her sideways.

Godfrey had the mail in his hand and went straight to the sink to run water over the plates.

'Seems like there are a couple of bills. Have a look while I do this, will you?'

He didn't really need to ask. Karl was a runner but otherwise he had bare manners. Just the staying and looking at fate, at the inevitable, the feeling the pain, waiting for it to hit you straight on was hard, not washing dishes or paying bills. Could knock you off if you weren't careful. Right?

He opened a window in the stuffy living room and sat by the small corner desk with the new laptop on it. It had come through some government scheme for single, disadvantaged

mums. Although he was almost an adult it had still counted.
They'd been eligible and after endless paperwork they'd
been hooked up with the essential twenty-first-century
gadget courtesy of the taking-care-of-those-less-fortunate
charity-type scheme. The cheap desk, which they had to
get themselves, was made of white, plastic-coated MDF.
IKEA madness but second-hand, so they'd been spared the
extended puzzling hours of putting it together. He opened
the drawer, looking for scissors. A pencil with a broken tip,
a sharpener, loose paper. Karl placed the wad of envelopes
on the desk. Godfrey shouted from the kitchen.

'How you getting on in there? Anything needing immediate
attention?'

The scissors were at the back. His hand reached but pulled
the drawer too far. The whole load dropped on the floor.
Typical.

'Wait a minute, man. I ain't no priority speedy boarding,
innit.'

The laughter from the kitchen was full and deep, in that
comfortable way that was sort of a bit too grandfather for
the age, but which Karl proper liked about Godfrey.

'You're too much. Get your groove on though, I got to get
back.'

Karl smiled. *Groove*, he smirked. *So last century. You getting
old, man. No swag at all.*

A letter fell under the table next to Karl's trainers. He
picked up the papers. Neat handwriting stuck out. Airmail.
Hardcore old school. Karl didn't bother to sit down, just
opened the thing. Quick.

Dear Rebecca,

*I pray this reaches you in the best of health. I'm writing today
to alert you of my brother's sudden injury. The doctors are
concerned. In the last weeks he has been unrecognisable.
A different man, as I told you on the phone. A few days
after our conversation, he spoke of you.*

*I have kept your promise until a few days ago but couldn't
keep it from him any longer. He himself had brought you
up. He now knows of the child and wishes to see him. Her?
It was not my intention to disregard your wishes. Please
forgive any shortcomings of mine. I will call you to discuss
further but as it has been difficult to reach you, I am*

informing you in this rather old-fashioned way. Please kindly send your email address.

Always Yours,

T.
Ikeja, Lagos
president@tundesfineclothingunltd.com

It had been re-opened; the torn bit of sello on the outside was a sure tell. Another pen colour scribbled on the side.
I'm in Italy from 4th until the 16th. Kindly call me.
And a number. Inside Karl, things sank. The heart, the stomach, the lung. All fell, crashing hard, pushing out the shallow bit of air that had survived his hasty opening-stuff-that-wasn't-his operation.
'I want to go.'
Karl's head changed to red, his arms stuck by his side.
Godfrey had entered the room and now stood next to him. He picked up the letter. His brow furrowed. His eyes had skimmed over the words, to get level playing field with Karl. Eyes wandered from thin paper to Karl's face, then back to the paper. Back to Karl.
'I will go.'
'I can't let you do that, Karl.'
'Godfrey.'
Karl was using Godfrey's weapons, one of his favourites: the calling of the name. Complete with dramatic pause. Very classic. They were eyeing each other, ready for the next round.
'Are you trying to say this isn't like major, I mean like proper? Don't give me your "just let it go" this time.'
'Karl.'
But Karl had learned from the best.
'Godfrey.'
Afternoon sun hit the open window right where the MDF fitted neatly into the corner. The window frame was old, wooden; it had started to crack over the years. It needed replacing.
'Karl.'
'Godfrey.'

Godfrey exhaled, his breath heavy from the opinion that
he had dropped on it. A tactic that people, especially oldies
like him, used when talking sensible shite to youngsters. It
was so much more important when you left the words out.
   'I heard you and Abu had some trouble the other night.'
   'You're changing the subject.'
   'Karl.'
   'Godfrey.'
   'Karl!'
   'Godfrey?'
   'But you did have some trouble.'
   'We did.'
   Both stopped. Paused. Looked away, then at each other.
Godfrey in his early-thirties-ness. Sporty Trinidadian, stocky.
That nice nice type of guy. Proper solid, who believed in the
right side of things. That you could find it with the right
amount of effort, the right amount of care.
   And that was exactly the sort of care he had for people like
Karl. For Karl in particular. Who he had taken home and
kept there when things were difficult. Before they had the
arrangement that involved calling him when things went
downhill with Rebecca. Before he got the special guardianship
and Abu's mum became a kinship carer. All of them tied in
by law. A group effort to get this thing safely to the other
side: Karl's growing up.
   They stared. At each other. Away. Godfrey, who was
through and through: there are no wrong kids, just wrong
outcomes. There were things to be grabbed with both hands,
opportunities to make one's own and so forth. In and out.
Like trains, his sermons. Karl didn't listen to too much of it,
not because he didn't care but because he had been hearing
it for a while. For the past six years. Godfrey's dark, almost
black eyes, coin-shaped and normally a little too large for
the face, narrowed and focused on the youngster's. His
tight-cropped hair shining, both from being proper black
and the bloody pomade he'd used. Pomade! *Twenty-first
century, hello! right?*
   'I'm cold.'
   'Then close the window.'
   Karl stepped to it. All casual, so shrugging-shoulders type
it amplified. And slowly he closed it, carefully. *Must remind
them again.* The council. Then out loud to Godfrey:

'Take a minute, a day, a week. Whatever. I'll ask you again.'
Full-on assault now.

'You know why, Godfrey. You understand. We both know it.'

Karl took the letter from Godfrey's hand. Pushed it into his back pocket.

'You always look out for me. You really do. And my appreciation is like crazy. For real.' He paused. 'Maybe you can't let me go legally but I doubt it. You can sign anything you want for me. You know that. I know that. I thought I had no dad. That mum didn't know him or he was such an arsehole that she couldn't even talk about him.'

Karl's voice was all screeching metal now, low volume, but still. It pierced your ears for sure. Godfrey pressed his lips together, trying to stay alpha.

'Be honest. Tell me that you don't get it. Forget even that mum lied to me my whole life, avoiding anything to do with the topic. Me and her don't have the same bloody life. If it's not the wannabes, it's the bloody police. 'Cause we're always causing trouble, right?'

Godfrey was still pressing his lips together.

'Would be nice to experience something else for a change. Not be suspicious. For a minute.'

Karl was looking at Godfrey. He waited, taking his time.

'I'll ask you again, seven days from now. If you can look me in the eye and say you would not go if you were in my shoes, I'll drop the whole thing.'

He continued on his sense-making, teamwork process. Looked away. Back at Godfrey. Arms dangling now, doing nothing with them, just loose and open and clear.

'I promise.'

He held out his hand, showing most of his rosy palm. Was waiting for Godfrey to accept the fair deal. And you couldn't say it wasn't fair. Made a whole bloody load of sense. Karl had cornered him. That's the thing when you train your people. Sooner or later they beat you at your own game. Punch. Strike. Defeat.

A week later Godfrey said yes.

4

___

**When we speak of nothing
we don't end the silence.**

The way she walked in gave her mood away. Karl hid in the
living room. Hiding was pointless. You couldn't get lost in
their one-point-five-mini-bedroom mansion. Everywhere
was present. Like over the top. When Rebecca entered, he
pretended to be tidying up. But there were no stray papers
or clothes, nothing to put away or straighten. Nothing. It had
all been taken care of. The day before yesterday. The day
his mother came home energised. Ready. Because it hadn't
been a relapse. Karl stood with half of his back to her. His
face towards the TV. Rebecca waited. It was rude. You didn't
treat your mum that way. Ignoring, pretending, avoiding.
    'I thought I'd skip counselling this time.'
    It wasn't a laugh that came out of his mother's mouth. 'And
you failed to mention it beforehand?'
    'I thought I'd give you time. So you could have proper chat
and all ...'
    She left the room. Not pleased. So not pleased. Karl
could hear her bedroom door open, then the water in the
bathroom. He sat on the small couch and checked his phone.
No messages. Abu was out with the twins and his mother.
Visiting relatives. He was stuck with his own life.

     gesture /ˈdʒɛstʃə(r)/
     noun
          1. What you show.
     verb
          1. How you do it.

He could smell the bath oil from here. His mother returned, already in her bathrobe.

'We don't have to have these sessions. It's something we're doing for the both of us. If you don't want to go, say. But don't take me for a ride.'

Karl was staring at the TV. 'Sorry mum.'

'Sorry? Can you explain yourself? Much more important than your apology. What were you doing?'

'Nothing.'

It was true. He had begged Godfrey not to say anything and Godfrey had agreed. For the time being. And then his mother came home all chirpy and ready to proper gel again.

'Karl! I'm trying to talk to you!'

She had loosened her hair. It was falling over the top of the purple robe. He hated that thing. Or seriously disliked it, if you wanted to be more therapy talk like. It looked too cheap, too old, too unglamorous for his mother. Rebecca always laughed. 'It's perfectly fine, does the job,' she would reply. She would laugh even more when he claimed it didn't do her justice. But there was no use buying her a new one. She didn't need one, didn't want one, loved this one. The softness from endless washes. The familiarity. She wasn't wearing it to show off. She wanted to be comfortable. Rebecca retied the belt, held on to the loose ends.

'Karl, I'm waiting for an explanation.'

'Just ground me or something.'

Rebecca's mouth would have hit the street if it had been big enough to make it through the lower floors. It flapped open, heavy. 'You want some form of punishment?'

Karl shrugged. He was pushing the boat out, major operation. He was already lost but once you ride a wave you have to keep bending your knees and go in, all the way.

'For what?'

He had been grounded once. In seventeen years. And that was because of Piers. Aunty Sarah had insisted because Karl had broken Piers' tail light. The grounding consisted of not coming along to an outing with them, which is what Karl had gone for in the first place. Piers gave offensive lectures while eating, walking, breathing. Basically he couldn't stop his mouth from hating Karl. Ever. No therapy could soften that.

His shoulders moved up and down again. It wasn't easy to be whatever on his mum. Not easy at all.

'I want to know what's going on.'

She grabbed her book from the table next to the couch. Her legs brushed his as she walked by.

'I expect you to explain yourself. It's not OK to leave other people hanging. You have a mouth; use it. We're all reasonable people.' She had been looking at him but walked out of the room now. 'If you want, consider it your punishment.'

A text came in. Abu. On his way home.

'We can talk tomorrow. Properly. You're right, I should have come to therapy. Let's talk about it next week.' Karl, in the hallway as well, took his jacket off the wardrobe.

His mother was only a few steps away, hand on bathroom door. 'I thought you wanted to be grounded? I expect you to stay here until you have given me a reasonable explanation. Suit yourself when you want to do that.'

The door closed and the radio went on. Jazz FM had some old-school hour. His mother had probably waited for it. He could hear the water, and her skin settling in on the enamel.

Godfrey came by the next day. Agreed that the joint therapy sessions were to be joint. Like they had discussed and agreed. All of them. Unless Karl said so beforehand. Or his mother did. It was worse. They really hadn't done any sessions for a while. This one was supposed to be a catching up to see if everything was still going well. They did that from time to time. How was it with their alternative-style family? Were Karl and Rebecca still on track, meaning close? How was Karl doing in general? How was Rebecca? Did they spend enough time with each other or did they get lost in their own lives? Especially when Rebecca was ill a lot. It helped. The checking in, Rebecca stayed main parent that way even in those rare times when a depression shut her away for weeks.

Karl had simply forgotten. A father looming on the horizon can make you do that. Especially when you intend to keep that new intel from your very clued-up mum.

'I was just dealing with some stuff. Got caught up.'

His eyes were glazing over. Now a proper reason. Twenty-four hours and he still hadn't come up with a good excuse. He wasn't unreliable, so people, his people, asked to get an answer, not for rhetoric.

'Probably the stuff with the bullies from your year?'

Godfrey could throw a lifeline like no other. Didn't agree one single bit with the not telling his mother, but he could understand it, somehow, could feel Karl on this one.

'Yes, yes. Distracted. So much going on. I need some time out, for real. Don't really know where my head is at.'

He was trying to work his Karl magic – smiled sheepishly, dimples and all – but Rebecca waved it away.

'Don't try your cutesy face on me. I gave birth to you. Been seeing it since.'

They laughed. The air had lifted a little. Godfrey got up. He needed to be off, had just dropped by because of being in the neighbourhood, which was true. He left out that he was glad to leave this situation behind, withheld info and all. Rebecca walked him to the door; Karl followed behind. They both watched as Godfrey descended the stairs. Rebecca put her arm around Karl's waist. Would have been the perfect time to bring it up. To start with the beginning. Of the story. Of what he was planning. But Karl lowered his head to her shoulder without any of those explanations.

'Really mum, I just don't know where my head is. Let's leave therapy for a while.'

deception /dɪˈsɛpʃ(ə)n/
noun

> 1. The act of not showing what is but what looks good.
> 2. Better than what you want to hide.
> 3. Missed opportunity.

'If you think so.' She tried to get a view of his face. 'If you don't think we'll get anything out of it at the moment ...'

She wasn't entirely happy. Karl wasn't letting her in. But that was how teenagers were, wasn't it?

5

We always think much higher
of ourselves, when we have
good reasons for our actions.

Godfrey agreed to a slow proceeding. *Let's start with a call.*
Tunde – who said, laughing, on the phone to Karl, 'Ah!
I feel I know you, just call me Uncle T!' – was in Italy on
business and happy to detour to London – his UK visa from
a trip earlier in the year still valid – introduce himself, make
his sincerity known and hopefully carry Karl swiftly to the
fatherland. Sometime soon.

What turned Godfrey around wasn't just Karl's *I can
knock you sideways with your own game, any time.* It was the
lot. Sandwiched between Uncle T's excitement and Karl's
calculated reasoning, it was difficult to get a straight thought
in. Godfrey's enthusiasm was *so yeah sure that makes sense
if not stupidly risky* and *I don't know that man from Adam.*
Anything could happen. Anything. And Godfrey wouldn't be
able to do shit about it.

But then Uncle T came to London and told Godfrey how
he had stayed in touch with Rebecca. And how Rebecca
had tried to cut even those ties. From day one. Tunde told
Godfrey how he had begged Rebecca to let Karl's father at
least know about the child. Even if she didn't want to speak
to him because that much was clear. Always said 'the child'
until Godfrey corrected him:

'Karl. Just say Karl. Please.'

And Tunde startled, his body stopping for a moment, the
arms and hands left frozen in the air. Then realising, laughing.

'I never knew. Even that, she never said. It was only the
child, if she answered at all.'

'First me alone,' Godfrey had said to Karl. Suss it out. He and Tunde had spoken for three hours straight. Top to bottom. Gone over the details, verified the security measures. You had to. This was bloody this century, not no trusting 1960s. If they had been trusting. At the end of the mega-interview the uncle had said 'Godfrey,' extending his hand, 'it will be OK.' Godfrey almost thought it was a genetic thing. The *truss me* gene.

Uncle T wanted nothing from them. And he had not miraculously inherited/been given/made 200 million (of any currency that was impressive, thus not naira), which were now sitting in his account needing rescue, urgently.

Instead, Tunde came with a picture of Rebecca with Karl's father, taken a bit more than eighteen years ago: a snapshot, a small bar in Lagos. The two sitting under an aluminium roof that shaded the few plastic tables and chairs. Behind them, a guy on a barbecue – 'He's making suya,' Tunde said – giving his thumbs up and grinning. Tunde also brought Rebecca's short replies to his letters, always on postcards that showed some variation on the Queen, or a similarly monarchy-type motive. Always ironic, the choice of card, always cryptic, the writing, always short, never mentioning anything specific about Karl whatsoever. *Fine. We're well, thanks. Baby is fine. Child is fine. Mother is fine. Now eff off already.* Last thing implied. *Please do not send money, don't need any, we're fine. Will not use it. As you returned it the last time I sent it back I'm keeping it aside now. Come for it when you're ready. Yes, secondary school now. Fine. Fine. Fine.*

Godfrey sat for a long time with all the cards. Nineteen of them. The only reason she replied was because Tunde kept bullying her, which is what it said on one of the cards.

'They call me the sentimental one.' Tunde was smiling now. 'And wonder how my business is as successful as it is. Sentimental people don't make money, they say; they make soppy lovers.' He laughed, throwing his head back. 'Well I cannot, or better, I should not, speak on that part. But we make good business partners. We are loyal. We don't forget you. Sooner or later one big fish or another is hooked. They want someone reliable. Who cares. Either to do a good job, or about them. If there is a common interest, it turns out one can even make some good money.'

He stood in front of Godfrey, who was still staring at
Rebecca's cards. At the photo. Both were quiet.

Uncle T came back the next day. Karl and Godfrey together
this time. Uncle T's smile was so proud Karl had to look
away. When they sat on Godfrey's couch Godfrey studied
Uncle T's face. Open. Excited. He was fully present, facing
Karl from the armchair. Karl was examining his fingernails.

'Well, something to drink would be good; where are my
manners. Tunde, can I get you a coffee?'

'Yes, thank you.' Never taking his eyes off the young man
in front of him.

Godfrey left and they could hear him running water in the
kitchen.

'I wrote to Rebecca.' Uncle T's voice was low. This was
something between them. He had Karl's attention.

'I mean your mother.' He took out the postcards and laid
them on the table in front of Karl. Karl had heard about
these from Godfrey. 'These are her replies. She wasn't, how
do you say it? Feeling me that much, it seems.' He wasn't
trying to be funny. Karl could see that. 'But I was feeling
you. I tried, Karl, I tried.'

'Here,' Tunde said, and brought out more than nineteen,
a whole lot more, sheets of paper.

'I kept my letters as well. For you.'

Karl's hands reached for the small bundle. 'I knew she
wasn't giving them to you. I have copies of all of them.'

Tunde tapped his hand on Karl's shoulder and followed
Godfrey into the kitchen. Karl stared at the paper in his lap.
Picked one up.

14 December 1994

Dear Rebecca,

I hope this finds you well.
I am deeply saddened that you are not returning my calls.
Adebanjo ... He is not the most reliable man. I have tried
to warn you. Please do not think we are the same.
The baby must have arrived by now. Kindly send a picture.
I cannot wait to meet my niece or nephew. Please allow me
to visit. I understand that you will most likely not return
to Nigeria but if there is only the slightest chance, allow
me to be of assistance.

I enclose $100 but will send more next month.
How are you?

Eagerly awaiting your reply,
Tunde

It was the shortest letter.

  Rebecca's reply was on a postcard with the queen waving at crowds during a procession. She was smiling and holding her handbag in the other hand. On her head an abomination in purple. Who chose those hats?

T.
We're all very fine. No assistance needed. Your money is in an account I opened here. Please let me know how to return it.
R.

Uncle T had written about his business. About the country. About his imagined relationship, the relationship he wanted to have with Karl. The Karl he had never met. The Karl he didn't know of. He wrote about the time Rebecca had spent in Nigeria. About England. About what he heard in the news. But mostly he asked, always asked: how is the baby? When can we meet?

12 September 1995

Dear Rebecca,

This is to inform you that I am coming to London! Kindly send your address. I will arrive on 16 October and stay …

The next letter was posted in London. From London to London. It started with 'Since you refused to see me …'

It was difficult to see the writing now that Karl's eyes were leaking. Uncle T was at the door but turned around again and complimented Godfrey, who was behind him, on an award that hung in the hallway. It was a five-a-side fun-league win

from three years ago. Uncle T aahed and oohed his way
through, asking details about how many teams, where did
they play. Etc. Karl wiped his face and folded the letters
carefully. Uncle T and Godfrey entered with cups in hand.
Godfrey handed Karl a glass of Coke, surprised. Uncle T
said nothing, just sat down, studying Karl in a friendly sort
of way. The silence. Uncle T leaned into it. Metaphorically
speaking. There was no awkwardness. It just was. You couldn't
always pick up words to flourish the unsayable. It would be
a waste. Too much. Sometimes moments had to be allowed
to be themselves. To breathe or not, to be bearable or not.
You couldn't always change it.

   Karl's head was still low. Letters in hand, postcards on top.

   'I need to make some calls,' Uncle T said. 'Maybe I can
meet you, both of you, for dinner later?'

   Godfrey searched for Karl's eyes. Karl nodded, head
unmoved.

Uncle T left the next day and went back to his business
dealings in Italy. Manufacturing new shea butter products.
Expanding his business portfolio.

6

**What are false starts
if not a warm up?
Question is for what.**

Karl's eyes stretched so far he could feel his lids hit the back
of his head. They had talked about Karl's father so often;
why was Abu not jumping up and down now? Abu got up to
close the curtains in the small room.
'You staying tonight?'
Since when did he ask? Karl was already on his folded-out
mattress, trainers neatly positioned next to the wardrobe.
'If it's not too much of a problem?' Karl was getting annoyed.
What the eff?
Abu shrugged a shoulder and opened his laptop. The tinny
music got louder and louder. Tinie Tempah's latest. Abu was
singing along. *Wonder wonder wonderman.* Azizah popped
her head in.
'Mum says you should turn it down.'
Abu didn't respond but tapped on the keys until the music
disappeared. The door closed. Karl could hear the twins
running in the living room. He opened his bag, got out a pad
and started scribbling. He could have fooled someone he was
writing if the doodles hadn't been that large. Too obvious.
Abu put the laptop next to him on the bed. 'So he wrote
like, the whole time?'
His voice sounded like it was being squeezed through a
strainer. Karl turned and crossed his legs, facing Abu, who
towered over him on the bed.
'First more often, and in the end, once a year. Proper letters.
And once he even came. Just to find me.'
'That is deep man.'

In his voice you could hear that Abu meant it. His shoulders were hanging low, his upper body hanging forward. His face was not participating in his approval. His lips started moving again. '*What kinda person should you be ...*'

Karl rolled his eyes. How many times was he going to listen to the same song? As if Abu had heard him, he changed mid-verse and opened the laptop again.

'There is this new exercise thing. You can get like, major fit, six-pack and everything. Arms proper strong.' He showed Karl a YouTube video. 'You see that guy? Even has muscles popping on his shoulders.'

Karl didn't get it. Was this all they were going to say about his father? But if Abu wanted to change the subject, whatever. Abu was holding the laptop in front of him so that Karl could see. He was narrating the whole thing as if there wasn't someone doing that in the clip anyway. Karl pulled the laptop off him, looked at the video for a minute and put the music back on but on low volume.

'Afsana wants us to all go to the movies at the weekend.'

'Why?' Abu slid forward and undid his shoelaces. He kept the trainers on, holding his nose with his thumb and index finger, smiled, pointed at Karl's socked feet and scrunched up his face.

'Haha,' Karl said. 'Mine don't stink. Unlike someone's. What's your problem with Afsana?'

'Have you noticed how much that girl can talk?'

'Woman,' Karl replied. 'Look who is talking.'

'It's not the same.' Abu wanted to smile but it didn't come out. There wasn't really anything wrong with Afsana. Maybe she didn't talk too much but when she was with them there was hardly space for anyone else.

On the weekend Afsana had to babysit so instead they met in the little green bit between the estates, her baby brother in tow. Nalini was holding on to his hand when Abu and Karl arrived.

'I have him like every weekend now, and even in the week I have to pick him up. I said to my mother it's not fair. My older sister never has to do it. She can stay at home. Maybe I want to do that, you know. Think. Chill. Do my nails. Whatever. Not always with Rahul on my arm ...'

Abu nodded and gave Karl a look. *Told you.*

'But she's helping with your dad, Afsana. Don't tell me you want to stay inside taking care of the house. So not you. Just saying.'

Nalini let go of the little hand and Rahul ran off.

Afsana followed him with her eyes as he ran to the large tree in the middle. They stopped by the bench nearby. Afsana's father had had a stroke last year. Her mother was working now and both Afsana and her older sister needed to help out more.

'I guess. You're right. It's just … I mean when am I going to do my thing? Without Rahul. He's cute and all but you can't do the same stuff all the time.'

Karl gave her the look. Abu called it the wrap. Better than a hug. More intention than an embrace. It was the sure announcement of a whole fucking eternity of useless going over the same thing, as far as Abu was concerned. They were going to sit down and talk the whole thing through. Eyes on Afsana. Understanding all the way. It just took a little too long. Karl had to take it to some stupid level. Always. Afsana had already said how she felt. A little *aw* and a tap on the shoulder would have been enough. Not for Karl.

'It's a bit cold but you want to sit here? Just for a minute?'

So predictable. Afsana and Nalini sat down, eyes still on Rahul, who was running around the tree for the third time.

'Anyone fancy Chicken Cottage? I might get something.'

Abu couldn't hear it again. Afsana had complained about her mother and how she had to babysit all the time last month. He got it. Life was shit. But she was always exaggerating, as far as he was concerned. Most of the time Rahul was at home. But he knew better than to get involved. This was about the talking. Not the destination. It wasn't about some solution to the problem.

The others nodded and Karl and Nalini handed him some coins. Abu turned and walked off but Nalini's hand held on to his sleeve. What now?

'Hey, you don't want the fiver?' She pointed to Afsana's hand.

'Of course. Sorry.' Now he looked like he had a problem with her.

'Family bucket? Rahul needs lunch anyway. We can all eat.'

Abu nodded and took the money from Afsana. 'Thanks.' He strolled out of the gated green bit to the little street. Two guys from sixth form were standing by the corner shop. Kyle and Mark. Harmless. Mark nodded and bent back over the little screen Kyle was playing with. When Abu got closer he briefly looked up.

'Yu'aright?'

'Not bad. New?'

Mark looked proud although it was obvious he had not held the thing one second. 'Nintendo 3DS.'

'Cool.'

Abu wasn't interested in games but with Karl going all lady talk what was he supposed to do?

'What game?'

'*Super Street Fighter.*'

Abu shook Mark's hand and looked at the tiny screen. Kyle was all in, absorbed, didn't even feel the chill. There was a lot going on and from behind Kyle he couldn't really see all that much.

'Wicked.' Abu was bored but he shuffled closer.

'What're you doing anyway?' Kyle returned to the game and Mark looked at Abu.

'Going to Chicken Cottage in a minute.'

The pair of them stood either side of Kyle now. Abu could feel something behind him, someone coughing. Mark pointed at the screen. Something amazing seemed to be happening. His legs gave a little, pushed from behind. He turned around. An older man with a Zimmer frame was stuck between the entrance to the corner shop and Abu. He had that shaking thing that made it hard for him to walk. There was a lot of sideways for every centimetre forward.

'Taking over. Everywhere.'

'Excuse me. Didn't realise ...' Abu stepped out of the way.

'Typical. Bloody Paki.'

You could have missed it. The last bit. It was that low. Just a bit of breath. Pressed into form by tight lips. Not tight enough to draw attention beyond Abu. Not meant to at least.

'Whatever.' Abu was tired of it.

Mark turned. 'Wow, what?'

The man didn't take his eyes off Abu, walked off, frame tottering over the uneven pavement.

'I think that's my cue.' Abu shrugged. 'See you later.'

It was busier now. The rush before the Saturday evening. King's Cross would be full of people trying to have fun, people who did have fun, and those who had to take them home. Afterwards. But here, a few streets behind, it would die down in a couple of hours except for the occasional stray. The youngsters of the area would hang in little groups. Either in the shadow by a corner somewhere, almost invisible, in the estate entrances or at home. Abu wondered where he would be. Where should he be? Afsana and Nalini had to be home early. They would walk them home. And then what? Talk about the life Karl had waiting on the other side of the world? Just to let Abu know that he was defo not going to be part of any fun on that front? That was not just depressing, it was pointless.

Uncle T called to let them know he was leaving Italy for Nigeria. He returned to London six weeks later. Accepted that he wasn't meeting Rebecca. Still not meeting her, after all those years. That for some reason that was out of the question. Either way, it was about Karl now; it hadn't been about Rebecca for a very long time.

It was finally getting a little milder outside. Uncle T wore leather loafers that looked smooth, as if they would caress the ground. His linen trousers were black, ironed perfectly. Abu was curious and Karl jealous. How did he keep it that way? In the plane. Uncreased? Linen! The fabric seemed to fondle his legs the way the shoes touched the ground. Everything well-mannered, gentle, well placed. The man had it down. His skin looked healthy, treated with just the right product, no greasy spots.

'Godfrey, I understand your concerns. Very much. I am not a father myself but I understand. I am an uncle. A family person. I understand.'

They were sitting in Godfrey's living room.

'Metrosex-something type innit,' Abu mumbled, out of earshot.

Karl looked at him, nodding. 'He's well trim.'

Uncle T didn't hear them. He continued. 'You have to come as well, Godfrey. That is the only way. We have a guest room, en suite. It would not be a—'

'No!' Karl shouted. He sat at the edge of the couch. Hadn't moved since Godfrey had invited them to settle in, done the pleasantries thing, the 'how was the flight'. The smiling a little more trusting towards each other, now that relationships were forming.

Abu jerked his head around. *Wtf? Bruv, what's your problem?*
Godfrey was warming up to a shutting the shutters any
moment now.

And Uncle T? Smiled. Rose from the armchair that faced
away from the TV. His trousers fell back into straight lines,
skimming the cream loafers. He walked over to Karl, all
calm, like nothing had just blown up a bit. Even if it was a
mini-outburst it was so not Karl. Of course, Uncle T had no
clue about that. All new to him either way, but he sensed the
shock in Godfrey and Abu. Uncle T just smiled, touching
Karl's arm, looking into his eyes. Karl avoided him.

'I just need to do it my way. Something for me. Just me.'
Calm again and not looking at anyone, face in high-alert
mode. So devastating. The longing. Belonging.

He didn't have a choice. Godfrey. He knew that. Knew it
since Karl said *I'll give you a week*. He could be the hero,
the one that *got him*, teamwork and all.

Or he could go all authority on Karl and say no. See him
disappear courtesy of the eighteenth birthday that was storming
towards them in two months. Karl would just vanish, not only
pounding pavements but straddling continents without any
contact, without any sort of bond left.

It was possible. He could see it in Karl's eyes. The way
they were further away than ever. The way his ears were no
longer listening, as if tuned to a different station.

Two sleepless nights later, Godfrey took the number the
receptionist gave him to queue with Karl and Tunde for a visa.

7

**Missing is still
a presence.**

Karl's father, Adebanjo Balogun, lived in Port Harcourt in the
week, while Uncle T was in Lagos full-time. Tunde suggested
that after they became acquainted, they could both come
to Lagos, so he could also get to know Karl better. Because
that is what he wished, had always wished: to get to know
his young relative, Rebecca's child. Godfrey nodded absent-
mindedly and did his arranging, the type he did best without
a giddy Karl, all shy and out of breath at the same time. Out
of outbursts, out of eruptions, out of saying anything but
how excited he was. Nigeria. For real.
    Abu's mum had not been saying much. She was happy
for him, but looked sad. The type of look that held back its
thoughts but broke your heart trying to figure out how to
rectify it.
    Mama Abu wasn't on the decision-making team, not
this time around, because she was against it. Not just the
dangers, or yes, the dangers, all of them. And she didn't
mean the foreign-travel advice. She was talking emotions,
the sensitive shit Karl processed behind his beautiful face.
And there was more.
    'Rebecca ...' then she stopped. Picked up something
the twins had left in the kitchen and put it on the counter.
Busied herself with something or the other, although she
had finished the cooking and the tidying up before Godfrey
had come. Karl couldn't see her. They were waiting for her
to continue. She turned around and looked at Godfrey, her
hands touching each other. No words. None at all. Godfrey
moved around on his chair, uncomfortable. Unsure, all of
a sudden.

'I know. We should tell her.' His fingers tangled in and out of each other. 'I know.' There was a defeated tone there. 'But stress is so bad for her. The doctor says it all the time. It triggers relapses.' It was meant to be convincing.

Mama Abu kept her eyes on him, eyebrows raised so slightly you wouldn't have noticed it if not for the clear message in her stare. Everything was in that look. The *it doesn't make any sense. Like this, you don't build any trust. At all.*

Instead Godfrey and Tunde resolved some details. Karl was to fly back with Uncle T and the father would be there, at the other end.

That evening Karl heard his father's voice for the first time.

'Excuse me? Could you repeat that, please?'

And his father's puzzled laugh pushed nervously through the phone. Puzzled because this youngster was a surprise to him. Had fallen into his life like the hail did in June. Completely random.

'How are you? Karl.'

'I'm fine.' Karl's words tripped over each other as if he was wearing someone else's too-small, two-of-the-same-side, trainers. All awkward and not at all smooth.

'We look forward to welcoming you here in Nigeria.'

'Thank you. I look forward too.' And was quiet.

What should you say? That it was, like, so exciting and amazing? But that you were shitting your pants just that little bit? Or just go with the polite angle and wait for the father to make a move?

The father's voice was deeper than Uncle T's. A bit strained, a bit faint, as if he was speaking through cotton wool. But with an echo. Courtesy of the connection.

There was time, two weeks, as Uncle T continued on his journey to the south of Europe. Business again – 'I'm doing this trip a lot lately' – before returning for Karl, to take him to Nigeria.

Karl was staying at Abu's again. Rebecca was 'struggling', as they all called it. Karl preferred to keep away. Give her space. To deal. Like himself, she had her own support groups. Sometimes she went once a week when the depression was starting. Often she wouldn't continue them. Just kept to herself. Took the space that everyone gave her. Except Mama Abu, who would drop by and check on her. The staying in touch. Connected. Then she caught another infection and was back in hospital. Second time this year.

Her cheeks were flushed when Karl walked in. Her eyes opened, like a curtain drawn back. Her room was cramped. A woman with busy wounds – oozing stuff, like real heavy-smelling, thick stuff that coloured the bandages in a burnt toast manner – next to her had moaned all night, Rebecca told him. There was a catheter attached to his mother's right arm.

'They say only a couple of days, not serious this time.'

Karl didn't look. Like he didn't look *anywhere*.

'How is the pain?'

'Not that bad really. It's mainly just the infection.'

He nodded, head bobbing up and down.

'How is college? And Abu?'

He straightened her small side table, the awkward aluminium nightstand on rollers, and walked to the sink with the flowers his aunt had brought in the morning. Aunt Sarah had come down from Sheffield, which was rare these days. Karl would have come earlier to catch her, but her husband had come along this time. And things never ended well when Piers was there.

Karl topped up the water in the vase although it needed none of that. There was that smile, hitting him like the cold water. Hurting inside as much as it filled every bloody bit of him with mushiness. Tenderness, you know that one. Rebecca's smile. The *all will be well.* The longing for it.

'Mum, I'll be away for a couple of weeks. Godfrey and me thought it would be good for me to go on this programme-like thing. Get some perspective on where I want to be with my life, you know. I have been saying my head is all over the place.'

'He didn't tell me about it.'

'We didn't want to worry you. Horizon-expanding. A workshop for kids like me.'

'With college?'

'Not exactly.'

'With the support group?'

'No.'

'Then what is it? I'm not sure I can give my consent like that. I need more details.'

'No need to worry, really, trust me. Just some time away, sort of learning by doing experience. I'll be back in no time. Give you a chance to recover. It's been a very bad year.'

'Yes, I guess it has.'

She wasn't finished. Hadn't finished protesting the way Karl took independence to a new level. But things have a way of unfolding at the worst moment. Creases folded over her face, contracting the skin as she pulled close all the muscles in a sudden jolt. When it came, that sharpness, the razor-like precision that carved her muscles, her mind blanked. White light switched on in her brain, a high-pitched humming sound. Karl rushed over. His gangly self swayed slightly as he stood helpless next to her bed. She smiled like a rare alien. Same way he felt. Rare. Everything pulled tight.

8

And the seeing ...
It is always more.
More than the obvious.

Nalini pulled on Karl's T-shirt. He turned around just as Miss
Martin started writing on the whiteboard at the front, his
shoulders raised. Nalini moved her head back, pointing to the
table behind her and slipped him the folded piece of paper.
  So we ain't good enuf for u now
Miss Martin was going on about social media, its rise in
the past few years, and how it had changed communication.
Talk about trying to get a captive audience, capture the mood
of the time. Karl swivelled around, looking straight at Abu,
a text already on the way.
  Thot u hated this class
  What u on about
  Piece of paper ... really? U from the stone age or sumthin
  'Karl, anything you'd like to add?'
He had forgotten to turn around again, his head red now,
sending messages of being caught into the stuffy classroom
instead of firing rapid texts at Abu.
  'No, sorry, miss.'
Abu's hand shot up.
  'Miss.'
You could see the pleasant surprise. Miss Martin came a
step closer, encouraging. 'Yes, Abubakar?'
  'The way I understand it miss, is that we used to spend
more time together, innit. And now we ain't even in the same
place any more. So although it's called social media it's, like,
social but not really, cause we are leaving each other ...'
He pulled his legs, which were sprawled out underneath
the table, up and straightened his posture.

'... alone.'

Karl's mouth opened and something tumbled out. A laugh, a cough, difficult to tell. His head turned from red to purple, his eyes staring out of the window, arms folded.

Miss Martin took up the point – and what a good one it was indeed – and a heated debate started. Afsana said she loved, like totally loved bbm and texting but to be her real friend you also had to show up in person.

A dark-haired one countered, 'But I feel like you can be freer, really say what you mean. I'm not embarrassed when I send a message. And also, that way there is always someone.'

Some nodding, some mumbling, probably to make some other point but not up for joining the discussion in a too obvious way.

Nalini said she also liked to hang out in real life.

'That way I can really tell my friends what's going on. Can't really do that messaging. I don't know if they're really paying attention.'

Abu nodded. Just his point. That girl had a thing or two going for her. Not just cute she was. If only Afsana wasn't always taking up all the space.

Leicester, who was sitting close to the window that overlooked the inner yard of the college, started. That should be interesting.

'Don't really matter.'

'How do you mean, Leicester?'

'You can hide on social media or you can pretend to be someone else in real life. It doesn't matter.'

'Care to elaborate?' Miss Martin was back near the whiteboard. Looked like she wanted to hold on to something.

'If you're a faker then you're a faker.'

'And what is a faker, in your opinion?'

Miss Martin's eyes focused on the traffic light she could see from the window. Five more minutes. Dangerously long if someone was up for stirring up some shit. Not long enough to have a sensible discussion.

'Nowadays everything is allowed, right. You don't have to say who you really are. Not in school, not on Facebook, not anywhere. Same as social media, if you ask me. Not real. Fake.'

Another one from his gang stood up, leaned forward and slapped him on his shoulder. A couple of others egged him on.

'Go on Leicester, break it down.'

Four minutes left. Miss Martin went to her desk and put her bag on the table. Picked up the papers that were on top and carefully placed them inside the bag. 'I hope you don't forget to be respectful. With your commentary.'

Leicester looked around the room, smirking. 'Respect is when you don't tamper with nature.'

Karl's slender limbs looked like they were imploding, making themselves scarce. And invisible. Someone in need of disappearance, as in *now this sec.* Abu was ignoring the whole thing and had started zooming in on his hands, finger by finger, like there was some secret he had missed so far.

'Shut up, Leicester.' Nalini looked like she would burn him. Her eyes were smoking.

Afsana rallied behind her. 'No one wants to know about your issues.'

'That's right.' Two of their friends at the table next to Nalini spoke at the same time. Leicester's friends jumped up. A row of them, in the middle of the room. One of them, one side of the head shaved with a little cut (the barber must've slipped), almost shouted.

'Freedom of speech, innit, Miss Martin. He can say what he wants. He's not swearing, he's not calling names. It's just his opinion. For the debate.'

Miss Martin looked around the room. Nalini and Afsana's supporters sat back down but eyes were on her. Expectant. Nalini raised her hand.

'Miss, can we do this another day? There is no time now. I have a feeling, correct me if I'm wrong' – she looked at Leicester – 'this is not really about social media.'

'Thanks Nalini. You're right. We'll leave it for today. All of you consider what you want to contribute to the discussion. Remember, we're talking about the effects of social media on our society, and your generation in particular.'

The bell rang. She stepped out, bag under her arm as soon as the sound finished. Behind her the air was thick; you could have made bricks out of it.

Mark, who hadn't said anything during the class, rushed past Karl.

'Sorry Karl.'

There was some laughter. Some embarrassed silence. Some complaining. Pairs and little groups ready to debrief.

Another one of those. The discussions. It seemed it had got better lately.

Karl stomped out, almost running, all the way out of the building. Abu followed but made no eye contact and went left once they were outside college.

'Karl, wait.' Nalini and Afsana caught up with him. 'What's up with Abu?'

They turned around, and caught the last of his red sweater turning into a small side street at the far end.

'Ask him.'

The air had followed Karl but the heaviness went mush now. He wiped over his eyes. Afsana looked the other way, polite like that. No words. Nalini just stood still and felt him, like in giving him some space. It was a moment. Then the noise from the gate bubbled closer and when they looked back, the wannabes, with Leicester at the front, were coming up behind them, shouting and laughing, spreading out over the width of the pavement.

'Ignore them.' Nalini pulled Karl by his hand. Afsana skipped in front of them.

'Are you both also like, so tired of them? OMG I could like die, for real, that's how tired I am.'

She walked backwards while watching them. The gap was closing.

'Where is your spokesman? Didn't have anything to say for yourself in class, did you?'

'Oh, you got something to say again Nalini?' Leicester was cocking his head.

Nalini was warming up. They had been here before, facing each other, about other things. She was ready to let him know a few of her thoughts.

'Leave it.' Karl let go of Nalini's hand. 'It's not worth it, Nalini. If they want to get me, let them.'

'They ain't even going to do anything. Not while we're here,' Nalini replied.

He was turning into the street where the estate Abu lived in lined up nicely with the other buildings. It was quiet here, just resident traffic, and not many cars at that. You could hear the big junction, King's Cross, heaving away a couple of streets down. But here you were in the shadow. Not all that clear.

The group caught up with them. One grabbed Karl's bag.

'You can try but it ain't the real thing.'

Karl didn't seem scared. His eyes glazed over and he disappeared. Lashes all cute and curved. Didn't look like a dream, but he was far away, that was for sure.

'Where's your Abu? Finally left you? I might ask him to join us, now that he has seen sense.'

'Yeah right.' Karl pulled his bag back and focused his dreamy eyes on the other side of the street. 'I see you later. Thanks you two.'

When he arrived at Abu's, Abu wasn't there. Mama Abu was playing with the twins so Karl went into in the kitchen. Abu's father was standing by the window, looking over to the other estate.

'Good day at college, Karl?'

'Not really.'

Baba Abu was a serious-looking man. Kind eyes but tired face that made it look sad, always looking at you slightly too long. You'd get all shifty. There was too much seeing there, too much space. Space you couldn't hide in.

'You know, I never thought I'd end up here.'

'I thought you were born here.'

'I was. I mean here. In a little council flat where you can see your neighbours doing all sorts of things.'

Karl followed his hand. One floor down, in the corner apartment opposite a young man was doing a headstand. It was impressive; completely straight line. Except, he wasn't wearing any clothes. There were two others behind him. Naked as well.

'Last week they still had on swimming trunks. It's obviously getting too warm. Or this is the advanced class.'

'It is obvious, to me at least, that this is far from advanced.' Baba Abu's eyes didn't move. The two behind the man kept falling back down.

This time the tears were from laughter. Karl blew his nose.

Baba Abu turned around. 'At your age people are not always very understanding.'

Karl shrugged and sat down.

'I'm not even sure if patience will help so I'm not going to advise you to be patient.' He sat down at the table. Karl got up and stood by the door.

'Sit with me.'

Karl sat back down. It was hard. This staying. In the moment.
Here, now. His legs were typing Morse code on the kitchen
floor, if you could still talk of Morse code.

'I have no idea what it means, how to do it.'

'What?' Karl's bopping stopped for a split sec.

'Being alive, being a man.'

That was the thing with Abu's dad. Too deep for a mid-week
afternoon but Karl fell for it each time. So many questions.
Good ones. Sometimes just asking was enough.

'In a way there is no sense to it. Everyone does it the way
they think is right. For some it involves inversions without
clothes on. Now are we going to get into a state just because
their private parts are hanging the wrong way? Or are we
going to let them get on with it and focus on our own lives?'

They were sitting next to each other, staring at the window.
From the table they couldn't see the naked headstand class.
That was the thing with views. It depended on the angle.

'All I can advise you is to get on with your own life.
Everything else is not doing yourself a favour.'

Karl nodded. Yes, it was sound. The advice. And he had
heard it before. Minus the naked blokes opposite of course.

'One thing I think you do need to do is talk to your mother.
Going off like that ... I don't think that is the right decision.'

And the nervousness returned.

'You are not good at that. Addressing the things that need
addressing.'

Everyone knew it but it was rare that Karl sat through a
whole laying it on the table.

'Sometimes in life it doesn't matter if you're good at it or
not. You just have to do it.'

The older man raised his arms, the palms facing away from
his body and folded over, his head following. It was meant
to be the start to a headstand. They both laughed. Then it
got all sober again. Proper.

'I don't agree with Godfrey, Karl. She deserves to be talked
to. Confide in her. Your mother ...' He was waiting for Karl
to look at him. Karl's eyes only passed his, couldn't settle to
exchange anything. Baba Abu lifted himself slightly. 'There
is no need to make this a secret. You are disappointed with
her, I understand that. But this is your chance to talk.'

The pattern of the kitchen floor was rubbed out by too
many chairs scratching over the linoleum. The brown and

beige geometric pattern had become indistinct. Washed out. Karl could hear the twins competing with each other for their mother's approval. Outside, the afternoon noises got louder. More people on the road, start of rush hour. Traffic would be thick. The warming of the weather meant even in this slow street there was more commotion, more walking, more cycling. It would die down in a couple of hours.

'Where were you?'
'Not your business, is it?'
'Like that? Wow.'
'What's your problem, Karl? What is it?'
'You're asking me? What's yours?'
Abu's bag went flying into the corner of the tiny room. He followed it with a dramatic plonk on to the bed. Overacting all the way. Karl pulled out the mattress from underneath the bed. Placed himself on it. Folded his arms behind his head and looked at the ceiling.
'Not leaving *you*. Just going. Going *to* Nigeria. I have to.'
'Some guy appears out of nowhere, some guy you don't even know and in one minute all you talk about is Uncle T.'
'Chill man, that's not even true.'
Abu stretched his legs over the edge of the bed. 'Did they bother you?'
'You care now?'
There was silence, both of them thinking, waiting, gauging each other, waiting some more.
'You are a baby, Abu. Man, I can't even believe it.'
'Shut up. You're not the one who has to stay. They're going to deal with me when you're gone.'
'They don't really care about you.'
Abu shook his head and scoffed. 'Is that why I get punched every other day? Sorry, must have got that mixed up.'
A knock at the door, then Mama Abu's face appeared. She held the door open with one hand, her body still in the hallway.
'Are you two ready?'
Dinner time. She studied their faces.
'Oh no, I wanted to help. I'm sorry, got carried away.' Karl jumped up and smoothed his T-shirt.
'You don't have to try so hard. She likes you already.'
'Abu, what is that for?' His mother was not having it.
'He's always trying to impress you. It's not necessary.'

'Abu, I said what is that for.'

In other words: leave it. The mostly silent-communication mother could, when she wanted to, throw some very well placed words. Both of them uncomfortable now. So much stuff hanging in the air it was making you feel all tight in your chest. How could you sort through it all?

'We're coming.'

Mama Abu waited. Wasn't going to leave like that. She didn't raise rude kids, no not at all. Abu got off the bed, avoiding his mother's eyes, head turned the other way.

'Sorry. We're coming in a minute.'

Behind her the silence returned. Karl. Abu. The neighbourhood. Karl got beaten less because Abu stepped into the line of fire. It had become a thing of pride for Abu. You don't leave your bestie to be attacked. You take care of that shit, as he liked to say. Not that he could; one dreamy Karl and one Abu against a bunch of haters ... too much even for Abu's big mouth. But still. You tried. Best friend's honour.

9

**Coming and going is easy;
arriving is an art.**

Karl finally stepped off the plane in Port Harcourt. There had been a wait when they stopped in Lagos but those flying on were not allowed to leave the plane. He needed to stretch his legs. Properly. Not the tight walking up and down the aisle one. Uncle T was behind him, already on his phone, already doing what he seemed to be doing all the time: business. He had chatted to Karl about it. About the Italian leather loafers he imported, and the handbags and dresses. And the shea butter products he was so proud of. New thing. Would take off. Once he got it right, he would manufacture in Nigeria, but for now he was working with someone in Italy. Old business friend. Uncle T had talked about all the nice things he brought to Nigeria, which could be bought for very nice prices. The shop he had started with and the wholesale he was now doing, which included shipping containers and frequent trips to Italy. Had made an effort, sincere and all, to draw the teenager in, show him his world.

But Karl and his inner thought process was busy with the voice of his father, which he had heard a few times during the past weeks. Always short, awkward conversations. Had learned that he worked for one of the oil companies in the area. Piping field engineer. Karl asked, 'What is that then?' but he answered in *it's obviously designing and maintaining pipes and doing stress analysis innit,* which meant zero point zero to Karl. No bloody explanation. They did not have the same flow as Uncle T and he did. Adebanjo did not have the same pulling-the-youth-in, all-warm-and-cosy style. But then Uncle T had a seventeen-year advantage. Godfrey said it like

that. Uncle T had known about Karl for that long. Adebanjo
was still catching up.

Karl had no clue about his father's work. What made sense
were Uncle T's spotless outfits. And his well-moisturised
hands and face, the good-smelling body. Uncle T was about
to launch the whole cosmetic range. He was a caring-about-
appearance guy in more than a few ways.

Karl was heading into the gooey air Uncle T had warned
him about. The seasons. Different to the UK. Even the rain.
'Normally it is very hot, but it is rainy season.' He laughed.
'You will see. Sometimes the cars look like they are swimming.'
The sky was cloudy. A blanket of white hung low as if it
was going to bang down on the people underneath. Force
them to lie down. Have their arms spread wide, like in an
ambush. A bit like the police trying for the brown youth.
Uncle T had told him about the downpours that could make
water levels rise in the city because there was nowhere for
it to escape to. Traffic stopped as it rose calf-high, drainage
not prepared enough. An hour later the water would have
done a runner, metaphorically speaking, and people would
be on their way again. Often it was better to wait it out. Stay
somewhere until the rain stopped, until the water had found
nooks and crannies it could escape through. But not now.
Maybe it was his welcome, spare his good trainers from
getting soaked. He walked, leaning forward into the humid
wall that was the air, holding tightly to the backpack from
Godfrey.

'Return it, please. And I want to see you back here in two
weeks.'

A cheesy smile in reply. It had almost pushed Godfrey over,
it was so sudden, after all their hard-fought battles. Just like
the heat was laying its heavy arm on Karl now, trying to push
him, trying to get him to lose control of his gangly limbs.

'OK then,' Godfrey had return-smiled. 'And updates. You
hear me? Daily updates. Text messages when you can't call
but phone calls if you can. And that is not a question.'

Uncle T gently pushed from behind to help him along, so
Karl raised his shoulders quickly, the bag positioning itself
neatly (enough) on his shoulders. He looked back. Uncle
T was talking fast – it seemed urgent – but he was smiling
at Karl, apologies in his eyes. Karl walked through the
boarding bridge and although he was warm and muggy and

with luggage, he felt light, floaty. All romantic, blurry-eyed, you know how that shit gets you. He was *here*.

The phone found connection almost immediately. A text. Roaming rates. Expensive. Super expensive. Karl was relieved he had let Abu talk him into getting a Blackberry the previous year. He hadn't been convinced at first. They were ugly, man, nothing for style as far as Karl was concerned. But it was cheap. The messaging. Free. That's if you had data loaded up. You couldn't do better than that. At least he would be able to keep Abu in the know. He wasn't so sure about the others with other phones. Godfrey. Rebecca. But he didn't plan on making himself available to them so much. Baba Abu's words kept repeating on him like a heavy dinner since that day they sat in the kitchen. *There is no need to make this a secret.* But Karl hadn't told her. All this talking they had done. All the *how close were they* and *was everything going fine, family-wise.* And not one mention of Uncle T. Who had come to see him. His mother who was all *we're equal and in this together.* He had nothing to say to Rebecca.

It was cooler inside the building, but he wasn't prepared for this. The people! The chaos in front of him made his vision blurry. He couldn't make out where to go. Everyone seemed to know what to do, where to be, and one-sided conversations raised the volume levels. Phones. Everyone on theirs, talking, telling of the arrival, asking where pickups were. The lot. At least that's what he thought. The noise. As if a tap had been turned on. Gush. In one go.

Uncle T caught up and pushed again. Karl had a hard time moving. There was a family of six, mother with a baby in one arm and a stylish handbag in the other, father with two oversized carry-ons and the other three kids, varying in size, with a matching set of adult backpacks, brand-new, attached to their backs. One of the kids was so small that Karl couldn't see the back of his head, just the rounded zipper bit of the backpack. There was a group of friends, students, Karl assumed, in the trendiest sportswear, speaking into the latest mobiles, pushing past him while joking and egging each other on. What Karl didn't know. Their words were lost in the rest of the commotion. There were purposeful people with determined looks who didn't deviate from their way out. They pushed through the crowd with long strides. Karl's head was spinning.

'Let's go.'

Uncle T had finished his phone call. He pointed ahead, past the sea of black people.

'You queue over there.'

It was hard enough to stay level with this much newness. The sounds, the smells, the colourful outfits interspersed with sports and business wear. He felt lost. And scared. How to fit in here? How to even try?

But this part, immigration, produced even more dizziness. This was only sweat. Nothing else. No question mark, no slow trying to catch your feet. Just bare panic. He closed his eyes for a second. *Breathe man, just breathe.* He could hear Abu. The visa was approved, the Port Harcourt address verified. All he needed was for it to go quick. No overzealous immigration officer, aka gender police in the making. Karl took out the mobile again.

heat man!!! no rain in site. @ passport control. Im here. Cant believ it. All gud so far. wish me luck

An officer in a beige uniform walked along the queue that was forming. What his role was supposed to be was a bit difficult to see. The foreigners from the plane were lining up with Karl. It was easy to spot the lot of them, either white or light-skinned, like Karl, almost as if they were carrying signs: *really not from here.* They were all older than Karl, mostly male, travelling by themselves with little luggage. Their faces were getting sweaty, like Karl's, but theirs were changing to much deeper red tones. There was a general wiping going on, a couple of chequered handkerchiefs, back of the hand wipe – that sort of thing.

Uncle T had disappeared to the other end of the small hall.

Karl's eyes followed the officer who stood next to a burly bloke with one large bag hanging over his shoulder. They were shaking hands and a few notes were slipped from one palm to the other. The officer caught Karl staring and Karl focused on his trainers instead. The burly man proceeded to the raised immigration booth and exchanged a few words with the officer behind the glass before leaving the queue and the airport altogether.

'You have something for me?' The man in beige appeared next to Karl.

Karl shook his head. 'Sorry?'

The line was moving faster than he had thought. A lot of the white men in the queue had someone waiting for them, someone in uniform who would fast track them down the line, past the raised booth and out.

The officer looked at Karl. 'What did you bring for me?'

'I'm sorry.' Karl swivelled around. Where was Uncle T when you needed him?

'Anything.'

'I'm sorry? I don't understand. It's my first time. My uncle ...'

The officer didn't hide his pity and waved him forward. He had arrived at the raised booth and the man took his passport from his shaking hand and gave it to the man inside the booth. Another officer. He took the passport, looked at the picture, looked at Karl. Karl made himself scarce, pulled himself away from his skin, disappearing inside his bloodstream so that nothing on the outside could touch him. But the guy was still looking. Staring. No bloody subtleness at all, just full-on fixation. Curious and shit but unmoved, no smile, no softening, no invitation to exchange a few pleasantries. Nothing. Then waved to the supervisor behind him, who disengaged from the guy he was chatting with, in slow motion. Before he could make it to them, officer number three arrived, a guy who had been inside the building, further down, closer to the exit. Number three placed his folded arms on the rim of the small cubicle. He was about to tell officers number one and two, the one walking Karl over and the one in the box, something funny. You could see that because he was already smiling about it, like he knew this was a real good one. When he opened his mouth officer two shoved the passport in his face.

'Ah ah, they no know how to dress demselves. Dis one, no be woman ...'

Officer number three, unimpressed, still smiling, licked his lips. Looked at the picture, but didn't really. Didn't care one single bit.

'My friend, leave am now. No be our problem.'

Karl smiled. That shy, *I'm so damn unaware of my charm but I'm throwing everything your way* smile. *Because right now I need it to work, I need that charm to charm you out of asking me too many questions, out of extending this, making it obvious for everyone around. Embarrassing me. Hurting me. Making this unbearable.*

And dangerous.

That's it. Someone had sense, he would be moving on in no time, just like most of the white dudes who had been in the queue before him. All he had to do was get some damn oxygen into his body so he wouldn't collapse right here. Before he had officially made it to Nigeria. Breathing in, breathing out, one two, one two. Focus on pairs instead of the throng of officials shuffling around the little cubicle. Officer number two was flipping through the passport pages, thumb cinema-like. Officer one was casually looking at it and then at Karl again. Only Spain, otherwise no other country had ever seen this gathering of well-stitched pages.

The supervisor arrived.

Four of them now; officer number three still shrugging his shoulders, ready to move on, finally drop that story. Who cared about whatever it was; it was a long time until they were off; why make life harder by winding yourself up like that? And right at the start of their shift?

'Wetin worry you? Leave am now. De family will tell am.'

Karl looked at Uncle T, who had walked through the Nigerian citizens' line and was now far ahead. A questioning look. Karl quickly shaking his head, vigorously. Number four, the supervisor, followed his glance.

'Your father?'

'Uncle.'

The officer looked back and forth between them.

'But my father is waiting for me,' Karl added, the word unfamiliar, almost sideways in his mouth. The puddle of sweat on his lower back was descending, trickling between his cheeks into his underwear. Father. Even more foreign than his first experience of the country. 'He is outside.'

Number four's face stopped doing what it was doing midway, the expression frozen. And like his face, time was now freezing over, sucking out all movement until everything became unreal, dangerously flat, a wall that would collapse and bury you in its debris.

Number three was looking around, trying to find someone else to chat with because this was defo no chatting whatsoever. Not what he had in mind when he had come over. Number two was still staring at Karl. At the long T-shirt that was hanging over his jeans. The trainers that were holding the jeans up, as it seemed. Number one? Had nowhere else to be, nothing else to do.

It was a bit much. The attention. The waiting. The not saying much. A whole group of people, yet again focus on Karl.

'Your father is outside?'

Number four seemed to have recovered. Karl nodded, eyes sending nothing cute and charming any more just good old *please*. Pleading. But number four was already reaching inside the booth. Fumbled around. Then a quick stamp. Officer two shook his head. Supervisor handed the passport to Karl, 'Welcome to Nigeria', ignored everyone else and walked off.

Officer two annoyed. Disapproving.

'Na crazy, dis one.'

But there was nothing else to be done. The group dispersed. Karl was through and out the other side.

Uncle T, who was already close to the exit, talking to a man slightly shorter than him, his round face much darker, a tone that glowed attentively, a bit like Nalini's make-up on a fresh winter day. He had a kind of stiff appearance, not quite as confident as Uncle T.

Karl slowed down. Stopped. The air fell, dropped on to him. Again. The weight of it all.

Uncle T turned around. He was speaking very fast with the dark-skinned man, who in turn inspected his shoes, then travelled with his eyes to Uncle T's face, looking like he had done something, his shoulders pulled up to his ears. Uncle T's hands were rotating like windshield wipers now. The man looked younger than Uncle T, as if he was barely making it out of his twenties. Fresh-faced and nervous.

Karl? Transfixed, stared at the exit door, holding on to his backpack. No one had said what he was supposed to do. Stand next to them? Wait? You would think there were instructions, that they would have thought about that. You would think these things were clear. Arrival. The father. And *then* improvise. But it was sort of before all of that. Arrival, yes. But to what? Didn't the father say, 'We look forward to welcoming you'? Why did the welcome exclude him? And why did it piss off Uncle T?

fear /fɪə/
noun

1. Emotion alerting you: there might be a threat
   of danger, pain, or harm here.

verb

1. Feeling that something that is to come, either
   by or through someone or an action, is likely to
   be dangerous, painful, or harmful.

Uncle T saw Karl standing and turned around. Took Karl's
hand, grabbed the backpack with his other, and started to
walk, pulling Karl along.

'Why is he not coming over here?' Karl asked. 'He doesn't
look like he wants to see me.'

'Karl.' Uncle T stopped before they reached the now smiling
man with two rows of very evenly formed if not oversized
teeth.

'Karl … This is not your father.' He paused for a second,
his assuredness wavering for the tiniest bit. You could have
missed it, Uncle T was that good, but it was there. Worry.

'This is John, your father's driver and assistant.'

In the way he said it, the way he had stopped walking and
held Karl's hand, looking away slightly, it was already clear.
Something was off here. If Karl hadn't sweated so much at
immigration, he probably would have smelled it all along.

'Where is he then? At home?' His voice was croaky. The
words hurt when they forced themselves out of his mouth.

John was walking towards them, dragging Uncle T's
supersized rolling suitcase behind him, squashing the
protective space between them. Soon there wasn't anything
left, no buffer whatsoever. Karl felt like turning back, running
back through security, telling them to not worry, he would
not upset dress codes any longer. Instead he would be sitting
in the plane, waiting for it to refuel, then straight back to
London. To King's Cross. To Abu.

John extended his hand, his lips parted, the smile
overwhelming. Those teeth, *wow!* They came forward in
one coordinated long jump.

'Welcome Karl. I am John. I am a distant cousin of your
Uncle Tunde's wife.'

Uncle T was nodding. Yes, family, distant, but still. Without
thinking, Karl took the hand, like a robot, and shook. His
eyes full of questions, the shoulders so low now they could
have mopped the floor.

'Your father couldn't be here.' John shot a quick look at Uncle T, then smiled again.

Panic rose in Karl, making his feet itch. He needed to clear his head ASAP or he would explode.

Uncle T put his arm around his shoulders. 'My friend.' He drew him in. 'Nephew. Ah ah, the new addition to our family!'

He smiled here, waited for a second to cement his sincerity. Impart it on to Karl. The *you are welcome here. I will take care of you. I promised.*

'Don't worry, it is well.' And he looked at John. 'Your father had to take care of a few things unexpectedly and could not be here. But you are welcome. Very welcome! Now the two of us will have time to get to know each other even better.'

The smile became a laugh now, meant to snap them all out of the awkwardness that had descended so suddenly it popped your ears. His hand patted Karl's shoulder.

'Don't worry. It is well. We should be moving on. You must be hungry. And tired.'

Karl nodded absentmindedly. He should have stayed home. King's Cross. Safe. Take some out-of-control youths any day.

His mobile beeped and buzzed. A text. His hand went for the phone in his jeans, fingers automatically unlocking it, pressing view. You could think they were born that way, the young'uns, movements coordinated in response to the latest tech in their front pockets.

so whats he like? Abu.

Karl stared at the screen, then at John, who was smiling, taking him in, somehow already down with Karl, already sure that theirs would be a good connection. Karl thought about the father who was MIA. And his mother. Had the father done a runner on her as well?

'Please let me take that.' John took the backpack from Uncle T, swung it on to the giant suitcase, and smiled at them both.

'Let us go. The car is over there.'

And walked off. Uncle T pushed. Karl's legs responded, unconsciously, obedient.

And now it was here. The Nigeria. With Karl in it.

The heat slapped him. He felt like holding on to something and grabbed at Uncle T's shirtsleeve, but the well-dressed man's stride was too quick and Karl missed him. And there was the noise again, like a swarm of bees on steroids. Miced up to the max. All was quick and slow at the same time.

Loud and muted. The walk to the car, through the crowds
of people, unorganised but all on a mission and not shy of
explaining so, in raised voices and accents and languages
Karl didn't understand, meeting their relatives who were
waiting, or their friends who were overjoyed to see them,
past the porters who rushed over and tried to grab their
bags but who both John and Uncle T waved away, past the
only people who were not rushing or loud or purposeful: the
airport personnel – they stood or leaned or sat in slowed
timing, dragging out every second leisurely to make it meet
the end of their shift sooner. People were staring at Karl
and smiling and saying things he couldn't hear because his
ears were not cooperating. He couldn't make out individual
sounds, then it faded away, and he saw moving mouths in
slo-mo, the volume turned off.

They pushed through the exit door, past the taxi drivers
who offered their services, offering all sorts of rates and
making all sorts of promises. Karl shook his head and shook
off hands that were grabbing him and kept himself upright.
Here. He. Was.

Finally they entered the vehicle. Karl in the back. John
driving, Uncle T chatting away from the front seat.

*This is the airport road. This is this. This is another this.
And this info belongs to this another this. It is related to that
(story etc.) and ah you will understand later. You see here?
Another this.*

Karl couldn't hear his words properly, brain racing so hard
there was no space for them to enter, but he tried to take in
the scenes, the sound the crickets made in the fading light.
Chirping, charging the air that started to feel less heavy, as
it was cooling now. The people, the noises, the roads they
bumped over, the holes they tried to avoid and sometimes
proper rattled over. The houses that looked like they were
shedding skin, like they needed moisturiser, TLC. A lick of
paint.

There were low-level buildings that looked like shacks, set
back from the road, large puddles in the dirt in front. Rusty
cars parked aside. Then some real shacks with aluminium
roofs. A few high-rise buildings in grey with no windows or
doors, or anything at all once Karl looked closer, nothing
but its cement shell. Blocks of missed opportunities, some
wood scaffolding still attached. Flats to be.

The traffic put King's Cross in the shade like proper. They were moving but Karl could see other large streets with several rows of cars in one lane. Completely chock-a-block, complete standstill. No movement whatsoever.

Uncle T was commentating on everything. The first images of Nigeria. All Karl could see of him was the back of his head, turning when explaining why the roads were so bad, which area this was. The wind that entered through the car windows was soft and lukewarm. It patted Karl's face like the gentle caress his aunt would give him when she visited his mother and found him in the flat, in his room for once. That was, of course, before Piers, her proper lovely proper asshole husband, spoiled things for them, aunt–nephew-wise.

When they arrived at the gated estate, it was completely dark. A security guard sat in the small booth that flanked the large iron gates, which had to be opened in the middle. A candle was flickering, casting shadows through the window opening. Was all a bit suspense thriller. You could hear the music. It would be proper slow, creepy.

The other guard had his foot on the cement step to the booth. His arm was leaning on the narrow wooden plank drilled into its wall. You could hear the piano banging on the same note now. *Ti-ng ti-ng*. Still slow though.

Both guards had been looking at a magazine. One turned and walked towards the window. John had already opened it. The guard pointed his flashlight inside the car, waving it around as if he was saying something with it. Now the music would be getting ready for some real tempo. *Ting ting ting*. Some sonic landscaping ambience shit in the background.

'Good evening sah.' He nodded towards Uncle T.

'Good evening.'

'Sah no dey?'

'He no dey.' Uncle T replied. *Ting ting ting ting ting*.

John took the guard's hand and started shaking it while his stare was planted firmly on Karl's face. He was saying something to John in a low voice, chuckling.

'Na so.'

Then the hands left each other and he stepped back. Sound would drop out here, completely. Danger averted. Although it seemed that no one but Karl had felt any anyway.

'Good evening.' The guard tipped the rim of his cap and John pressed the button at the front panel. The window glided back up until there was just a little slit at the top. They pulled up at another set of smaller gates, only for the house, not the whole street. A young man jumped up and ran to unlock the metal chain that kept it closed. John drove into the space next to the house. It was completely dark. You couldn't even see your own thoughts.

'NEPA. Dis country!' John muttered with disappointment.

'Our electricity company. NEPA. Karl. That is the name. We used to call it Never Ever Power At All.'

Like I'm supposed to know what you mean. Went over his head, like most of Uncle T's comments since their arrival. Uncle T slammed the door shut, cursing. All one swift action. Bang. Door shut. Body in absolute darkness. Frustration exploding now. The young man disappeared to the back and then a motor started and light flickered into action, showing them all where they were. John opened the door at Karl's side.

'Come.' His hand briefly met Karl's T-shirt sleeve. Karl flinched. 'Please. This is your father's house.'

There wasn't much to see yet. It looked more like a bungalow than a house. One storey, a front yard that had a terraced entrance with large sliding doors, a regular-sized wooden door at the side. Plants in tiled squares flanked both edges of the house. Uncle T was talking to the young man. Karl could now see his washed-out trousers. The grey had patches of dust and dark marks on them. His once-white shirt was now a grey/beige/brownish affair, unbuttoned.

Uncle T waited for John, who had got the large bag out of the trunk. He nodded a greeting to the guard and quickly strode up to the tiled terrace to the wooden door. He took a key out and opened it.

'Karl, come.'

Uncle T waved him closer. Karl took a step, then another. Time stood still. It was partly the thick air, the loud crickets, the arrival, the tiredness. The body dragged across an ocean, from one continent to another. Dragged because Karl hadn't slept the night before, but spent it talking with Abu. Abu would have been at school today, last two weeks before the summer break. Jealous that Karl got holiday early.

'Is only 'cause Uncle T can't come back again before the winter innit.'

'Still. I will have to sit through the whole thing when I could be checking the Nigerian ladies.'

Karl rolled on the mattress, laughing. 'And since when do you speak to the ladies? You, who never shuts up, as soon as a girl comes your way, you're pissing yourself, or off into the sunset. By your bloody self.'

Abu let that one slide. Was true, no point dwelling on the fact. They imagined how this Nigeria would be. How Karl's father would be. There was no getting around that this is where Karl was at, metaphorically speaking, and would be at, physically speaking, so Abu just had to get on with it. Get over himself. Enjoy the whole thing. Like they did. Even when they were not together. Sharing.

What should Karl ask him, what should he look out for? They had laughed, moving from their backs, their eyes staring into the dark room, at the ceiling. Abu on his single bed, Karl on the guest mattress. At the exact same moment, they both turned to lean on their forearms. They giggled even more.

'Oh my days. Imitating me, are we? Got none of your own impulses?'

'I was first.'

'What are you looking up for anyway? Too dark.'

'Why are you?'

'You keep talking. I'm awake.'

'No point sleeping now. Not long till you have to get up, bruv.'

Karl had gone to see Rebecca early. Had told her what they had all told her over the past weeks, minus Mama Abu, who said: 'Leave me out of it; I won't lie to her.'

'So, I'll be off, mum. Text me any time. I will be in touch anyway but probably not call. Just to be away like proper. Really immerse myself, you understand?'

Rebecca looked at Godfrey with that same *this makes no sense whatsoever* look that Mama Abu had about the whole thing. Only Mama Abu had not told her either. She just avoided her altogether. Still called, but didn't drop in that often. That morning, Godfrey busied himself in a cheerful manner. Smiled his fake smile and left with Karl as quickly as they could.

Uncle T was still outside. Karl could hear him talking with
the guard in the courtyard. He was standing in the spacious
lounge, unsure. The smells were different. The crickets were
still at it, proper concert.

'You need anything? Water, food? There are things in the
freezer. The cook was here the day before yesterday. Let
me get something for you. Please sit. Sit.'

'No, water is fine, thank you.' He was here. How mad was
that?

John sat with him.

'You work with my father?'

John turned towards him. 'Yes. For many years now.'

'What's he like?'

Uncle T came back before John could reply. He was all
business mode, nodding, already starting on a new phone call,
which he left to take inside the bungalow somewhere. Karl
was on a white leather couch that faced the large flat-screen
TV on the wall. John handed the water to Karl, switched on
the TV and left him sitting alone.

'Has John shown you the guest room yet? I will be sleeping
next door to you. We share the bathroom. Your father's room
is at the other end. John showed you everything?'

'No.' Karl sank into the cushions. His feet a couple of
centimetres off the floor. It was good to have some space after
the cramped flight. 'He went to do something at the back.'

'Ah yes, he is checking the generator. Whether there's
enough fuel.'

'What for?'

'Light.' Uncle T looked like he didn't quite get it, then a
light switched on in his brain. 'The electricity, it goes off.
Often. The people who can afford it use generators.'

'Makes sense now. The noise.'

'Yes, that noise,' Uncle T seemed to be relaxing now. 'You
will get used to it.' And with his confident stride he marched
to the kitchen to get water for himself. 'Or not.' He laughed.
'It's just one of those things.'

Karl nodded although Uncle T couldn't see him.

'And all the security?'

'That's another of the things. You will get used to it as well.
A lot of problems in this country, a lot of security is needed.
If you can afford it.'

'I see.' Although Karl didn't get shit. Gates to lock off the whole bloody street?

'This is a gated community. Only employees and their families of the oil company your father works for live here.'

'My father ...'

'Don't worry about that now. It is well! We will take care of everything. Do you want to eat? Are you ready to try our food?'

'I still have the sandwich from the plane. I probably just need to lie down soon. Very long day.' Karl looked around. 'Is he coming tonight?'

'No, not tonight. I will explain. Don't worry, trust me. It has been a long day.' Uncle T nodded. 'Come, I'll show you the room.'

There wasn't anything spectacular to it. A small landing led to a door left, a door right, and a door ahead. The bathroom was ahead. The bedrooms either side. His room was covered with a mosaic pattern made from stone and had a wall-to-wall built-in wardrobe. The bed was in the middle, pushed against the wall, facing the window, which had proper heavy curtains. *Keeping shit out* curtains. *No peeping here whatsoever.* A small desk on the side. Uncle T picked up a remote from the table and pointed it to the air conditioner at the wall.

'The two rooms are for when his ...' He broke off.

'His children?'

Karl had already seen the toys stacked neatly at the bottom of the right side of the wardrobe. A cardboard box with a remote-controlled car pictured on it. There were other things. A football, some PlayStation games, a children's encyclopaedia (a matter of seven books). Uncle T followed Karl's look.

'I don't think he plays with them any more. Maybe the football. He's much too old for that toy car.'

Karl nodded. There was a gap, another one, between the bringing him all the way here, and finding what was here. Those were two bloody different things.

'If you need anything please knock on the door. I don't sleep very much. I will hear you. Don't be shy. OK?'

Karl nodded. 'Thanks.'

'The bed, all is fresh. The house help came yesterday.'

More nodding.

'The soap, towels: in the bathroom. Everything you need should be there.'

Karl smiled; there wasn't really anything else to do. It was bloody awkward.

'Thank you for everything.'

'I'm sorry Karl. This is not how you imagined your welcome in your country.'

'No, it's fine. Thank you for bringing me. Three months ago I didn't even know that there was such a thing as my country. Obviously it's not my country, I just mean ...'

'I understand.' He paused and sought out Karl's eyes. 'Try to rest. I will do anything to make your visit here as perfect as it can be.' His face changed. This was a dangerous thing. What he had just said. You shouldn't set out to fail like that, to drop all the way from perfection to reality. It had already flopped in less than twenty-four hours.

'Karl, I will be at your every service, as they say. '

The pause megaphoned their thoughts; it was all very obvious. The tension. Bloody hell. Uncle T patted his back again. Karl cringed. It had already become a rather unwelcome habit, this play-hitting. However gentle Uncle thought it was, it was also proper strong. Like in hurting you a bit.

'Good night.' Uncle T's good-trouser-cladded legs carried him out of the room. That was defo close to perfection. His walk. Idris Elba as Stringer Bell had nothing on him. He turned one last time and smiled before closing the door.

Karl went to the bathroom. He undressed and stood in the bathtub. Although he had only turned on the cold tap, the water was lukewarm. He could see himself in the mirror over the sink. His lanky body. The puberty blockers meant the breasts hadn't developed. Tiniest buds. With a tight vest you couldn't see anything. He didn't even need to bind them. The day washed off him. The sweat, the panic, the newness, fled his body straight down past the triangle of hair, down his legs into the drain. He was glad for the quiet in the flat. It seemed like Uncle T had gone back to the living room.

The next morning, Karl woke to the sound of the generator. It worked itself into his dream and instead of the buzzing his mother said: *But when will you be back? What is it you're looking for, Karl?* She was lying in the bed like when he had visited her on her last stint in hospital. Her voice was different, rhythmic and even, without any breaks and with authority that was unusual for her. Karl wasn't sure if she could see him. He was looking at her from the ceiling, floating above her, his back scraping against it.

Some things can never be found. They are not what they seem.
The generator seemed to spurt. Then it was quiet.

The light rose, revealing a dull morning, the sun concealed by the clouds again. Karl was thirsty and warm. The sheet was tangled up in-between his legs. There was a strange quiet now that nothing was coming from the backside of the house.

10

**What is being, anyway,
if not the way we are
measuring the absence?**

Uncle T knocked. He wanted to take Karl along to a business meeting. They could talk then. Could he get ready?

Karl dressed in his loosest jeans and a plain grey T-shirt. What was the effing dress code?

John arrived, walking in with a plastic bag, leaving his worn-out slippers at the door. He waved and greeted Karl, who couldn't follow the exchange. The words climbed, played some melody before they stayed open, then left.

'Yes sah. Yes sah.'

The phone rang and Uncle T disappeared with another apologetic look.

'We call him Blackberry Plus.' John winked. 'Don't tell him. Just a little fun, you understand. Because he carries so many phones.'

Karl laughed. 'I noticed.'

'His business is going well, so his phone is ringing. He works hard but he likes his phones too much. Each time he comes back, a new one. Blackberry, iPhone, Samsung. Everything. When a new model comes out, sah, he wants it.'

'What does "sah" mean?'

John stopped mid-flow, startled for a second. Then the healthy teeth moved out of the mouth with his smile. The teeth were something one could hang on to. Very assuring.

'You say it to a man, when you give respect.'

'Oh. Just *sir*?' Shit, how simple was that? Karl was losing his touch.

'Yes. Nothing special. Just "sir".'

John twisted the word so it sounded closer to how Karl had said it.

Karl's skin scrounged up, like one of Abu's T-shirts tossed into the back of the cupboard. Embarrassment.

'I will bring you something to eat when we are at the office? Or, you are too hungry?'

Karl shook his head and sat down. John nodded, still smiling.

'Just waiting for your uncle.'

'Yes, I understand.' He went back to the room and sat on the bed. His backpack was neatly placed in the corner by the window. The clothes from the day before hung on the back of the chair, trying to lose some of the panic-sweat smell. Karl would wash them out later. Once Uncle T told him where the washing machine was. Or washing powder. Karl could do it by hand. He had options. Uncle T called from the front of the house. Minutes later they were all on their way.

'It's one of my business partners. Friend, really. I often conduct meetings there when I'm in town.'

John weaved the car through the tight traffic. They were drowning in a sea of vehicles. They had to crawl forward bit by bit. It cleared once they made it to their exit and there was more to see. People were on their way to work. Obviously, it being morning and all. They passed a small shopping centre in terracotta. Karl wouldn't have known it was one if he hadn't caught the sign. A few metres past the wall that separated it from the street was a little congregation of people, a couple of battered minivans pulled in, young men hanging out, shouting. Some of the people responding, the congregation divided, everyone rushing in, filling the van to the max.

At the office, Karl was introduced to everyone. It was painful. Uncle T's business friend, a large man in crisp clothing, looked like he was modelling an *African American Golfer's Digest* outfit. They were obviously a good match, friend-wise. It was good to have things in common. He shook Karl's hand and asked him about the football season. Karl knew only that it was not on in July. Parked for the summer. Heads popped up from nowhere and multiplied like no man's business. All curious, all smiling, all talking and shaking Karl's hand, all eyeing him, enquiring, Uncle T showing him off. The vendors in front of the building smiled just as brightly as the office personnel, as the visitors and the office neighbours.

'Welcome. You are welcome.' He was very welcome. He
smiled and smiled and spoke proper English. Some of his
teachers would have missed a beat and stumbled if they
could have heard him over-pronounce his *very well indeed.*
How are you sir/madam?

Uncle T and his biz bro, aka fashion twin, excused
themselves. They were heading for a quick meeting. Karl
should remain; they would be back in no time whatsoever,
and also he hadn't had breakfast yet, which John would be
getting for him, as soon as he finished some other, quick,
very quick errand.

Karl sat down. No one had talked about his father. He
was stuck in the stuffy office. The secretary gave him
todayz paypazz. As if he had a clue about local affairs. The
half hours that usually flew by in London swelled, attached
to the heat, unwilling to move just the slightest bit. Each
second passed over the fake gold hands on the clock that
hung lopsided over the secretary's desk. One by one they
silently *tick-ticked* away, sometimes, Karl was sure, stopping
altogether. Just like the MIA had stopped being mentioned.
At lunch time the secretary brought red rice with meat. It
was hot, like in burning-your-soul-straight-to-hell pepperish,
but Karl polished it off in no time. Three glasses of water
gulped down afterwards didn't help with the burn but made
him burp. The secretary nodded approvingly.

Uncle T returned in the late afternoon, in a rush and
wanting to leave straight away. Double standards, *hello!* He
was meeting someone at the house. Was he ready, Karl?
Did he have good day? How did he like this Nigeria? And
the food? Had it been too spicy? And they should/would/
(could) go tomorrow to buy material and make clothes. If
Karl wanted to.

Karl tried to fake a smile and said nothing. Somebody would
have to talk about his father. At some bloody point.

But his uncle had already climbed back into the waiting
cab, and while nodding and smiling through the window
reassuringly, waved for Karl to get in on the other side,
the phone on the ear, talking to someone else, somewhere
else. When they arrived at the house, Karl was shattered.
Exhausted from all the nothing. He greeted the man who
arrived as they did and made an excuse to freshen up. Change

the sweaty T-shirt. The cold water that was only slightly cool
was well nice on his clammy skin.

He went back to the room and lay on the bed. The phone
was buzzing.

*Hey! Update me. How are you? How is it? We're missing you
here. Be safe. G.*

Another three from Abu. He replied to Godfrey: *All safe,
all good. Karl.*

What to write to Abu? What to say? He lay on the bed and
used the remote to switch on the aircon. His body slowly
relaxed as the coolness dried off the water. Heaviness took
over. It felt like it was in the middle of the night when Uncle
T knocked on the door. Karl's eyes were glued shut. For a
moment he had no idea where he was.

'Karl. Are you awake?'

The voice sounded familiar. It was warm, used to him, like
they had already shared something. The door moved. Uncle
T's head stuck through the opening. Karl jumped, the thin
fabric in hand, covering the length of his body. He landed
on his feet in front of the bed. Uncle T tipped backwards,
back against the wooden door and hit his head lightly on
the frame.

'Sorry. It's just me.' He looked at Karl. 'Uncle T. Your uncle.'

'Sorry,' Karl mumbled and sat down on the bed, the fabric
crunched up into a large ball, protective in front of his body.

'I was sleeping. Must've been dreaming.' He rubbed his
eyes, the sleep that had collected there smeared on to his
finger until it looked like it was gone.

'It's OK. Sorry it took so long. It was an important meeting.
If you are awake … we should talk.' And he grabbed the
chair at the slim desk and sat himself down. No waiting, no
courtesy of front-room gathering. Karl sensed another drop
in time. A lapse, a spin, a funny angle.

'No problem. I mean with the waiting. The heat knocked
me out anyways. As you can tell.' And he pointed to the
crumpled up sheet that served as his blanket.

'Let me just wash my face. Wake up properly.'

When he returned Uncle T was still on his spot on the chair,
remote in hand. He had lowered the temperature and it was
getting colder here. Or maybe it only seemed like that. Uncle
T was slouched over, didn't see Karl coming straight away.
Comfort was slipping out of the room.

Battles. You didn't even get to choose them. They just descended on you like jet fighters. Every time. No prep whatsoever before another bomb went hailing full speed into your brain. Mash up the whole thing.

Uncle T's face had crashed to the floor and was looking for some way to make itself proper sparse. His moisturised skin split like torn paper. His eyes looked like they hadn't closed at all the night before. Proper catastrophe like. Karl hadn't seen it. Hadn't got enough face time to notice. Uncle T motioned for him to sit. Worry in his face, all *let me diffuse this before I get on with it*.

Karl felt spikes attack his stomach. Mind racing, he wanted out, out of this situation, out of this stupid, stupid being here waiting for a man who wasn't.

'He died right?' He was still at the door. That way you could run, you could fucking leave this small bedroom that had nothing inside to distract you. 'I'd rather just know.'

And Uncle T jumping up from his chair now, suddenly, just like Karl minutes before. One large stride towards the door. Arm flung around the youngster, pulling him close while Karl tried to resist, tried to bloody keep the distance between them, between things. Both struggling. Karl inching out into the small hallway in front of the bathroom. Uncle T trying to reach, trying to keep bonding, physically, you know how that goes, the contact, trying, just trying to keep Karl, keeping his feet on the floor. Put. And level.

'I need to … I mean do you mind if I go out for a minute? Just outside. It's too cold in here.' Karl still trying to pull loose, his feet already making towards the living room.

'I need to go. Please.' His voice like a whisper, almost not there if it hadn't been shaking like proper, heavy from tears that wanted to press out of the eyes and spray all over.

'He didn't die! Karl, he didn't die o.' Uncle T let loose and Karl stumbled forward but his hand grabbed the doorframe. He turned around, angry now. You really don't want your *new never-knew-you* uncle to see you cry. It doesn't go that quick, the trusting, the opening. Those tears were supposed to not happen. At all.

'What then? Why is he not here? Why hasn't he called or spoken to me? Where is he?'

'Karl,' Uncle T had pulled himself together. Tiniest bit of a front, he was defo putting it on. His face went back to *smiling for the nephew* default and he straightened his trousers. Cocked his face to the side, doing the thinking about the right words thing. As if it wasn't better to just say it already, get it over and done with. Quick exhale, one of those sorry-ass laughs. Resigned.

'Your father. He has disappeared.'

You could hear it here. The way it went all flatline, tone not dropping out but going on and on and on. High-pitched and screeching, attacking your effing brain.

'He had come back. Had not been here since he contracted the infection. He had taken time out to be with the family in Lagos. But he was here for two nights. The house help came to prepare for your visit. He was here when she came.'

There are gaps and there are cliffs. There are sudden changes to the ground, whether for real or in your panic.

'But where … why … what's going on?'

'I don't know. Karl, the truth is we don't know where he is.'

That exhaling thing happened again. Quick shove of air out of the nose.

'At the moment, I don't know anything but that he isn't here.'

11

**To convince a fire to stop burning
you have to make sure
it ceases to rise.**

There is news that strikes us boldly, head on, pushes us violently off our feet. Hits us unshielded, unexpected, and then finds us responding unguarded, wailing. This was not such an occasion. Of course not. This was nothing yet.

Karl jerked in a funny way. You could see it. Inside, thoughts speeding, mind flying all over. Like major fast.
   'What do you mean, disappeared?'
   'Karl.'
   It was sad. This name-calling thing everyone seemed to do. Was it a grown-up thing, like a proper issue, or just a way of stalling time?
   'I don't know exactly what to tell you. We don't have the details.'
   No details, no/know nothing.
   'He came back to Port Harcourt a few days before your arrival.'
   'But then what? I talked to him the day before I left!'
   'Exactly. He was ready, he had prepared everything. Then on the day of your arrival ...'
   Uncle T gestured for Karl to come to the living room. John was sitting on an armchair close to the front door. He flashed a smile (without the teeth thing, didn't open his mouth enough). The man Uncle T had been meeting with was still on the couch. He rose and shook Karl's hand. He was a business partner of Uncle T's. More importantly, he was a close family friend, a close friend of Adebanjo. Karl

sunk into the armchair right next to the couch, facing the man, Mr. Layeni. Uncle T poured water in a glass and placed it on the little side table next to the armchair. Karl's glass. A weak attempt of keeping a rising fire in check. Fear, such a powerful accelerator. No need for fuel.

They had thought he would be back by now. Hoped so anyway.

The security guard emerged from the dark spot by the entrance, positioned himself close to the armchair John was sitting in. Hands clasped in front.

John came to the bungalow on the day of Karl's arrival and found the house quiet. The door locked. The car in the driveway. The man himself gone. The security guard said he left early that morning, long before John came. That it seemed like he had gone out to service the other car. The one he hardly used. Nothing suspicious really; he sometimes left that early. Traffic. To beat it. Before the morning rush hour.

The other car. An old one. 'Na de small one,' the security guard said. One that was parked on the other side, where there was another driveway, a narrower one, and another gate but that one was just locked shut and never in use. Unless the car was moved. Which was not often. Not often at all.

When John had come, ready to drive to the airport, to pick up Karl, there was no father. The security guard looked uncomfortable.

'Him neva come back. We wait small but sah neva come.'

'I couldn't call anyone. It was too late. It was time to get you.' John's teeth were in competition. Which one could make it out first? John used the car keys he had. Made sure there was a welcoming committee at the other side when Karl came through the gates at the airport. Only without the main man there was no committee at all. Totally unspecial.

Uncle T had been on the phone to John when he left the plane. Had raced ahead so he could catch him first. Find out what the heck was going on. Grateful that John had made an executive decision and come to pick them up.

'And nothing has been found out? No word at all?'

'Nothing Karl. Nothing.' Uncle T looked deflated. The entire facade crashed.

Mr. Layeni's eyes were narrow, piercing. 'I've called his work. They are not expecting him back yet. I didn't want to alarm them so I couldn't ask too much. It is best to keep this between us.'

Karl thought about the secrets of this story. The father who required so much silence. It had been a bad idea. It was, like, so clear now. Out of control, knee-jerk reaction, so totally romcom it wasn't even funny.

Mr. Layeni cleared his throat. 'I saw him on Monday, the day he returned. All was well.' He exchanged glances with Uncle T. 'He had called the mechanic the day before. To service the other car. So it would be ready for you. Karl ...' And he shot another glance at Uncle T. 'He worked for the oil company.'

It was supposed to be an answer for something. Give a clue about the situation. Like *hello!*, say what you have to say or leave it, right?

'Yes?'

'Sometimes there are complications. Usually it involves foreign workers.'

Karl's trousers buzzed. He put his hand into his pocket and grasped the phone. How comforting that gadget could be. Direct line to sanity. All you had to do was treat it right, give it juice, keep it charged, and it would recharge you.

'I don't understand.'

Mr. Layeni shifted in his seat. Uncle T got up from the couch. 'We are making some more calls, waiting to see whether your father will get in touch. The country ... many things happen here, Karl.'

'You think something happened?'

And Karl's face went from one to another. Uncle T, Mr. Layeni, John, the security guard.

'No need to worry. We wait a bit. Things will resolve themselves. It's only been a day.'

'And a half.' It shot from Karl's mouth. 'A day and a half.' His voice trailed off, not as sure as it had started.

'Yes, a day and a half,' Uncle T confirmed. 'Not long at all. He probably got stuck somewhere and his phone ran out of battery.' It sounded like a lazy effort. Uncle T continued. 'For now we have to figure out what you will do with your time here, eh?' His tone, supposed to be light-hearted, dropped flat on itself. No one smiled.

'Do you not go to the police or something?'

The four men all looked at Karl.

'Yes.'

'I mean at least they can register it, right?'

'Yes, they could.'

Uncle T looked tired. Of course it wouldn't make any sense. They wouldn't register anything. Not here. Not now. And why would they? If not for some large sum, nothing would be done.

'It is late. Try and get some rest. Tomorrow is another day. John will take you around. Show you Port Harcourt. Then, in the evening we figure out what needs to be done.'

Karl was relieved. At least he wouldn't be trapped inside all day again.

John rose and extended his hand. 'I come for you in the morning. You get up early?'

Karl nodded. He didn't need to sleep in on holidays. Although it wasn't so clear what exactly this was. Not pleasant, not holiday-like at all. What to do with this?

Mr. Layeni got up too. 'If I have news I will let you know straight away. Very nice to meet you.'

And he put his hand on Karl's shoulder. When everyone left, Uncle T showed him the fridge. It was full. Bottled water, soft drinks. The house help was coming back the following day. She would cook.

There were too many questions. He felt numb and without energy.

'What if he doesn't come back?'

'He will, Karl. He will.'

It almost sounded convincing.

12

Junctions are not made for all-round vision but for choosing the way ahead.

It would have been a good time to call Godfrey. To mention the detail of the father's disappearance. Naturally neither Uncle T nor Karl thought of it. Conveniently blanked that part out. They would not be thrown by a little hitch, not in the first week out. Things were just getting started.

Both made their way to their rooms for the night. *Their* rooms. Meaning one of them was Karl's. For the time being, but still. He was welcome here. For Uncle T at least. Karl was thinking what to do about this journey. A bit of fear bubbled to the surface. The excitement drowned it straight away. He, the father, would appear. Uncle T had said so. He would know. He was from here. He had known that this would be the best thing, to come here. The best thing for Karl. Meanwhile it was time to find out what the city was like.

It was getting late. The numbness was making his body heavy, very heavy. Time to sleep. He wanted to be up bright and early so John could show him around. So he could get a proper taste of this city in case this was going to be over much sooner than anticipated.

'I will just send Godfrey an email tonight, OK?'

Two minds. Karl nodded and smiled.

'Thanks. Was just thinking that. Can you let him know I'll text him tomorrow, please? I can't text him like all the time otherwise I'll run out of credit too quickly.'

Uncle T nodded. 'Maybe we wait a couple of days before we call. Until we know what to say.' He laughed. It was like the name-calling. A bit helpless.

'No need to wake sleeping dogs.' God, Abu would crack up if he could hear him. Now there were half-arsed sayings as well?

'Goodnight, Uncle.'

Both doors closed. Uncle T tapped an email into the laptop that spoke of the good arrival. That he was staying a little longer in Port Harcourt with Karl, so things could settle in properly. How interesting Karl was finding everything, already taking to the food and to the distant but much trusted cousin of his wife. That he might take Karl to Lagos for a few days, to spend time at Uncle T's own house. Meet Uncle T's wife. That they would call as soon as possible. Probably not the following day because they had planned a full day. Quite full. Very, in fact. Probably the day after. The calling home. That things had been very busy since touchdown. Business. All that business.

* * *

Abu brushed off the dirt. Leicester, Connor and Sammy were at it again. Had been quiet for a while, busy with other targets. When they'd remembered him, they'd run past him, snatching his bag, pretending to be on their way somewhere. Meaning from some building to another, between all the glamour that the new King's Cross still left them. This was a back-of-a-building road. Small, no reason for many people to be here. Shortcut but also a trap.

They threw the bag in a dried puddle by the side of the road. 'Whatever.'

It was quieter without Karl. He was an even easier target but the wannabes' interest had halved. At least he hoped so. He got a few of those words thrown at him that were supposed to make him twitch with anxiety. Like the 'C-word'. And 'want to be close with the pavement again?'

'Whatever. You've been there. Do it again. I'll live.'

The last bbm had been cryptic. *cant really say much*. Abu had no clue what that meant. *More details soon.* Abu had replied, *landline number pls ur starting 2 wori me. need more info. Ill call u.* It was as if his left ventricle had decreased in capacity. Blood flow stagnant. He was missing his main man. What if something went wrong in Nigeria? What the

eff would he do? They were an organism that worked best
in close proximity. In and out. Ying and yang. And so forth.
He got the getting to know yourself Karl was trying to do.
But still. King's Cross was already promising a very dry
couple of weeks. And dryness was the least of his problems.

Abu arrived at the tech shop. The wannabes hadn't followed.
Too lazy to make it out into real daylight. Cowards. It was
much busier than in their little forgotten quarter behind the
fancy-pantsy King's Cross major reconstruction mayhem.
How much building could you do in one effing junction? Talk
about out of control. The construction sites spread further
and further, some of it unrelated, some of it inevitably part
of the whole area regeneration.

The junction by Warren Street tube was busy and it felt like
he had suddenly woken up. His street was like, forgotten.
Sleepy. Here it was speed galore and pushing your way
through people and past major traffic. Rows and rows of
cars, different lanes colliding almost, the typical London
pedestrian pushing forward in tense hurry as if behind them
the world was breaking off into nothingness. Buses weaving
in and out of traffic, overtaking each other, unnecessarily,
just to make it two seconds earlier to the next stop.

Abu's mother wanted him to pick up Skype headphones.
A little present for Rebecca. You couldn't be more obvious.
Make sure she clocked the whole on-the-other-side-of-the-
world thing straight away. Karl had asked him to go see his
mum. Take her some of his mother's food. Make sure she
was OK.

Abu was glad there was something to do. It was cramped
at home. The twins were in some loud phase, omnipresent
and noisily enforcing their own personality, like they were
one single character or something. They were constantly
teasing him. *See? This is what we've both settled for. You will
have to deal with it.* And in a couple of weeks, when school
was out for the summer, they'd proper drive him mad.

Too much for Abu, who was used to offloading and hanging
with Karl. All the things he did, he did them with Karl. Listen
to music. Check up on those bands they liked, online. Internet
window shopping. Walk around the block, the neighbourhood,
Karl's house, youth centre. Talk to the girls (or *women* as his
bloody highness kept insisting). With Karl. Karl was good
with the women but Abu liked them too. Just too shy to say

much, to even stay long enough, but amazed how they drew their lashes wider and longer, gazing into Karl's eyes just because he said 'let's talk about it' to them.

Abu's body was getting grown. His round face started to get longer, losing the baby fat on his cheeks, and it featured a few stray hairs on his chin. It was still brand new, not real growth, but he was liking the way it felt when he caught a glimpse in the mirror.

Abu walked through the aisles of the tech shop. The new phones were wicked. He held a Samsung Galaxy in his hand. *I wish.* The headphones were further back. The customer service person had followed him. Abu turned around.

'Looking for something?'

Customer service person just looked at him. No answer, no laugh, no nothing. Just stood, waited. When Abu moved further and tried a few headphones he finally found some words.

'These are for customers. You have to buy shit if you want to try them on.'

'Oh really,' Abu replied. 'And I'm just wasting my fucking time, yeah? Because I don't got no money to pick up some bleeping headphones?'

Another man in a T-shirt the colour of the chain came closer, concerned.

'Everything OK here?'

'Your colleague needs to keep his stereotypes to himself. Fucking racist.'

The person looked like it had happened before and he wasn't happy about it.

'You need to stop that, you know. I will report you. No need to follow anyone on discriminatory assumption.'

The first customer service guy whatevered away, leaving a cloud of effing and blinding in his wake.

Abu pressed the intercom bottom. He could hear noises from the open windows. Mothers telling their kids off, someone else on a very loud phone convo. Rebecca's voice sounded happy when he said, 'Hello, it's me, Abu.' She hadn't seen much of them since Karl's disappearing act. Mama Abu was on strike. Kept saying she wasn't going to lie. She wasn't going to sit with Rebecca, pretending. Now Abu had to come up with some bullshit just because everyone was avoiding her.

Rebecca held the flat door open, smiling. A woman had
followed her to the door, still talking.

'Such a waste.' The friend's dress was bright green. 'It's
not just fans; we are all shocked. I cried yesterday, Rebecca.
I really did.'

Amy Winehouse had died unexpectedly, after relapsing for
the umpteenth time into heavy drinking.

'Such an amazing voice. Just bad habits,' the friend
continued.

The city was on pilgrimage to her Camden home.

'Do you listen to her music, young man?'

Abu just shook his head. Not so much. Not his style.

'Such a waste. But you knew it would happen. You know it's
inevitable. Unless you change your environment. When you're
in that deep, and I mean drugs here, you need to go cold
turkey all the way. Even leave your man behind. Anything it
takes to get you out of it. Everyone can have another chance
but you have to grab it. You really have to want it.'

She didn't need breath; she was able to yak on without any
pause or visible use of her lips. The words just catapulted
out in her nice but non-stop voice.

'Coming back to that Norwegian murderer ...'

Rebecca stopped her. 'No no no, I do not agree with you.
Since when does the terrorist get all the attention? The
victims should. Not his sorry excuse of a being.'

Abu closed the door. The two women were already back
on their way to the living room. Rebecca looked better, the
chalkiness gone and her eyes alert again.

The woman in the green dress responded, 'But it is important
to understand him, why he has done such a horrible thing.'

'Why?' Rebecca was unconvinced. 'What do you get out of
it? Other than him spewing more of his hatred on national
and international television.'

Rebecca went into a proper rant. She could get like that.
All righteous. Could break it down like no man's business
and you had to be quick to keep up and find your own shit
to say. That's where Karl got his *the order of things* and *how
they are so out of order* opinions from. Not that he agreed
with Rebecca. Most of the time they didn't. But they liked
to reason.

Now Rebecca was going on about white supremacists taking
over, etc. etc. She got well heated up saying that normally

a terrorist wouldn't get so much airtime but of course, because he was white and shit, we got to know all about his bad childhood. About why and whatnot and his inner life. No time for the actual monstrosity. Or the victims.

'There is some understanding that needs to happen. On society's side,' her friend offered.

'Not on that level. Not by giving room as if his sick mind had some justifiable reasons. I don't think so.'

Her friend stopped and smiled. 'I think your young friend needs some attention.' She pointed to Abu, whose body was all inward-pointing, shy. It always happened around Rebecca. He was still standing at the door to the room, bag in hands. She stopped herself, motioned for Abu to come closer, hugged him.

'How are you dear? Mum and dad? The twins? Haven't seen any of you. If I didn't know better I would think you are all avoiding me.'

Abu looked at his beige boots. His denims were folded over. On his waist, a leather belt with a shiny buckle. Armani. Karl thought it was a bit too much. And embarrassing. Not the buckle itself but the free advertising Abu was giving. Whatever. It looked wicked.

'Everyone is well, thank you. Just busy, end of term, you know. My mum asked me to bring some food. Just something simple. Rice and vegetables.'

Rebecca perked up. The Tupperware opened with four separate clips.

'Your mum is such an angel. Please tell her how much I appreciate it.'

She patted Abu's arm and put the container on the side table.

'And you? How is everything? Have you heard from Karl? He texted me yesterday and said he was getting on well.'

'Haven't spoken to him yet.'

Rebecca doubted the story everyone was keeping up about Karl's whereabouts. He had been on weekends away with one of his support groups before but two weeks was taking her for a ride. During term time. They had caught her in a low phase. Was easy to play her then. She had just gone along, with those questions in her eyes of course. But Godfrey shrugged it all off. Avoiding.

'Will you tell your mother that I'd like to speak with her?'

Abu felt the room close in a little more. Why did he have to straighten out all of Karl's bull? Why?

'I'll tell her.'

'If she's busy I'll call her. The twins are off already?'

'They're breaking up next week. Starting summer programme the week after. Here, my mother also wanted you to have this.' He gave Rebecca the plastic bag with the headphones and mic inside.

Rebecca was pleased when she opened the box.

'Look, I'm going to be a cool mum now and stay in touch with Karl, in an up-to-date way. I'm finally arriving in this century.'

Her friend laughed. Abu was all like *why me* inside. But he smiled as well. Awkward.

'Yes, they are quite handy. If you get good Internet. Not sure Karl has much connection actually.'

It was proper awful. Rebecca's excitement. Abu made his exit. Yes, he would pass it on. All of it. For sure.

* * *

In the morning Karl was determined to speak to Abu. Before he could follow John to yet another unknown place he would have to use the phone. The landline.

i'm goin 2 call frm my numba. call me bck NOW.

When John returned, Karl was sitting sideways on the large armchair, legs dangling over one side, chatting away. His face relaxed, his cheeks rosy in excitement. He was laughing.

'I'm not sure,' came through the receiver. Abu was shouting. 'Godfrey is going crazy, man. He's worried sick. You need to call, like for real.'

'I'm here, innit? No point to run straight back. How's mum?'

The last bit had an edge to it. Like when they saw the wannabes strutting down towards them and they quickly checked, left, right, behind them and in front, to see whether anyone else was on the street. Anyone who would help.

'She's good. Karl, call her. It's not fair, you get me.'

'Thanks man. I will, I will.' It wasn't that easy. Who and when to call. And the what to say? What could you say? Better just let that shit take care of itself, right? Karl saw John and straightened up.

'Need to go bruv. We do the same again soon. I'll bbm you when you can reach me on this line.'

He jumped off the armchair, still laughing.

'Well, you got Internet at your disposal. Cheap calls. Use it.'

All of his gangly self was swaying from the abrupt movement. Abu had told him funny things. Nalini was teasing him. In a good way. Giving him proper lip and everything. Was it his ears that made him shoot off each time they came closer to him? If he thought they were for flying she would have to tell him that they were just cute. Something, something distinctive. Winked, walked off. Afsana had been off sick the last few days and Abu had caught Nalini alone. Just the two of them.

And now Abu, of all people, started talking to her regularly. First shy, then *oh OK you* do *like me*. Karl couldn't believe it. Abu, who'd push him forward when they bumped into the women. Who was fascinated but would run off to class instead. Things were changing, for real. He had only been gone a couple of days. Ha. Abu. Wasted no time. Karl didn't think he had it in him.

'I'm ready,' he said and John looked up from the paper in his hand. A blue taxi was parked in front of the bungalow. The driver was leaning against the door, going through his phone. Still had the thin plastic film to protect the display. The man looked up and nodded, opened the door and sat in the driver's seat.

'Your uncle is using the car today so I booked a taxi,' John said.

Uncle T appeared on cue on the little lawn in front.

'Call me, Karl. If there are any problems, you have my number. I know John is already waiting for me to get back inside.'

It seemed true. John was cheerful. It was proper moving. All because of him? Some strange teenager who appeared out of nowhere? Maybe he was just a morning person.

'John. Ahbeg. Make you take care of dis boy very well o. Anything happen, me I dey find you. You hear?'

'Yes sah.' He looked mischievous and winked at Karl. 'Nothing go happen sah.'

Was just like Karl, like Abu, and a whole lot of other peeps: John liked to have himself a main man, someone to roll with. And since working and trying to build his own business and

his wife having their first baby and all those damn things that
needed taking care of there hadn't been much time for any of
that sort of thing. Karl was welcome, very welcome indeed.

They went to John's place. An apartment building located
on a wide dirt road that heaved with activities. Small traders
lined the length of the street with their little ramshackle
stands. The sun climbed from behind the edges of a city
that seemed to burp, constantly shaking and pushing out
more. People, vehicles, dust and commotion. Hectic. It had
something of rush-hour Tube service. *We are stuck in the
tunnel before the one in front moves.* Karl smiled.

Only here it was so much louder, shouting and horns beeping
and arms swaying upwards, exclamations, frustration. The
taxi driver didn't participate. He had something very, very
cool about him. When the taxi got stuck for a good twenty
minutes between rows of other vehicles, he got his phone
out of his back pocket again and spoke in a low voice to what
sounded like his wife or girlfriend.

Karl sucked in the scene. The stalls at the side of the dusty
road with women sitting behind them, legs apart, leaning
slightly forward on their thighs, mostly chatting to each other,
or fanning themselves with a bit of cardboard. Pyramids made
of tomatoes, grains, beans, smoked fish, vegetables and tins.
All perfectly balanced on enamel trays. Customers in front,
haggling. Kids with or without clothes running in-between,
playing and shrieking and waving and looking at Karl with
open mouths. Karl aware. He was the main attraction. The
one sticking out, being random in all the chaos.

People were in bright outfits with so many colours it was
unreal, let alone the patterns and textures, sometimes all
proper coordinated, matching purses and shoes for some of
the glam-looking ladies. Others were in faded, washed-out
clothes that had probably never gone together in the first
place. Some of the women walked so slow they were, like,
floating. For real. Heads perfectly straight. Hips swaying,
left, slow, right, slow, step, slow. If you didn't concentrate
you would think they weren't moving at all, their bodies just
hanging in space. Karl's eyes followed them. They were fully
inside. Their own skin. Nothing spilled over, nothing shrank
inside. Comfortable. Abundant. Themselves.

Men in suits. Men in long shirts in the same fabric as their
trousers and small bags in their hands. Kids, women, men,

shouting, trying to sell Karl a hand vacuum cleaner or CDs or handkerchiefs or second-hand books and magazines or 'pure water' (which John said was not as good as bottled and not for him, just for the locals), or crisps or sweets and a million other things. The car completely surrounded, drowning in the sea of people trying to get or sell something. And watching him with open mouths. Beggars with all sorts of limbs missing, waving half an arm or a deformed leg in front of the window. Looking straight at Karl, hands asking. For money. Karl frightened. John just waving them off.

'Don't mind am.'

Then suddenly there was an opening and traffic moved again, slowly, but at least they were in business. The house was near, at a street corner, a short way from a small, local market.

'In the day the activities here are too much,' John said. He turned around once in a while during their journey, like Uncle T had done when Karl first arrived. But John was stiffer, never jumped or anything, even when the car jerked them all around in sudden moves. Instead he moved up and down, all graceful and shit, as if he were advertising perfect posture and the smoothest streets ever. Not as smooth as the women Karl had seen, though.

'I will show you tomorrow. The market.'

The house had a cemented parking area in front and a woman was selling small items from an overloaded wood stall, which was positioned at its edge, where the property made friends with the dust road. Little packets of coffee and laundry powder dangled in portioned sachets from both sides of the wood edges. There were a couple of shops at the bottom of the road. Between them the way inside the building. He couldn't see much; it was dark. Stairs led up, probably to the occupants' flats, and as they walked closer he inhaled the smells that called for attention: breakfast, brunch, almost lunch. Some people were already cooking. A dark woman with hair in shiny, spiky twists, greeted them with two perfect rows of white teeth.

'Good morning. How are you?'

Karl couldn't be too sure. The words felt familiar and strange at the same time. He wasn't required to respond. Was he? He nodded instead, only so much he could do, shy or not.

John answered and they exchanged friendly words, her
eyes wandering to Karl, looking at him, just straight at him,
not even once taking the bloody time to blink. It wasn't a
bad look though; it was something else. Like in, good. Like
in doing something, something inside of Karl. His palms got
sweaty. She stood in front of the shop, which John explained
was a little canteen, some aluminium pots in her hands. Water
dripped off their sides.

'You come eat here. Later. I'm Mena. We go talk small.
You're welcome. Welcome to your country.'

She looked at Karl, smiling. Her face all open. Her black
top was cut deep enough to show cleavage. Karl was staring
too. She had the usual wrapper tied around her waist. Karl
threw his best cute boy smile her way, eyelashes patting
each other. Hoping – you could only hope – for maximum
effect. She was probably a good few years older but seemed
like she was up for teasing him as if he was her equal. She
winked and laughed, from deep inside her tummy. Karl didn't
know what was so funny.

'See you soon.' And she took her pots, turned around and
went inside the shop, waving with her free hand.

Karl confirmed, 'Yes. I will try your food soon.' His heart
slightly giddy. And *defo*. Without volume. *I'm going to be
back here in no time.*

John was waiting at the bottom of the stairs, reading his
folded paper. 'She only does lunch. She closes in the evening.
Now she is busy preparing. We call it bukateria. Or buka. A
small place to eat when you are not eating at home.'

Karl followed him up the stairs. Uzo, John's wife, opened
the door, baby in arm. It still had the undefined, young-baby
face, all plump cheeks. John put his paper on a little side
table. He grew in size as if his feet were soon to take off and
he to hover over Uzo and the baby. Funny noises and funnier
words came out of his mouth. Karl had to bite the inside of
his lips. So much for the properness and perfect posture.
Levitating would count as quite the feat but the baby talk
and creased face probably didn't. He shuffled out of the way.
You had to know when to give a bit of space, right?

The living room was a lot smaller than his father's. Three
armchairs facing each other with a small table in the middle.
A TV. His father's place felt too proper (other than the
bedrooms). All white leather and whatnot, all showing off in

that *I'm understating here!* way but blowing it all up in your face. John's was just warm. You knew you could hang here; this was for being in, not for showing to someone.

Uzo's relaxed hair was pulled back into the shortest ponytail ever. Her face and hair almost one thing: from chin to nose to forehead to hairline.

'Her name is Rose. We are so happy. My wife was very sick but by the grace of God …'

They split apart slightly and his wife extended her right hand, the baby still on her arm.

'She is beautiful,' Karl contributed, fingers stroking the infant's cheeks.

'You must be hungry. You like our Nigerian food?'

'I'd love to try whatever you're making. Thank you.'

He followed her into the kitchen to show that he could be very useful, master dishwasher in fact, helping mothers in England and Nigeria alike. Reel them in and impress was one of his transferable skills. He was still waiting for his career advisor to pick up on it. At least that would make for a useful session.

Abu always said that. 'If nothing else, you could make a living with that. Mama's boy gets a whole new meaning with you, man, although you do forget your own, you know. You should offer services; take the whole mother-pleasing thing off the shoulders of stressed teenagers. Let us get on with business.' And Karl always replied, 'Whatever. I do take care of mum. It's just different. Someone has to show that not all is lost with our generation. I'm doing you a favour.'

Usually they would be on to a lengthy discussion then. The state of the youth. Why not all was lost but why some were acting all gangsta all the time. You know the type that rules the street and makes things difficult, whether you were Karl or Abu or just bloody in the way. And mostly why Abu felt like he had to pretend sometimes as well, even when they were smashed into gates and metal fences together, and not only on snow days.

And Abu would hurl back that there was no place for no black or Asian youth in London. You didn't even have to be smart to know that. But you didn't have to be all political analysis all of the time. All that talking didn't change a bloody thing. What was Karl going to do about it? And how come all his sense-making came with running at night, and why was he

not doing the one thing, calling Godfrey, when he did? What
was that? Wasn't even meant to be an insult or anything.

Karl didn't take any offence. Was just that they knew their
shit. The stuff they did. Like Abu being all mouthpiece. And
Karl all Nike advert gone proper inclusive. There wasn't
anything to do about it but accept and keep being friends.
The 'fag boys' from around the corner. 'Pussy boys' as the
wannabes liked to add. Both their words. And Karl would
be all, 'You know you can just tell them you ain't gay and be
done with it. It's just me this is for anyway.' And Abu would
be, 'For real? Bruv, do I look like I have a problem with gay
or anything? They know we ain't gay. I'm not even going
to go there. When have I ever let you down? Tell me? Do I
really look like I will talk to some pisshead? Got better things
to do with my time, mate. If you want to preach again find
yourself someone who doesn't know how to act. Ain't me.'

Would shut Karl up 'cause it was true. No one had a thing,
not one single bit of competition, nothing at all, on Abu. That
guy was major correct, knew how to brother from another
mother like nobody else. If Karl wanted to talk he could, could
tell Abu all about what and how, the whole *how* Karl wanted
to be Karl. But you couldn't pretend like you were better
because you had read some books on the topic. Abu had
too. Abu who hated anything college with a passion, which
meant he hated anything book-related, had been first to say
to Karl, 'Look mate, found this online. Anything of interest
there? Should we get it?' From there they passed each other
the brochures Karl got in the support groups. Karl teasing,
'If only your teachers knew that you can actually read.'

And Abu, 'If only yours knew you're not as nice as you
seem.' And kicking Karl with his bare feet.

Uzo handed Rose to him.

'I have cooked yam. I will fry some egg.'

Karl got all cosy; the mushy feeling poured over him as if
Uzo had always known he was coming. He wondered if she
could smell he was a runner? Not good at sticking to things
in the moment. Not when they came head-on.

After the food, John sat down and explained a few ins and
outs about Karl's father's work. It made Karl's head dizzy. It
was all hot and bothered, humidity like there was no bloody
tomorrow, coming through the open window, full-on assault.

Not one bit of draft. With a full stomach Karl could feel
how tiring the last days had been. The flat had a keeping-
the-outside-out-ness about it. Proper relaxing. There had
been a lot of info lately. Too much push and pull, everything
different and new. And those endless questions. Had this
been the right thing? To come here?

The words John used didn't seem familiar. Maybe he was
speaking his own language? Had forgotten that this was Karl,
yes, new mate and all, but London through and through.
Or maybe, again, it was just how he pronounced them. He
interrupted him every other sentence.

'Pardon me. I'm really sorry, I didn't quite understand.'

Didn't take long before his mind drifted completely and
he just installed the *listening intently, yes very much so* look.
Was so much easier when you just let your face do the job,
your mind resting, total peace.

'Mmm, I understand,' Karl nodded. To not leave those
eyelids lying on top of each other too long. That was the
trick. But of course they did their own thing, as if they were
freelancing, and not part of the whole team. When he opened
his eyes again he heard John and Uzo talking in low voices.
She was sitting on the armrest, Rose held close. Both looked
up as Karl stirred.

'I'm sorry. Not sure what happened.'

Karl looked around. Uzo was smiling.

'Ah, please Karl. Be at home here. We have a small room
at the back, you can use it if you are still tired.' She winked
at John, who seemed to gel with the whole thing. What was
it with the guy? Karl liked him too but it had been like, two
minutes. You couldn't really call that deep connecting. John
showed him the small room. Looked like it was used to store
all the stuff that had nowhere else to be. Proper full up and
cluttered. But there was a single mattress leaning against
the wall.

'It's not much. But if you like to rest properly, you can
sleep here.'

Karl had to laugh. Not like loud – that would have been rude
– just it was too much *I've been before* in a whole different
setting. The single mattress thing on the floor seemed to be
the new global language of friendship. *You just crash here.
Any time.* Maybe it was a shortcut to making ties.

'This reminds me of home. I sleep in my friend's place on a mattress like this.'
John nodded. It seemed to make him happy.

> **bond** /bɒnd/
> verb
> 1. To fix/bind/connect or be joined, quite firmly (as in securely) to something else, especially by means of something (glue, heat, pressure or similar. Could just be circumstance.)
> 2. Become connected to, link up with someone. Could be described as teaming up if you wanted to.

Instead of more sleep, Karl asked if they could go out. The taxi was hired for the day; might as well get the most out of it, right? Like throw yourself into the mix, check out the scene Port Harcourt-style. He was thinking about Mena, the cook. She might be out again and throw him some attention.

John did not telepathically get the thoughts in Karl's head one single bit. He was all business now, excited about showing him the Garden City, the one that was known all over Nigeria for its beauty. He rushed Karl past the yard; Mena was waving from her little eatery but John, not wanting to stop at all, just threw back one sentence, totally lost on Karl again.

He entered the waiting taxi. John was into sharing mode, info sharing, big time. Karl had already missed that bonding session earlier when he had snoozed off. Now John was all about trying to make some context, for the missing father, the oil, the city, the Nigeria. How the beautiful city had lost its beauty. How oil money was not invested properly. How developments were not for the general population. How the city was bursting. How this and that wasn't and hadn't and wouldn't be done. The foundations for a monorail, an electric inner city train, had begun. It was supposed to ease the congestion problem. But it was going slow, very slow. Like so many other things that were supposed to happen. How it was off, really off. How the father was working for an oil company, meaning not part of any developments, not good ones in John's eyes, either. Not for the people. But how he was making good money, and that was something. And because the father was making money John was making money by working for the father. Karl just wanted to drive around.

When they pulled back up at the flat, Mena was serving a late lunch. A young girl in an old white dress was cleaning the used plastic tables, making space for the next customer. Mena waved again.

'Karl. Come and eat,' she demanded.

'Hi.' He was pleased. She remembered his name. That's what you get when you got it, you get me?

'You look busy. Should I come back later? Make it easier?'

She nodded.

'Easier for what?' John mocked but she had already turned away, her hands dishing up the latest order. Karl followed John into the dark hallway, then up the stairs.

It was late afternoon when he bounced back down the uneven cement steps in the stairwell that divided the building in half. The girl in the white dress was sitting in front of the buka on a small stool. She was soaping plates in a large plastic bowl between her outstretched legs. Inside the small hut-like shop, Mena was packing away large pots.

'Hi. Hello.'

She turned around. 'You're back.' She seemed pleased. 'Karl. Come and talk to me. Sit.'

Karl's throat felt scratchy. The blood had vanished from his face and upper body and was now pooling in his feet. It was difficult to make the few steps. This wasn't a girl from college down the street. His 'wow' eyelashes might do nothing at all here. He managed to make it to the bench she pointed at without knocking down the whole stall. It was low, wooden; he sat down carefully. Mena came closer and put her hand on his arm. She looked at him for a while, nodding but without movement, internal, if you know what I mean. As if she recognised him from somewhere. A tiny bit of a twinkle in her eyes, narrowing them the slightest bit. Karl could feel her thoughts on his skin, whatever they were. One thing was clear: she was defo not teasing him schoolgirl-crush-like. Not one bit. She was probably Godfrey's age. Like Godfrey, she was black-don't-crack all the way. She could have fooled you, looking like a teen.

'How do you like dis our Port Harcourt?'

Her hand was still on Karl's arm but she was watching the girl outside.

'A lot. Very interesting.' Karl was all *what now*? No game, no plan, nothing.

'John don show you de city?' She lifted her hand, turning.

'A little.' Karl didn't know where to look.

Her blackness was that rich and deep kind that reflected back. She waited for a bit, thinking, then, she looked at him. 'At home everything na fine?'

What was she on about?

'What do you mean?' This was turning out to be weird.

'You come for visit, first time, from far, very far. Then your father no be here. I hope dat at home, everything is fine?' She laughed. 'Nigeria, I mean, how do you say it? It never make a good impression.'

Karl laughed too. 'It did. Sort of.'

'No!' she was adamant. 'Not like dis. Dis no be de way. Sorry for John telling me. We talk sometimes. He say he like my special opinion.'

She laughed again. Karl nodded. The going-along type.

'I am not a special person. I just cook. But John' – and she winked at Karl – 'him say I can see more than de junction. Maybe because so many people I see every day. I get used to seeing more than people show. Sometimes at least. You ask him what is there to see at the junction. He will laugh. He will not reply. He will not know what kine junction he dey talk.' She rolled her eyes, still laughing. 'Don't mind John. He is special. Junction, no junction. Your father. They will find him. For de rest, dat be your own story. You will do it de way you want. You understand?'

Karl nodded some more. Like what the heck was going on here?

'It is OK, really. John has been very good to me.'

'Anyway' – and she rose – 'all I want to say is it is well. Don't worry. It is well.'

A young man rushed in. 'Good afternoon, auntie.'

He almost bowed respectfully, then laughed. He looked at Karl and folded his skinny, stilt-like legs, swinging to sit next to him. All had taken a split second. Much less than Karl's complicated journey from the steps to the inner workings of the hut.

'Here you dey chop well well,' and he smiled at Karl. Then back at the woman. 'Ahbeg Auntie, anything.'

Mena's face lit up. She obviously knew this guy and she went behind the counter and lifted a plastic cover. Underneath was a full plate, dished up, all ready and just waiting for the right dude to come and ask for it. Chunks of meat in a thick stew on top of a whole lot of boiled rice. Karl, now used to the dim light, saw that there were several portions lined up on the narrow counter.

'Nakale, na late. Time don pass too much. You never finish before?' She looked up at Karl. ' Dis one him no go eat.' She hesitated. 'Or you wan try it?'

Karl swallowed. His mouth was still too dry. And now he was proper confused by that random convo. Which junction? And what was supposed to be going on at home? Or was it here she had talked about? He would choke, for sure, proper, if anything required salivation. Like speaking, coughing, doing anything else but sitting here, concentrating on keeping his body arranged, his torso upward, his legs un-shaking, his hands steady. Independent, he was for the first time hanging in this Nigeria. Now this was the real shit.

The young man, Nakale, had got up as soon as Mena lifted the plate. His grin looked childish, his face a shiny schoolboy's complete with sweat bumps and greasy skin.

'Auntie, I de thank you.'

His hand lowered as soon as he sat back down, now opposite Karl, the plate in front of him. He attacked the food in a precise manner, not wasting any time, full spoon straight into lowered mouth.

'Karl be him name. John brought am. He come from London.'

Nakale looked up but didn't move his face any higher. The spoon kept shoving rice and stew, in even movements. He was still chewing but he stopped for a second. His hand reached for another spoon and handed it to Karl.

'Come and eat.' And he was silent again. There were no words but a lot of noises. All of them appreciative.

Mum, it's like proper cool here. Learning lots. Don't worry, all is good. Will call soon. Karl

* * *

Abu would have liked her to say something about him. Nalini was still talking about Karl and him being so understanding, sweet, different, etc. etc. Since that first time she had said nothing about him. Nothing at all. No sign at all. He was hoping, despite her reeling off Karl's better attributes, that she also noticed how *he* was growing into a man. The halal perfume (fakes he got from his mate down the road that matched all the latest trendy smellies almost accurately) he dabbed on in the morning, at first break, after college and sometimes in-between; the clothes that showed he knew his stuff. Well put together. Outfits that were proper coordinated. Karl would have made a double flip had he seen what happened to him in a bloody week. Anticipation that made him wake early on Monday and without Karl to talk things over with, left his thoughts trailing, always ending with the image of her face.

'It's a shame if he doesn't make it back for his birthday. Remember last year? We ended up going to that place at the Brunswick.'

Her eyes widened, reminiscent of the grown-up experience, when Karl and Abu had spontaneously invited her and Afsana to go for a cheap lunchtime-deal meal when they had accidentally run into each other on Karl's birthday, almost a year ago.

'We could look out for any of these offers this year, you know what I mean. Groupon. Get a proper deal. Like a proper three-course meal or something.'

Abu nodded. 'Not sure he's going to be back. You know how it is.'

Karl. Nothing to say here.

He was aiming for mature and world-knowing, as if he was assessing the larger state of things. He didn't even know how anything was, let alone Karl's latest doings. All he knew was friendship didn't seem to be all the same to Mr.-quickly-getting-occupied-otherwise.

'Where is he anyway?'

These were things that no one had bothered to brief Abu on. He had no idea what he was supposed to say. Neither Godfrey nor Karl had given any real instructions.

'Taking care of business, innit.'

Nalini fell for it. Impressed, she glanced at Abu sideways, her cheeks flushed from the cold this time.

'Tell him I said hi and I hope everything works out well. You gonna talk to him?'

'Defo. Sure thing. I'll let him know.'

Afsana was almost catching up with them at the gate. She had forgotten the paper that she had done for college and didn't want to miss out on the praise. It was on the local history they were all working on. Nalini and Abu had chosen Slavery and The Bloomsbury Group, with a few others in their year. It had hit home for all of them.

'He would never believe I actually did it on time and OMG I did so much work.' Afsana had been in overdrive, her mouth babbling away. 'He's just gonna think I'm being funny. No way. I'd rather come late.'

And she'd rushed back. Now she was swaying in a skipping motion down the street towards them, winner's smile on her lips, her silk headscarf reflecting the bright day's sun.

'Can we, erm, do you, I mean, what do you think of ...?'

Abu's lips tripped over the words that came out of his mouth without his permission. Nalini waved at her friend, *come quick, almost time, you're still gonna make it*, and directed her attention back towards him. *What was it?*

It was time. Time to grow up, Abu figured. Karl wasn't here to help him through the endless days now. And even if, they couldn't act like conjoined twins for the rest of their lives.

'I mean, maybe I can walk home with you after college?'

Afsana arrived, running the last bit, and swung her arm around Nalini.

'Got it.' She patted her bag proudly.

A small hand squeezed Abu's. Quick. Nalini looked at him.

'So those ears do pay attention.' And she pulled Afsana towards college, looking back once over her shoulder. Smiling.

13

**The balance, the balance.
Isn't it to be equal?**

'I couldn't sleep. It was on my mind, like, the whole time.'
 Nalini was standing outside the estate, waiting for Afsana to join them. She had bbm'ed that she had to get Rahul ready but her sister was dropping him at nursery. Could they wait for her? It gave Abu a minute alone with Nalini. He'd waited at the corner since eight, not wanting to miss them. During the week he had seen her here and there, usually surrounded by at least three other confident girls, all of them in some major debrief. He never managed to catch a quiet moment with her.
 'You know,' she added, looking at him for confirmation. 'It's just like so intense. I never knew this could be so close, like here yeah, right here. I mean, everyone knows about slavery but it sort of has nothing to do with now, with anything we see, you know what I mean?'
 In the week it seemed like she had waved at everyone but him, her eyes always somewhere else. Smiling. He was just never sure who it was directed towards. Her crew, or any of the passers-by she engaged with?
 He shot a smile back, despite himself, despite thinking that she didn't even care enough to lift her hand or throw some comment towards him, like she did with everyone else. It stung, you know. Everything Nalini and no proper face time. His new mates – just some of the youth from around the area, acquaintances he had to quickly upgrade because Karl was nowhere near coming back and Mark and Kyle were going to be off to Spain all summer – were laughing about him. His stupefied, all-things-Nalini look. Too much for their taste.

'You stuck in time, bruv?' They banged into him when he stopped midway in his track, because everything her.

Now he shifted his legs left, right and back. 'Are you going to do it in project week?'

Nalini got excited. 'Yes, I think so. I mean we're practically on Leigh Street anyway. It's like our history. Like local. You know what I mean?'

Abu shoved his hands into his jeans. Then took them out again and arranged his T-shirt underneath the ironed sweater.

'I'm still waiting for this summer to start.'

Nalini laughed. Abu felt good. Maybe she had been smiling at him all along?

'What was the woman's name again?'

'Mary Prince,' Nalini shot back. 'I got the book out of the library.'

'I'd like to have a look at it some time.'

Anything Nalini. Karl would be *oh my days*, if he could hear him, *all of a sudden you are into doing extra college work*? He was changing.

Nalini pulled on his sleeve. Her hand stayed on his sweater, he wanted to shift but not for her hand to move. It took his whole willpower to keep still.

'Don't do it just to impress me.'

Why did she have to be so bang on the money?

'I'm not.' His head was moving left and right as if it was on rotation.

'Abu.' She was still holding on to his sweater. His legs were on their way to a major cramp and he had to give in. His knee released and his foot started tapping.

'What is the deal with you and Leicester?'

'Why are we talking about Leicester now?' Her fingers went from Abu's arm to stroking his hair.

'Everyone is scared of the guy. You always have something to say to him.'

'How do you know?'

She had caught him. He hadn't been around much when she gave Leicester lip, not outside class.

'I hear about things. Maybe I saw you once or twice.'

'That guy is an arsehole.'

'Everyone knows that, but he also has a temper.'

Nalini shrugged her shoulders. 'So do I. You just haven't seen me yet.'

She pointed at his face. 'Your eyes are about to pop out. You don't believe me?'

'I don't.'

The streets were getting busier. A woman in a grey skirt suit and brand new trainers was power walking by them, a laptop bag swinging with every step.

'I caught him in a vulnerable position once. He's just trying to get in there before everyone figures out his life is just as sad as the rest of us.'

She stared at the estate as if she could pull Afsana out by osmosis.

'What do you know? Help us out here. Leicester would be finished—'

Her hand caught his in the air. She pulled it down. She was so close now he could smell her face cream.

'You don't want to know.'

They were standing hand in hand but not like he had dreamt of. This was accidental, her thoughts trailing somewhere he couldn't follow and it didn't have all that much to do with him.

'Normally I wouldn't be all into the whole Mary Prince thing, you're right, and yeah it started because, erm, you know ...'

There was air between their hands again, she had let go. She turned her face towards him.

'Know what?'

'You know...' He nodded to a couple of guys on the other side of the road. 'But when you got all excited it made me think. You never really know what's going on, right were you live. I mean *was* going on.'

She narrowed her eyes and nodded. 'I'm so busy with this I can't even tell you. I mean what does it mean for a whole country, you know. For us. Like history. All the money here, in the country, so much is from that time. From slavery. It's like mad.'

Abu was biting his lip.

'And Mary Prince ... I'm just thinking about courage. About speaking your own mind. And then there is this black woman and she did just that. Being young now and having the courage to be who you are. To speak your mind. To be different. Things like that.'

His face relaxed and he nodded.

'Speaking your own mind ... I do that. Kind of.' He laughed.

'That's why I'm chatting with you.'

To say he was relieved was an understatement. He wasn't made out for this sort of intensity. Not first thing in the morning. But then it felt good as well, good and special. Exclusive. Afsana was waving from the door to the tower block.

'Leicester thought we could be an item.'

'What?'

'Not now, some time back. I went to his house once. Sad situation there. But that wasn't the reason.'

Abu could feel the anger rising inside of him. Bloody Leicester. He wanted to ask more but his mouth stayed shut, teeth pressing on each other.

'You're right. I don't have a temper, not like that. That's why I don't go out with arseholes.'

Afsana arrived and looked at them.

There was a silence. Abu and Nalini smiling. Things were on a roll. Just the two of them.

The next day Abu sent Karl a bbm. *waz happening blud, u callin me or wat? U wont believe this history project week. talk bout slavery rite where we live. @ leigh st! is like crazy.*

Karl replied *seriously?!!? call u l8r.* And when he did, that evening, Abu told him all about Mary Prince, the first black woman to write about her experiences of being enslaved. How she had been taken from Antigua by her slaver, to the bottom of where they lived, to Leigh Street, exactly.

'Same old bloody street we walk along all the time. Can you believe it?' Abu shouted, and it was a shock. His new vehemence, his new interest. Abu didn't tell Karl about the urgency. How it like, pushed through him. How he couldn't think of much else, but everything her. He had stayed behind, in college, after classes, to catch up and find information on the Camden Slavery Trail. Nalini would like that. She would do her attention thing again, right? Be impressed that he kept up with her. With everything her. They could check out the neighbourhood, *their* neighbourhood, together. His chest puffed up, filled with the importance, his new purpose. He told Karl he would forward him some stuff by email.

'In case you ever go online. I mean if you ain't too busy, all important and so on over there.'

Neither of them picked up on the fact that, like Mary Prince, they had been doing their own sort of running on that same street. Right at the bottom of Leigh Street.

He didn't tell Karl much about Nalini. It didn't feel right.
Karl should know by being there. Wasn't like Abu had to
fill in every detail before. Karl didn't ask much either, no
making up for missing out on Abu's most important change
this side of the season. Just listened and was *oh wow, slavery
right there, need to find out more, creepy, innit* and *Nigeria is
interesting.* Interesting. Like nice. No bloody info whatsoever.
You might as well say *don't feel like telling you anything*.

* * *

Karl woke and the sound of Rose was in his head. A muffled
baby cry. He remembered how he had picked her up the
previous day and how she had stopped immediately, looking
at him curiously. It had tugged so heavily, direct line to the
mushy part inside him.

Daylight filtered into the small room. There was no baby.
It was at John's. He was at the bungalow. Where his father
was supposed to be. But wasn't. Uncle T had got some people
involved. He had just said 'security people'. Karl should not
bother about it. All was going to be well.

Karl's shoulder was stiff, courtesy of falling asleep with his
mobile in hand. Abu. Nalini. And Karl. Here. There. Things
had changed in these past ten days. Time was speeding up,
like no man's business.

Nakale was taking him along today. Since their first
introduction in the buka, Karl met him there almost daily,
when Nakale wasn't at uni. Mena felt they would be good
friends. She liked Karl. She liked Nakale. End of story. You
could call it meddling but someone would have to show
him more of the city. The real city. And what was on the
outskirts, what was hidden. Uncle T was trying his best to
find the father while doing business. Meaning he was away
the whole time. John was trying to make up for the absent
father but also had business, even if that was coming along
rather slowly. And he was sort of that little bit too old for
proper youth type hanging. Mena – Karl now called her
'Auntie' like Nakale – wanted Karl to get to know the place.
Nakale wanted to show him what he did in the little spare
time he had. The recording of what was going on in the area.
The pollution and stuff. Karl was in sync with that. He could

not leave like some lazy tourist who had only seen the inside
of some fancy bungalow.

'Well, it's a precaution only. You are not from here.'
  'I get it,' Karl replied. 'I stick out like a walking cash point.'
That's how it is when you're light-skinned like me, Karl thought.
You don't blend with the locals. No fucking chance. However
annoying that was. He wondered how it had been for his
mum. It must've been much worse, the sticking out. He had
texted her that morning. Told her of the great time he had
(had left out where that was though), that he was learning so
much about himself, and that he would be calling her soon,
very soon but his credit was almost gone and he couldn't
reply that often. Rebecca had probably never expected it to
be different. Had known that she wouldn't be able to fit in,
period. Karl wasn't feeling her any more than he did when
he left. To keep a father from him for the whole of his life
wasn't softened by how her trip here might have been all
that time ago.
  Nakale's head turned. They were sitting in the back of a
blue taxi, discussing the day ahead.
  'Cash point?' Nakale giggled.
  'Like where you get money. With your card, innit,' Karl
replied. Then his face relaxed. 'You know, most people at
home don't carry much cash. We use cards everywhere.'
  Nakale answered, 'We just call it a bank.'
  Both laughed. Nakale was pleased. This was a *I got you*
reply and Karl nodded, *yes this one is yours.* His eyes followed
the passing scenery like, *hello, speed limit?* The tall palm
trees, the houses bunched up together all random, the small
villages that ran past the window. The endless stream of
petrol stations. One after another, like for real. Some of their
names familiar but others Karl had never heard of. Some
abandoned as if someone had left in a hurry.
  The highway was a bit more proper than most of the streets
he had travelled on so far. Better even than the road from
the airport. Almost no potholes. Between the tall trees that
shot into the sky and ended in heads that opened like bushy
green umbrellas, arms waving for attention when there was
the tiniest bit of breeze, were chimneys just as skinny. High
up, boring concrete pipes, nothing going for them in terms
of design. Also waving. But without any patience. Was all

deep orange, spitting around, tiny bits of smoke above. They stopped by the side of the road. Nakale on Karl's case. Wanting him to see this front row.

'Comot for car. You fit hear am.'

Karl stepped out into the heat. There was bush in front. The road was like a highway, without any railing, nothing between you and the effing cars. The tar bright black, smooth, looking all promising, very promising, for this Nigeria's future. The wilderness in front too thick to look through but in the distance those ugly funnels, making a whole lot of noise. Hissing. Burning. Spitting.

Karl was getting dizzy. Nakale had told him that the kids in some remote villages didn't even know what electricity was. Some company working right in the middle of their land, large turbines in the field next door, keeping the whole operation top level. The villagers? Nothing for them. Anything infrastructure was just for production. Sharing is caring, my arse. Flow stations, into which the oil was transported from oil rigs, on grass fields. Close by, two tarred strips, almost too narrow to fit a single lorry's wheel. Just wide enough so that you could carry away the pumped oil. Between the tarred strips, wild grass, up to your hip. It'd snap when the vehicle snuck away, carrying the totally local oil. Some kids knew electric light only from these skinny chimneys. The ones with the waving, spitting fire at the top. Their own village dark at night. Like, completely. They called that burning 'Shell light'. You didn't have to be a genius to work that one out.

Karl just stood, looked at the things. The chimneys looked like they were some major affair, even if ugly. Looked like someone was controlling the area from below them. He climbed back into the car.

'They call it gas flaring?'

'Yes. The village we are passing. Life expectancy only thirty-five years. Because of the flaring. The gas, it comes back with the rain. There's toxicity. Health problems.'

Karl wanted to return to the buka. To the 'it is well'. 'But at least people benefit a little? Like jobs, I mean?'

Nakale started another lesson about how the employees in the oil industry were mostly from other states of the country. Excuse being that the locals weren't educated enough. Although there were laws against it, it was still going on. It had to be all that doom and gloom didn't it?

Karl thought about his father. When he had asked Uncle T why his father lived in Port Harcourt but Uncle T and the rest of the family in Lagos, Uncle T explained that his wife's connections had landed Adebanjo his job here. Nakale looked old when he went all into the details. Karl sat quietly in the back of the taxi.

The next day, Nakale came by the compound after morning lectures. He often took his own samples into the outdated university lab and sold the reports to environmental organisations, trying to build relationships with some of the NGOs so they would help his career. Nakale wanted Karl to know the things that didn't make news. The way news was made here, or more effing precisely: there. Abroad. What was left out.

Maybe he could be useful, be able to help Nakale. Somehow. Being here felt like King's Cross was a piece of cake.

'I learn to look at the evidence,' Nakale said. 'The things you measure. Whether you take the sample of drinking water to our old lab or send it to some American place. It will tell you the same thing. It will show you that you cannot drink this water.'

His anger was so calm it woke you up. Was *are you not meant to be proper vex*? But Nakale was all factual, like the evidence he collected with the help of his university lab. He hadn't looked at Karl for quite a while. They slowed down and Nakale pointed to the gated premises. Security men with machine guns were all Terminator-style, protecting whatever was behind the high-fenced, barbed-wire walls. Nakale added how the village kids played underneath the Shell light, mesmerised by the spectacle, which did not even break for the night.

'They neva tell us how much de danger, what it go do for us. For our health. And this our leaders be too greedy. Anything whey come him way, him go take. Him no go ask wetin dey happen for later. He just think make me chop now. This money, the oil money, it has made our country. But de people here, who are suffering because of it, we have not enjoyed. We have not seen our share.'

'I get you but what are they chopping off?'

Nakale stopped in his tracks. Eyes wide open. *What the what?* 'I no understand.'

'You said someone is chopping something. I didn't get it. You mean like chopping off opportunities? The lifeline of the fishermen or something?'

Nakale startled. 'Chopping who? I just said the big man, the one in charge thinks make I chop now. Let me eat now.'

'Eat?'

'It is just the way we speak. Chop. Eat. Enjoy. It is just how we say it.'

'Because you like to eat. So to eat is what you do when you have the money to eat? So if you have more money you will eat more?'

Something like it. You could say it like that. But Karl was defo trying too hard. Where was the flow mate? Just hang. Be. Present.

They returned to the buka in time for the last batch of hungry customers. John had instructed Nakale quite firmly: 'Not later than five. You hear?'

He wasn't going to have Uncle T on his case. They still had to drive across town to get him to the father's house.

Karl quickly greeted Mena and thanked Nakale. He ran up the stairs, exhausted and sweaty, taking two steps at a time. Uzo motioned to the kitchen. There was food, he could wait for her, just a little moment until she had rocked Rose to sleep. Karl's phone was ringing. Rebecca. He excused himself and slipped into the little room that had been assigned to him. The display went back dark once the ringing stopped. He would text her later, before bed. Some things were better seen than heard. Especially when they were lies.

There was a small towel on the mattress on the floor. The boxes and bags and items had been tidied at the end, stacked as much as possible.

He went to wash off the dust and all the shit that came with standing at the side of secluded rural roads staring at the bushy strip next to the tarred street, witnessing the leaking gas, while the sun beat down on you. Faint puffs escaping through holes in rusty bundles of pipes that lay open. You could see it. The way the gas danced above the metal, disappearing into the sky while new fumes pushed through. All the bloody fucking time. And where was the fucking balance?

'Are you listening man? Karl?'

'Defo bruv.'

Karl could see the money ticking away on the little display in the Internet and phone shop he was standing in. It was a low shack in a row of five. The one right next to it sold everything from brightly coloured flip-flops (which he had got a pair of the second day he arrived at John's – it seemed like ages ago), to cheap two-piece dresses in plastic covers that hung from the back wall, to children's shoes. On the far end of the tiny shopping cluster, a dark woman sat on a low wooden stool. Her wrapper, tied above her breasts, left her smooth shoulders in view. She sold face creams and lotions.

It was quiet on the street. Electricity had done a runner as soon as Abu picked up on the other end. A little transformer, something Karl didn't know or recognised, was humming away, keeping the computers healthy by protecting them from the sudden power losses and surges.

'Well?'

It wasn't a question. It was a *I'm having enough of this. Pretty soon. Try harder blud.*

'So she was like impressed, right?'

'She was.'

The tension was clear. Karl's mind had been drifting throughout their conversation.

'Do you hang out all the time now?'

'I told you—' Abu blurted.

'Cool man,' Karl interrupted. 'I just mean like a lot. Are you like hanging out all the time?'

'Not all the time but yeah, I try to catch them on their way to college and she often waits after, innit. So I don't have to walk alone.'

Karl could feel the pride.

'Aw, bless. You're like married already.'

'Whatever. She is different. Got opinions, like you. Not just pretty you know.'

'Never said she was just pretty—'

'I'm just saying, Karl. I'm just trying to tell you my shit, you get me? Do you have a minute for that or not?'

They were so, like, doing the absolute opposite of bonding.

'I'm going to do project week with her. We can visit a team at uni who are doing major research about it. Not that you care. Was her idea.'

'Extra college work in summer holiday? Wow, you have changed.'

'Did you get my email about the slave thing? Here in Leigh Street, and all around here.'

A boy came back lugging a half-filled plastic container. The shop owner unscrewed the cap, both from the vessel and the small generator outside her shop, keeping the door open. Karl could hear the diesel gurgling into the machine.

'Didn't have a chance to look at it man. Been busy myself. That guy Nakale, I told you about—'

'Yes you told me about Nakale.'

Abu was unimpressed to the max. Nakale. Again. Almost two weeks of Nakale this, Nakale that. Karl could almost see his face, all *who the eff cares about your bloody Nakale. There is us. Me. You get me.*

'Sounds cool though. Project week.' Karl stared at the ticking timer again.

'Any news from your father? Or when you're coming back? People are starting to forget you here.'

'Not sure. Just going with the flow. They have heard from him; he is well but not back. Uncle T is on it.'

Godfrey was on his back. This was not the arrangement they had made and why couldn't he trust him? Could he not at least check in regularly as they had agreed? Why always this disappearing act? Rebecca was on his case, wanted details. He couldn't keep her out of the loop forever. Etc., etc. King's Cross was slowly fading away, like a painting left on the side of a street. Godfrey wasn't going to take his bullshitting much longer. He could see him coming to Port Harcourt. Dragging him back, making a big scene. 'Told you I'd find you,' on his lips. He chuckled.

'What? Ain't really funny, is it.'

'Not that. Sorry.'

Karl could hear the irritation in Abu's voice. Where was the flow? Why was it like hardening tar? Not moving. At all.

The storeowner yanked the string and the generator sprang into action as commanded. Karl applied some proper engagement in his voice, like caring for what was said and showing interest. He didn't tell Abu anything about his first trip to oil land. How it had kept him up most of the night thinking about thirty-five-year life expectancy. Godfrey's age. And Shell lights. And the fucking world that was out of balance. Felt like not the right time, to say that he wasn't really all that busy with King's Cross.

* * *

Abu moseyed back from the UCL library. Project week was already coming to an end. Nalini had left a while ago.

'My mother wants me to pick up something from the market. You tell me tomorrow what you find?'

'You don't even have to worry about that.'

It was how the professor related everything in the lecture they sat in earlier. He wouldn't know how to put it in his own words yet, but it made sense. A whole fucking lot of it. Compensation had been paid to the so-called slave owners for the freeing of enslaved people. She kept insisting, *enslaved*, not slaves. Abu remembered 2007. He had just started secondary school but it was the thing of the year, with older pupils organising events to commemorate it. The bicentenary. He felt different about all of it now that he sat looking at the large photocopied map the professor had given him. It was a bit out of control. All those events and no realness, not like now, like what he learned about the neighbourhood. About who profited after the great thing happened. The abolition of the slave trade. Not the freeing of the enslaved.

'So here are the buildings in which people who received compensation for the loss of slave labour lived. Here' – she pointed to the list – 'you can see exactly how much, what their names were, and how many enslaved people they "owned".'

She said that no one 'owned' anyone, that they couldn't ever. But that the system said so. Because it had been good for it. For the whole empire.

His knees bopped underneath the heavy wood table. There was something about the names. His fingers traced the lines, trying to read the tight handwriting. The number of people compensation was paid for. And nothing for the enslaved, for their forced graft. Can you imagine? Their names weren't even mentioned. The anger rose so suddenly it took him by surprise.

At home the twins came running as soon as he bounced up against the door, keys in hand.

'Abu. Godfrey is here.'

Abu looked up, his eyes tired from scrutinising the small print in the library. Godfrey was in the living room, all sports-clothed-up like he had sponsorship. Liked to wear his trackies whenever possible. Probably to feel more youthful. His hair smelling of whatever he used to get it all shiny like that.

'Yu'aright?'

'And hello to you. Don't overdo it on politeness.'

'What have I done now?'

'I need to speak to your man. Like now.'

'Can't help you with that. How's it going?'

'If not for Karl taking major liberties, I would be perfectly fine. '

'That's his own thing over there. Nothing I can help you with.' *Or want to*, he added silently. Why always him? Why always Karl? If he didn't want to come back, whatever. People would just have to live with it. He did.

'Abu. Why don't you speak to your friend?'

Perfect. His mother placed a small plate with snacks in front of Godfrey and looked at Abu with her eyebrows up. Killer look. He had to think of Karl and what he always said about his mum. He was right. She was totally on it, she could suss it out, any time. But Abu was growing out of it and if he was honest a bit tired of it as well. It wasn't fair. Too one-sided. The placing all on him as if Karl was proper damaged. He wasn't. Abu knew it. Everyone knew it. He had some issues because he was alone often, etc. But didn't they all have issues? Where was time for Abu's?

The two adults sealed the afternoon with summaries of Karl's inner workings, the way he ran yet remained always in tight circumference. How he just needed space.

'To breathe,' Mama Abu concluded.

'Lots of stuff, college,' Abu mumbled and grabbed the bag he dropped on the floor when he entered. Godfrey called after him.

'I need a number for him. He doesn't pick up his mobile.'

'Probably out of credit.'

'Well, I'll top it up for him then.'

'Why don't you top up mine instead?' He shouldered the bag and left for his room. It was stuffy in the small space. The bed unmade. He managed to keep his mother out, a leftover from Karl's careful tidiness, but he couldn't be bothered to keep it up. And of course, with making sure he didn't miss Nalini, he had started leaving earlier.

He opened a window and peered out. Opposite, through some high gates inside the next estate's inner yard, two men shook hands. He couldn't hear them. There was helicopter noise, coming and going. The London sounds he had grown up with. Every crucial football match, protest march or whatever, they were on it, from above. Doing their rounds. *Paranoid*, he thought. There had been many protests lately though, now that the country was busy with university fees rising and the words of the year: austerity measures and cuts. The cuts. He didn't get it all but that the banks had effed up, that much was clear. Worse, everyone but the banks was now paying for it.

He closed the window, pushing the blanket aside to sit on the bed. Godfrey was still upfront, his voice filtering through the thin door. Abu hadn't considered uni but since hanging out with the Godfreys of his generation, for whom there were no untalented youth, just misdirected potential, he had heard all about the opportunities on offer. Everyone believed in Abu, but he wasn't the smart one. Or the troubled one. Didn't need all that much care. Already had a good, functioning family.

Godfrey once promised to see about an internship opportunity at a small, local radio show. Of course everything was forgotten when Karl did the next runner. That time he stayed out all night, so alert was proper high.

The rotating sound got louder and louder, the helicopter approaching his area. After that night Godfrey was busy keeping an even closer eye on Karl. Wasn't much time left to remember Abu. When Godfrey finally did, one of the wannabes was doing the gig. Local radio programme, about what the youth want. But then no one cared what Abu wanted. Not even Karl. Not any more.

Abu wanted to tell Karl that do-goody didn't pay any more but he wasn't here anyway. Karl's good credit seemed to have crashed suddenly too. He didn't even seem to care.

Abu kicked a pair of jeans that he hadn't bothered washing for the past two weeks. Everything Karl. It could drive you up the wall, for real, even if you were proper loyal.

14

**Rules – they show you
which one is this side
which one is that side.**

Abu's mobile vibrated. *WTF?!! waz goin on in t'ham. where
ru? pickup!!* He didn't feel like answering. What was Karl on
about now? If he missed him or anyone else, he should just
get his sorry self back over here. Five weeks since he had
left, two weeks since project week had finished. Time was
standing still; it didn't even exist any more. He had barely
made it through Saturday by hanging with his new mates,
holed up in one of their bedrooms, to play the latest version
of Lara Croft. They half-heartedly invited him into their little
group because he could talk the talk like no one else. It was
entertaining when he stood up to older people with his *yeah
and that's what you get for the lost youth, told you no manners
at all*, and threw the fast food wrapper on the street. Wasn't
that much of a deal. Only he would take it out of the bin,
in front of the person who had just discarded it, and then
deposit it on the pavement, just to make a point (once they
had left, head shaking, he would be back to collect the shit
and put it back in the bin. He had manners, like for real, was
just feeling the no future thing). Something was changing.
Abu couldn't help himself. It blinded him. Loyalty is to be
in balance is to be equal. Isn't it?

There wasn't anything to do and his new friends drove
him up the wall. Nothing, nothing to chat about. No opinion,
whatsoever. The summer was drifting unbearably. He had left
them early and stayed up all night, watching *Dexter* episodes
with his father, who was off work for a few days (or nights, if
you wanted to be all correct about it), and wanted to speak
with him about the slavery thing. Interested. Intrigued. But

also just wanting to bond with this child of his, who was outgrowing his childhood.

But Abu used only words that had less than three syllables, and only one word at a time. They had sat lost in their own translations, aka, thoughts.

'He has been away for much longer than expected.'

Baba Abu had tried a different angle. Abu didn't respond.

'It must be hard. The sudden change. It is not like Karl to ...'

Abu's head moved back and he exhaled. Loud and deep and long. Looked at the ceiling. Kept his mouth shut. His father looked at him. They sat like that for ages. Nothing coming past Abu's mouth. The chatterbox. The not-keeping-it-in-when-necessary. The I-can-talk-anyone-into-their-grave. Silent. Not one single word uttered. His eyes fixed on the crack in the faded white paint above him until his dad finally went to bed. Abu had flicked through the programmes until it got light.

He was grateful to be sleeping and turned his head back to the wall. There it was again, the sharp smell of sweat and lack of fresh air of the past weeks. Courtesy of his feet, which were glued into his first-class trainers at daytime. One of the other things his pretend new mates accepted him for.

'Respect. You decent bruv.'

London warmed up finally. Summer was here. He pulled the duvet over his head and closed his eyes.

* * *

'Him no answer.'

Nakale was taking Karl to the lab for the first time. He had made his way to where Nakale lived so they could catch one of the motorcycles, an *okada*, together. He lived in a similar set-up to John, a few streets away.

Uncle T was fine with it. Basically Uncle T was busy. His shipment was on its way. The person who seemed to not be on his way was Karl's father. The security company was saying they were in touch. To be patient. It was the fifth week of his trip. Godfrey was angry. Very angry. He called twice a day, although Karl didn't pick up. The texts said it all. Most of them where exclamation marks. *Call me back NOW!!!* But Karl didn't want to leave. Was trying to be Nakale's sidekick.

Learn more. Be of use. Be here, just be here, you get me.
No shit from the wannabes, no past. Just now. What was
one more week? Summer holidays had started anyway; he
wasn't even missing college.

They were passing a dark shop next to an unpainted house.
Nakale's auntie owned the tiny spot. A young woman was
standing in front, raising her hand in acknowledgment.

'Auntie not in?' Nakale asked.

'She had something to do.'

Nakale nodded and waved down an okada.

'My cousin.' He rushed to talk to the okada rider.

Karl looked back. The cousin was fresh-faced, all clear
skin, defined cheekbones, lips that you wanted her to say
something with. Or lick. Or anything that would make them
move and show all of their fullness in action. She looked
him up and down.

'You keep calling your friend, Karl, until you reach him,'
Nakale insisted, and Karl nodded, absent-minded. The
young woman turned back. She stroked the fabric she was
holding, unfolded it, held it up into the air. Her hair was all
roughed-up Afro in a very, very cool way. Like you wanted
to play with it and say something even cooler. Her toes were
sticking out of some trainers that had the front bit cut off.
In a fashionable way. And a heel. Like sandals cum running
gear cum wicked outfit. It went well with her denim skirt.

'With friends you have to keep trying and trying. You don't
give up. Even if they are angry.' Nakale had to bring him
back to earth, didn't he?

> **absence** /ˈæbsəns/
> noun
> 1. State or occasion of being away from a place
>   or person.
> 2. A neither here nor there marked by not being
>   able to be applied, or defined.
> 3. That which is not present.
> 4. If present is taken as related to gift (that which is
>   bestowed on someone) it might resemble theft.

Karl nodded and sat behind Nakale, who had already climbed
behind the okada rider. Three of them on the bike, the two

friends with their hands backwards, holding on to the seat. Nakale's cousin waved. What was her name? Nakale hadn't even said. Karl didn't let go of the small motorcycle and just nodded.

Once at the lab, Nakale's never-tiring self showed him the whole campus before they settled in front of a workbench. He started on his samples.

'Look for here.'

Nakale took him through the soil sampling procedure. Karl wanted to know all of it. Know all the shit that was going on, but science wasn't his strong subject. His mind was drifting; he couldn't even fake it. Nakale said 'OK make we go see am.' Meaning, let's start with where he took the sample. Show Karl the site. Again. Maybe Karl would have a better attention span then.

Nakale asked the driver to stop the okada on the side of a small bridge. There were some proper dramatic Shell lights, just behind the village. He wanted to show him before they moved on to taking soil samples. The stretch of dusty tar made a tense intro to the dancing flame show ahead.

'Cashpoint,' Nakale had started calling him. 'You see am innit, or is London brain blocking your absolutely fabulous precious veew?'

'Bruv, ahbeg. No easy de way you de block am with your big Uniport head.'

They were laughing, Nakale appreciative – he had taught his friend well – when the five twenty-somethings appeared out of nowhere and surrounded them.

'OK. Bring moni!' they demanded quick, didn't bother with introductions.

Karl turned around, perplexed, but then the dimples smoothed when his jaw dropped.

'For what?' Nakale replied.

'For de thing you do.'

'For what?' he repeated.

Karl thought of King's Cross. Seemed like every place had their share of interrupting a-holes. Only these did not at all look like they were trying to be anything. They were. Like in completely. Already somebodys.

'You are journalists. De moni you carry.' The leader of the
pack was doing a good job being threatening, in your face,
hands too close to your body for comfort.

'Money for what?' Nakale wasn't having it. He gripped the
sides of the okada as if he was scared his anger would make
him jump off, volcano-like, throw himself on the guys, which
would so not help the situation.

The okada driver held on to the rust-dotted handlebars,
probably cursing the second he had accepted the job. The
young men shouting ignored him, the focus all on Karl.

Karl was all piece of wood slammed into the face.
Dumbstruck. Silent. Then, as the men's voices got louder
and louder, accusing them, well Karl, of working for an
overseas paper for 'whey him go carry big moni when him
sell de pictures,' trying to interfere. It took a while to get the
whole thing. Karl's Blackberry. That was the problem. The
super tech device that would earn him major cash through
first-class pics. He wanted to laugh because earlier that
morning he had had to take out and reinsert the sim a few
times before anything happened on the screen. Had to use
the second-favourite IT trick (after turn off and on again):
soft but persuasive bangs on the table.

But the guys were not up for a laugh, so much was clear.
They were like a phone upgrade to contemporary Londonites:
one more, and another one, attracting more of their friends
until it was twelve of them, all moving hands in the air, poking
Karl's shoulder, demanding explanations, demanding his
little bag (water, always carrying water but they probably
thought money), and of course his phone. Maybe these
were the without-jobs youth, like back home, or the not-
wannabes-but-for-real of the Niger Delta, he thought, while
his legs became soft and he became scared they wouldn't
carry him through.

Nakale totally unimpressed. He had remained all bored
expression and firmly on top of the motorcycle. The driver
tried to dismount a few times but with Nakale tight behind
him, wedging him in, all he could do was hold the handlebars
and hope for the best.

But whatever they were, job or no job, the men were also
healthy-looking, strong, fit. Like in punch you out in one.

'Come down. Come down for okada.'

Nakale stubborn, holding on to the bike.

'Give us de moni or—'

'You know we do kidnapping for here,' somebody interrupted and the rest got lost amidst the shouting that restarted, now, about what price Karl should pay for his release. The leader, a skinny dark man with taut muscles and a vein that wanted to explode out of his temples, screamed at the top of his voice.

'Undredtausand, undredtausand. Make he bring am!' He slapped his fist into the other hand and his face went all alien. Scrunched up. Ugly. Karl wanted to kneel on the dusty road. Do his swan-like fall, then hide under his arms, hands covering the eyes. You didn't have to be there for everything. You could just let it happen without you. Not even Uncle T or Godfrey could bail him out now. But the man's friends shouted back what type of nonsense he was on about. No one would pay that.

'Na small boy.'

And the negotiations continued.

'$5000.'

'Him no carry dat type of bread. Wetin be wrong wit you?'

'Two thousand.'

'Ah! Sey 500.'

'One thousand.'

Back and forth like bad table tennis, and Karl managed to stay on his feet, arms by the side. They seemed to forget their two hostages, who were still blocked up, unable to move, in the middle of their testosterone-oozing circle.

'Him no carry any moni at all. Na be school boy. Na £20. Make we move.' Nakale seemed to be immune to the danger. Or just too angry.

They cried out what insult, what this, what that. But they weren't proper vex; their voices had got softer. You didn't have to be a genius to see that, close-up, Karl was indeed a small college boy, unlikely to be connected to any of the oil giants, or he would not have been seen on some rattling old okada, in the middle of this lonely rural road. The phone was not the camera they thought it was. It was all ridiculous. Someone could come by any minute. Someone who would not participate. And as much as they shouted they knew they didn't have it in them to kidnap a small boy. Take him where? To their parents, where they lived and who would 'I go beat you' them as soon as they entered the house? They had not thought this out. Kneejerk reaction. Opportunists really. But not good on the improv side of things. They were not the ones who had joined any of the militant gangs more prominent on the winding creeks, far from the boring road that they could reach from their sleepy village. After almost an hour of shouting, there was nothing, just the effing dead end they wanted to escape.

'Karl, give him your emergency money,' Nakale hissed in a low voice while he locked eyes with the driver, who had turned around. And Karl slipped off his trainer, hands shaking, fished out the soggy £20 note he kept folded small in his socks. Held it out to Nakale who took it before anyone had clocked anything. When Karl hesitated he hissed again.

'Ahbeg, quick.'

And while the group were still effing Naija-style about the price, Karl put back his trainer, sat back on the okada. Nakale tapped the driver on his shoulder and whispered in his ear. He turned the key in the ignition. Nakale looked at the two reasonable members, a stocky man with a wide gap between his front teeth and a soft-spoken tall one with a faded red cap who stood directly in front of them. They had been ignoring the aggressive shorty once they had told him that his demands were ridiculous, but paid attention to their silent movements. When Nakale looked at them they nodded, and he squeezed the driver's arm. The okada jumped and gripped the tar and they fled from the dancing flames and the mob that was now angry with the two collaborators, their pride defeated, stinging.

Nakale dropped him a little way off John's home.

'Karl. I'm sorry. Just small-village boys. This thing never happen before.'

He reached out to Karl, who turned his back to him, all lost in his mind, no processing, just trying to keep it all out, banishing the pictures, trying to keep his eyes dry, his hands still, the sweat from pouring.

'Don't tell John. Or your uncle.'

'Course not. Am not stupid.' And he left Nakale, who looked worried; returned to the safety of the small back room at John's as quickly as his excuse of upset stomach, bad food, let him.

The next day Nakale and Karl went back to the lab. Pretended nothing had happened, took off where they had left it. It wasn't the first time Karl was jumped and, either way, no one had really touched him.

Nakale carefully recorded something in his chart that was made of neat, biro-drawn tables.

'The increase is here, you see. From that large spill a few weeks ago, the Christmas tree I show you.'

The structure of short metal valves and fittings had spurted gallons of oil high up in the air. Nakale had shown it to him on their first field trip because the huge spill had attracted international attention. He had also pointed out the clean-up procedure: a tractor had dug up the earth so that the fresher white sand lay on top, merely covering the stained, polluted soil underneath. That was it. Nothing else.

'You're going to pass this info on, right?'

'I better wait and show later what type of cleaning is done and that nothing has improved. At all.'

'Why can't you just take them to court or something?'

Nakale's forehead was shiny with all the sweat. He put the pen next to the paper on the scratchy lab table.

'Which money go help anyone believe me? And who cares about some small pollution here?'

'But it's the truth man. If you show them, I mean this is not some random shit. You have all the data.'

'Then some company's money will convince them that it is not so.' He paused and stared at the writing in front of him. He sounded exhausted and turned back to his papers and flicked through them, his eyes scanning over the figures he had taken during the past fourteen months. He didn't include Karl, didn't slide anything closer, highlight particular entries. Karl didn't seem to get how things were working here, or how they weren't working, especially when you were a nobody like Nakale. So much was clear.

No need mum. I can stay longer. Godfrey thinks it's a good idea too. Easier to be away than to call all the time. My credit is almost gone. But will text you soon.

15

**And always
things turn.
Upside down.**

'You're not going anywhere,' Abu's mother shouted after
him. He was standing at the door, keys in hand.

'I just want to see my mates. I've been indoors since
Saturday night.'

His mother stepped in front of him and put the chain
on. Symbolic. She was good with her gestures, like with
her looks. Abu defied her. Looked away but his body was
clear; he wasn't giving in, not this time. His face wasn't just
stubborn: there was hurt there. Something that everyone
seemed to miss had bubbled up to the surface. You could
smell it. You could even touch it. It was there. His mother
studied his turned-away face. She pulled him into the living
room. The TV was on. The same picture on repeat. A large
building. In flames. The silhouette of a woman, captured
mid-air, jumping to safety. From her flat. On the ground,
people with outstretched hands, reaching for her. The fire
ravaging the large carpet shop. Abu's mother covered her
mouth with her hand. He could hear her breathe before she
pulled the twins close to her, one in each arm.

'Watch this.' She was looking at him.

The news of riots, sparking in Tottenham and quickly
spreading across the capital. Abu got it, Karl's missed calls.
Six of them. Eight texts. *tell me waz goin on. wtf?!* News was
not on his programme schedule. He had no clue whatsoever,
had missed the whole thing like proper because he had been
tired of his new mates, who weren't really friends at all. And
Karl, who had disappeared from his radar altogether. And

the adults, who were supposed to be fair and shit, and not dump everything on him.

'You're not going out.' His mother was all authority, and released her tight grip on the twins. Mother and son stared at each other.

'You are not going out Abubakar, I mean it.'

The twins sat on the floor, eyes on their brother. His sister said, 'Mom, why are you angry with Abu?'

Mama Abu shook her head. No reply. Eyes on Abu. This wasn't even telepathic communication any more. It was clear and straight. She went back into the kitchen. Abu sat down and changed channels. The twins were up on him.

'Why is mom angry with you?'

'I don't know.'

The footage was changing but showed the same. It was everywhere. Mark Duggan, a black man, had been shot by police in Tottenham. The circumstances seeming like usual – dodgy. White police, young black man. Dead. Days later, anger was all out of control. Spread and spread, first across the city, then across the country. The twins were glued to the pictures, couldn't look away.

'Abu, why is she jumping?'

'She's trying to be safe innit. The building is burning.'

'But why is it burning?'

'Someone put it on fire.'

'But she'll hurt herself, Abu, right?'

'It's more dangerous to stay inside. The flames would get her first, for sure.'

'Where is she going to live now?'

'Don't know, maybe relatives.'

'Did she hurt herself?'

His phone was beeping. There was force when he replied to the questions that kept coming like a broken tap.

'I don't know. I'm not there, innit.' He walked back to his bedroom and checked his mobile. *man it's like going on evrywhere. out of control. what u up 2? like rite now … ;)))*

One of his new mates. Shame Kyle and Mark weren't around. At least they were decent. This lot was all group pressure and he didn't even know half of the guys bouncing along when they met up. He looked at Karl's messages and finally replied. *only jus realised. all gud. what do u hear ova there?* And Karl's reply came seconds later. *Omg. reply nxt time! where r u?!!!!* It was a warm afternoon. Another text, another mate. He sat up, his face tense. Brain working. His mother was preparing dinner; he could hear the water running in the sink, the clonk of pots. It was only one large step to the wardrobe. Under a few T-shirts he found the sweater he was looking for and grabbed his older trainers that were stored away with his other shoes. The fabric was cool when he slipped the jumper over his head. The trainers felt a bit odd. Stiff, unfamiliar but after flexing his toes a few times they gave in and remembered his shape, his weight. The twins were running past the door.

'You do, you do, you do!' the boy shouted.

'Never, never, never,' the girl shot back.

Abu sat back on the bed. He could hear his mother whistling. A song he knew from when he was just the twins' age. She just couldn't get over it, loved that tune to death.

sorry been out of it. city jus killin me rite now, like proper. home bt leavin now. hackney. catch u l8r?

16

**To close
is always so much more
pronounced. With or without a bang.**

am linking wiv mates man. no time rite now.
Karl was folding his clothes.
don't get involved Abu! Won't end well.
'We can leave now,' John shouted from the living room.
Karl jumped up and into the bathroom to check on his looks.
how do u know? u here?
Karl's hair needed a crop. He pulled the vest down and
tucked it into his trousers, the T-shirt loose.
seriously? like this?! whats goin on with u?
'I'm ready.'
*tired of cleaning up after u. all u do is disappear. whatevr.
movin on*
After five weeks of being at John's, Karl was going back to
stay at his father's house. There was finally news from the
missing in action.
*not quite like it. Only been few wks
my point
is what?
6 wks of baby-sitting
then leave the house, no one forcing u 2 stay inside
thats what im doin
not what i mean
why not
coz u goin 2 get caught. we always do. u know that
different thing altogether
really?
evryone going
since when r u evry1*

since im ur errand boy. always takin crap for u. and where r u?
wtf abu if u can't handle fship let me know. thought we were
tight

They arrived at the gated community and the security
guard waved once he realised it was John in the back seat
of the taxi.

'How far?' he tipped his head and leaned over to the window
John had wound down.

'I dey I dey.' John replied, showing those teeth. He slid a
little forward on the hot seat to come closer.

where r u now?
still here
stay home. come on abu
why? jus going 2 check it all out.
cuz ur not rough like dat

The taxi climbed over the speed bump, raised cement
that covered the length of the street at the entrance to the
community. They followed the curved street around once
the wheels had carefully climbed over the second hump.

tis evr1, evrywhere. all ur do gud. Is all pretend. all u do is
leave others 2 clean after u
wat u talkin bout?
ur mum, godfrey, evry1

It was getting hot in the car.

who the fuck is evr1?
mates school my parents. evryone
waz ur problem?

The security guard had reported that Adebanjo had returned
in the afternoon. Uncle T had boarded the next flight back
from Lagos to Port Harcourt.

maybe im tired of getting it cause of you. U don't even know
how 2 be a frien

No reply.

im sorry man. its too much evry1 is on my case and u ain't
even here

No reply.

Karl

No reply.

man i'm sory!!!!!!!!!!!!!.

No reply.

'For here,' John instructed the driver. He got ready to leave the car. Karl didn't move, did nothing, just sat. John turned to him.

'You're are not coming?'

bbm me plz

Karl

ur my best mate. i know ur going thru stuff but fact is everone is. fact is ur mumm ain't dead. you can spend time with her you know. rite here, rite now. she's cool and u know it. ur father might never accept u. i have no clue what it's like over there but u know the shit here. you lucky man. other kids might be dead just coz of bullying. i'll fight anyone for you, any time. i will step in front if someone is coming for u. it's my job. just like arsenal's is 2 score. sure, they don't always do so, yes i don't always win but what i'm saying is: IM HERE. all the way. Something is happened man, like for real. call me ASAP. Abu

17

**Gestures. Opening and closing.
To do both is saying
quite loudly: no not now,
not here, not you.**

John opened the door and stepped out of the car. Uncle
T was shifting from one of his loafers to the other, white
handkerchief in hand, wiping his shiny forehead, pulling on
the other door so Karl could come out too. Karl didn't. The
front door opened. He could hear the excitement in John's
voice. It was all relief and shit. Greetings were exchanged.
Words passed back and forth. Uncle T laughed. Happy, it
seemed. John laughed too. A joke. Apparently. Karl remained
in the taxi. The driver turned around. But John hadn't paid
him yet.
  'Excuse. Other business. You pay me.'
  Karl looked down at his shoes. The trainers were dusty.
He would wipe them later. The taxi driver poked him. John
turned around from the conversation at the front door. Came
back to the driveway. Handed money to the driver. Karl
looked back down at his trainers. He had checked the whole
scene out. It was a clear view. A dark man stood on the other
side of the door, on the inside bit. In the half-shadow, half
inside the bungalow. His cheeks were sunken in as if he was
sucking on a cough drop and he frowned like he needed to
concentrate to get the juices out of the sweet.
  'Excuse!' The taxi driver was getting angry.
  'Karl, the driver needs to go. We are not paying him to wait.'
  Karl stepped out. He stopped at the car bonnet. It was warm,
very warm. The heat and the driving. Lethal combination.
Uncle T walked and motioned for John to come closer. They
talked in a low voice. There were grooves in the dust on Karl's

trainers. The water must have splashed on them when he was washing earlier. John turned to talk to the taxi driver. Karl couldn't hear anything. His ears were hissing. John's voice seemed shrill. He was saying something. The colours were bright. They stung the eyes. The air blocked the ears. Uncle T was smiling. He walked towards him, placed a hand on his shoulder. It was gentler this time, no clap, no heavy-handed slap.

'I think you will need some privacy. We will be back in one hour.'

John hugged him. His smile wanted to blow up his face. 'Finally!'

They entered the taxi with a nod to the driver. Both smiled, so pleased. It was good when things came together. Karl stood in the cemented driveway.

'I believe we have some catching up to do …'

Stepping away from the entrance, the father entered the room, leaving the door wide open. He turned his head, scrutinised him, two deep lines furrowing the forehead, eyes a good stare in them. They were the opposite of Karl's, no deflection whatsoever, no putting things at bay first, the processing in small bits, nothing at all, no fucking warmth as far as Karl was concerned, but all getting into your business, getting into you. Straightaway. No warm up.

'… Carla.'

It was musty inside. No one had bothered to open the windows when electricity failed in the morning. Uncle T doing business and in Lagos, Karl helping Nakale take care of business and sleeping at John's as usual. It could have gone on like this, as far as Karl was concerned. Not quite forever but for a long time. It worked. Everyone was happy. So far.

'Sit down.' The eyes were looking from Karl to the couch he now knew well from watching TV in the evenings while Uncle T was still on his phone to this or that person. He sat at the edge. Where he never sat.

'What do you want? Water, soft drink? Do you want to eat? I can send someone.'

'I'm fine,' Karl replied. The thank you was stuck in his throat. There was a pause.

'This is not what I've been expecting.'

Things were funny like that. *And this is not when I was expecting you.*

'Maybe some water.' All was drying up. Karl's thoughts felt slow and lumpy, a bad vacuum seal job. 'Please,' he added, 'sah.' John had said it so he would just copy him.

The father studied him. In silence.

Eventually, 'How do you find Nigeria?'

He walked to the small kitchen with a window that opened towards the lounge. The fridge made that typical release noise. His father took out an old plastic bottle. The label had been peeled off. It was foggy.

'It should still be cold.'

The sofa was different now. It felt a bit like King's Cross. He knew it but any minute someone could spoil the fun. His father looked again. Piercing.

'So?' He handed him a full glass. The water swashed over the rim and made an uneven circle on the side table.

'Pardon me?'

'What do you think of our country so far,' the father repeated with more emphasis. Was Karl included in the 'our'?

'I love it. Really. Brilliant visit so far.'

He reached for the water and gulped enough to push down the lump in his throat. He shouldn't have said that, should he? It was odd to call it brilliant when he was here to meet the man himself. The one in front of him. He should have kept it vague, like open, so the father could know that everyone was really upset that he had disappeared. He could see his father's legs, ashy feet in leather sandals with a large flap covering the top of the foot, a small leather ring for the big toe. They were obviously different. Very different. Uncle T and him. No moisturisation on this front. At all. The father didn't seem to believe in Uncle T's shea butter products. Not for the feet at least.

The seat cushion shifted. The father leaned back, arms crossed over his head, touching the wall, eyes looking straight ahead. Very delaying tactic for emphasis, for drama, as if rehearsed, but then again he'd had quite some time since Karl's arrival in Nigeria, weeks of leaving everyone in limbo land, just so he could now come with effing heavy artillery.

'I was expecting a daughter.'

Karl wasn't sure; was this for effect or was he for real?

When you close something, something that could have been an opening, the manner is always more defined, more punctuated than any question you could have asked. It ends up hanging on the hinges, only for effect.

body /ˈbɒdɪ/
noun *pl* bodies
     1. The entire physical structure of a human being.
adjective
     1. Versatile.

'I was standing at the airport waiting for you. I left. I wasn't in the position to come back.'

It was a strange conversation. Stranger than any of Abu's ramblings, which were well strange at times.

'Uncle T said you disappeared the day before.'

'Yes indeed, something happened.'

What effing sense did that make? Karl thought he had been kidnapped. Had he come to the airport or not? What was going on?

'How is your mother?'

'Very ill.' Another adult who couldn't stay with the topic.

'Tunde told me. What is it?'

'Multiple Sclerosis. Degenerative. She gets a lot of pain. Loses her mobility.'

'I'm very sorry to hear that. She was very active when I … knew her.'

'Yes, she used to do lots of things.'

Points need to be connected or made here, man. You couldn't just keep it all casual like this. Because it would fall through the cracks otherwise, become meaningless, nothing at all. Then what's the point? What's the fucking point?

'How long has she been ill?'

'For long, but it got worse the last four or five years.'

'I'm very sorry to hear.'

That made two of them. Sorry. About a lot of things. Karl was getting restless.

'And your injury?'

It was Adebanjo's turn to be surprised.

'I thought it all started because of your injury. That is how Uncle T came to talk about me. Or my mum. Rebecca.'

He looked at him. The father. Karl wasn't focusing on his face but even with lowered lids he could scan the body. All seemed fine now, no cast or bandage, nothing. But of course it had been months since. Since Uncle T's letter arrived in London.

'I caught a bad infection. It was serious for a few days but the antibiotics worked. There are some very good doctors here.'

'I can imagine.' Karl wasn't sure what he imagined. The good doctors? The leg injury? The hospital stay? A softer version of the cold man in front of him? One that matched the phone conversations they had had. *We look forward to welcoming you, Karl.* That person. Where was he?

A mosquito was buzzing around, amplifying the silence. You couldn't not look. Karl followed it with his eyes, thinking about the inevitable, the having to strip so that some stranger in front of you could decide whether you were good enough for them. Or not. Might as well get it over and done with.

'Being trans ... I always knew. As long as I can remember. Mum always let me be myself. When I was eleven I just said I wouldn't pretend to be a girl no more. She understood. She knew. I had never been one.'

It was hot, no fan or air-conditioning to separate the time from the weight that crushed down. For some reason they hadn't been turned on. Karl knew for a fact that the generator had enough fuel. They had topped it up only last night. His father was looking at him. Then back on the floor in front of him.

'Is it the reason you disappeared?'

What difference did it make, right? The falling, the running, the leaving? When you open to something it gives the illusion of boundless possibility. But you know how these things are, it is difficult to say what, when and how qualifies as being a beginning. Or possibility.

The mosquito buzzed and buzzed like there was no bloody tomorrow.

'Who knows?'

'About me being trans? Uncle T should have known but I think he doesn't. He never mentions anything. Maybe he's just cool like that. In fact ...'

Karl thought about how cool he actually was. Uncle T. He pushed the glass, only slightly, on the table. It slid over the bit of water that had spilled. At last something went smooth.

'Tunde doesn't know. Your mother never told him.'

The father leaned back further, as if that were possible, really, but once you are making dramatic statements with your body, you have to go there, all the way.

'When he told me about you I asked him. Naturally I wanted to know. Is it a boy or a girl? He didn't know. All he knew was that there was a child.'

Funny how life foreshadows better than spoiler alerts on Internet gossip magazines. He was his mother's baby. Nothing else. No drama. It had been like that when he had started on puberty blockers. Rebecca hadn't made a big thing of it. Most kids in his support group had had a much more difficult time with their parents' consent.

'Who told you to dress as a boy? What is this?' The way it was said you could have used it to break down passive-aggro behaviour to others. It was done so well, so clear, so stinging. The body shouted, the father's body, all the things that he wouldn't say. Almost like the skin was foaming, all the unsaid underneath bubbling away.

'I just told you—' But Karl stopped. His father was walking him to the front door, metaphorically. It was as if he had the knob in hand, the door already half-open, the air impatient and ready for Karl to be swept out.

'I cannot accept your behaviour.'

No one had asked. No one had talked about behaviour. Karl had spoken about *being*. Being himself. About gender and truth. That bodies weren't the marker, for anyone. That things weren't all that clear-cut or obvious. Not even what constituted a man or a woman. Boy or a girl. He would have said more, even. Opened up right here and there just to get it out of the way. To show that he understood if it took him a while, the father, to understand the details of Karl's transition. But that Karl was willing to share with him.

The father looked at Karl, eyes squinting now as if they would be able to squeeze something else out of this situation. Karl thought about where to continue, what next to offer. He was tired of explaining. His lips parted. The next sentence was going to reveal more than he had planned when he left London weeks ago. Not at their first meeting anyway.

'I think it's best for you to return to London straight away.'
Karl's mouth stayed open, words stuck inside.

Adebanjo lifted himself slowly off the cushiony chair. It was
grand, the movement. Calculated for maximum impact. The
weight shifted slowly away from the seat back to full standing.
Respect me, hai hai, respect me, hai hai. One of the songs
Karl's mother used to listen to and tell him how great the
singer was. Adeva or something. How she used to make the
dance floor hot. Another of those whatever-mum moments
because, frankly, who cared about parents' club days?

'Send my wishes to your mother.'

The mosquito must have found its way into one of the
bedrooms. It was quiet. The buzzing would have helped.
Karl could hear Adeva's song loud and clear. He should have
asked his mother what 'hot' had meant in her days. What
were clubs like? More importantly, could he go without any
curfew?

'But how did you know?' If it hadn't been Uncle T who had
told him, who was it?

The father had already closed for the day. Moved on like
end of discussion and so forth. 'Your friend, your uncle.'
Feet moved apart. 'What is his name?'

No eyes for Karl. He looked at himself. Metafuckinphorically
speaking. Karl was all puzzled. Who? Nakale?

'Godfrey.'

He was taller than Karl, a squarer version. Solid, well-
proportioned. His *there are no bad kids* Godfrey. *There are
only bad outcomes.* Godfrey! Like this wasn't like the worst
possible one? Karl sunk deeper into the couch. There wasn't
anything to say. Nothing. Abu would have come in handy
now. To take the edge off.

The father did his steady, confirming authority strides, all
the way down the hall. Returned in record time with a small
plastic bag, folded. Karl studied him. Now that this part of
fate was sealed he had time to check for resemblances. The
face, yes, some of it, the body, in a shrunken kind of fashion,
but he had noticed the lashes. A little longer than usual and
curved, but nothing like Karl's.

'This is for John, for his help. You can stay with him for
tonight. Tunde told me that you two are close.'

He handed him the bag. It contained wads of bundled naira.
'There is no need for him to know.'

He looked at Karl again. Eyes all the way, straight into the mind. Something, wanting something. Something undiscussable.

'Or Tunde.'

'He will probably wonder why I am not staying here after all this waiting.'

'I will make an excuse. I will have someone arrange your return.'

One last look, brief, a trained inspection, then the father returned to his bedroom, closing the door behind. Karl could hear a car climbing back on to the driveway. There had been no embrace. Their skin had not touched each other's in any way. He left the house, door ajar, stepped out, into the air. There was no bloody relief. The air hung lazy and heavy, closing in on Karl's throat.

* * *

Mama Abu held the cup in both her hands and smiled at Rebecca.

'I thought all of you were avoiding me.'

Mama Abu followed the steam rising from the hot tea.

'Godfrey is not making himself available and Karl doesn't pick up the phone.' Rebecca sat down next to Mama Abu and turned towards her.

'What's going on?'

They sat for a while, Rebecca looking at Mama Abu. Mama Abu fumbled for a tissue in her cardigan pocket, blew her nose. Took her time with putting the crumpled tissue back. Her eyes were tired again. Not so much from the long days of taking care of a household but from having to sit here. The only one who made herself available to Rebecca. Karl had been gone for five weeks now. Five! She had pleaded with Godfrey to go to Nigeria and find him. Anything could have happened by now. And did the father call, at all? Hadn't called once. What kind of person was that? What kind? It was the first time Godfrey had seen her angry. She had raised her voice and asked again. 'Who does that? You tell me Godfrey. It is not right.' Abu behind his father, who stood at the kitchen door. Godfrey had started to cry. He had promised to talk to Rebecca but Mama Abu couldn't wait any longer. Abu had reassured her all was well with Karl. He just didn't feel them at the moment. Abu's words. But he was sending bbms. He could probably get him on the phone if he wasn't too busy with his new friends. There wasn't anything to worry about. Just Karl doing Karl. Doing a runner.

Still. Five weeks was too long to lie. She started speaking. First slow, then quicker until it all poured out.

'I don't agree. I didn't agree! I understand that Karl wants to find his father—"

Rebecca had sprung up and rushed over to the small side table by the door. She went for her bag and pulled out her mobile.

'We need to talk!'

Mama Abu stopped mid-sentence.

'Godfrey. We will really have to talk.'

Her mouth made a funny sound. Mama Abu was alarmed. She had never seen Rebecca like this.

'Aargh! I can't believe you. You all knew.' Then the phone landed on the armchair. Rebecca had flung it. She turned around.

'Are you out of your mind? All of you?'

18

**Only belonging defies
what's been given but responds:
how and where one places oneself.**

When the hidden and the unwanted, when all of that pours
on to the surface, staining it. Then you need to make sure
you got enough credit.

John looked excited. His legs mid-air, swivelling out of the
car. Karl rushing to the other side, another door shutting
firmly. The question on John's face would have to exhaust
or answer itself because he was well ready to drive. Like for
real. Like right now. Straight away. Uncle T was still sitting
in the front; Karl had jumped in that quick.
　'I'd like to keep staying at yours, John. If that's OK?'
　The air just stopped. Just stopped doing anything. Everyone
like *er hello what now?* Except for Karl who was all action,
all into getting the car to move ASAP.
　'Karl, what are you talking about? Of course you will stay
here.'
　Uncle T turned so quick his bag fell off his lap and slammed
on to the floor of the taxi. He was all *what now?* Karl couldn't
get into it. His father could tell him if he wanted to.
　'I forgot some stuff at John's anyway.'
　'I will bring your things tomorrow.'
　'I'd rather go tonight.'
　Uncle T stepped out and opened Karl's door. Karl sat. *Mate,
where's your loyalty?* John shrugged. Looked at Uncle T.
　'I can stay?'
　Uncle T almost jogged into the house.

Karl patted his trousers and turned to John. 'Forgot my phone inside. I'll be right back.'

Followed Uncle T into the house. He could see the mobile by the couch. It must have fallen out of his pocket. Uncle T had breezed through and was knocking on the door down the hall. Opened, entered. Karl could hear questions, Uncle T's excited voice. Excited as in puzzled. As in *what is going on here?* No answers. Karl waited. Was his father going to explain himself to Uncle T? He couldn't hear anything and put his phone back into his pocket. Uncle T returned and stood in the open area between kitchen and parlour.

'Something happened. Karl, you can tell me.'

Karl looked like he wanted to tree hug Uncle T. Lock him in in a big wrap then disappear under his arms. None of that happened.

'It can be difficult. For both of you.'

Karl nodded. Uncle T had no clue; why bother him? It wasn't his fault.

'Yeah, just need a bit of time. It's weird. You don't mind that I stay with John?'

'Of course not. I will come tomorrow. We can talk then.' He walked Karl to the car and paid the driver.

'It was good meeting your father?'

'Yes.' Karl had nothing to say about it. Nothing at all. 'Sorry, John. Something came up, I need to just—' He hadn't planned to reply to Abu but it seemed like the best way to keep John's puzzled looks, ready for proper probing, at bay.

call me now. help me distract sum1 plz. I rally really need u to do me that favour

'Sorry John, I have to take this.' And picked up after the first ring. 'Yes, Karl speaking.' He paused for effect. 'Really? That's awful. I can call the doctor directly? Tomorrow, of course.' And took down an imaginary number.

John looked concerned.

'Everything OK at home?'

'I hope so. My mum. She is not well. I will call first thing tomorrow.'

He put on his best good-son-major-concern face, which wasn't all that difficult. All he had to do was shift the crap he felt anyway. A 1-2-1 transfer.

The next morning he went to the Internet shop. First on the list was Godfrey, who wouldn't have much of anything to stand on, in terms of being pissed. It was hot in the little phone booth, like that was new, but Karl felt cool, very cool. And calm.

'Hi G man.'

Godfrey all over the place. Relieved and happy, his voice, like, tumbling over itself.

'If you ever ignore that many of my calls, and I know you have been ignoring me, or take that long again just to give me a little update—'

'Thanks for selling me out. Didn't expect it from you. Of all people. No bad kids right? Just bad outcomes. Seems like you helped that one along pretty well.'

'Karl, I was just trying.'

'I know what you were trying. I ain't stupid. Point is you had no right. Ask me, or leave it. It's none of your business.'

'You're right. I've been—'

'Ahbeg, leave it. You put me in some serious danger as if you have no clue. I had a good thing going here.'

They both fell silent. The small boy who had carried up the canister with diesel the other time was looking at him through the square in the cubicle door. A small window should've probably been in there to ensure some sort of privacy but the thin door gave enough illusion of separation. He was slender, limbs ongoing, hair cropped very tight. Skin ashy, needing some lotion or cream to bring back some shine. Uncle T would have been able to help. Uncle T. He had spoilt it for Karl. All was now measured by how well people slapped cream on their bodies. Not that there was anything wrong with that. The boy looked at Karl from the other side of the small shop, his back leaning against the wood, balancing on one leg, the other propped up, resting on the wall. His eyes didn't move but the lashes flickered up and down as if sending Morse code. Karl stuck his head out of the hole.

'So what do we do with this, Godfrey?' These were all Godfrey's lines. The one he used on the youth. 'What now G?'

'I don't like it when you call me that. I'm not a gangster.'

'No one said you were. It's short for your name. What now, G? What?'

'Well how did it go with your father?'

'I'm not talking about my father, I'm talking about you. Me. Trust. All the things you hold so high.' Karl was about to stick out his tongue. The boy was straining his ears to listen intently. His eyes were popping out of his face, trying to soak up the scene. Karl stopped his tongue midway. The boy could probably not even understand his accent. His cheekbones were high, the face was drawn backwards. It looked elegant, like it would make the perfect kind of profile. The lips carefully drawn, a slight rim framing upper and lower lip.

'Pretty boy.'

'What?'

'Not you, Godfrey.'

'I'm sorry, Karl.'

Karl pressed the receiver into his ear. A few tears rolled down his cheeks. It was hot, too hot; he was sweaty and uncomfortable. He was alone and useless.

'Why, Godfrey?'

'I wanted to protect you. I was scared, man. If I was to let you go halfway around the world I had to know that someone was going to look out for you in case ...'

'In case what? What Godfrey, what?'

'In case—'

'In case someone didn't believe me? That someone thought I was a girl?'

'Your passport! Karl. It was hard enough to justify to myself that it was the right thing to do. To let you go with a stranger I hardly knew anything about. That I was not letting you run into danger. Your father, I actually spoke to him for a long time. Asked him how I could trust him. He was excited. Reassuring. If he was picking you up he needed to know in case you had trouble at immigration.'

'No one knew. The first time in my life I'm able to walk around and just be. No hassle, no questions. No pity or sympathy or harassment or being beaten up. Just me. You get me? Bloody fucking *me*. The first time. And of all people it is *you* who spoils it.'

'But I didn't know that.' Godfrey's voice was soft. 'I had to make sure someone is there who will look out for you.'

'Well, it ain't my father. He told me to go back to London. That there isn't any place here for someone like me.'

'I'm really sorry to hear that. He said he would take care of you.'

'Weird way of doing that by disappearing before I even arrive.'

'He what? What are you talking about?'

'I will have to tell you another time.'

'Karl, where is your father?'

'He's here. In his place. At least now he is.'

'What exactly did he say?'

'I don't really want to go into the details. He just doesn't want me. He is disgusted …'

'I'm so sorry, Karl.'

There were tears on both sides. Both angry. Each more helpless than the other.

'I can't forgive you, not like that.' Karl paused. 'But I believe you.'

He could hear the older man breathe.

'I'm almost eighteen. You can't interfere like this. It's not your right. You understand? You put me in danger!'

The last bit came out slow and heavy, and the small boy's eyes widened. He understood Karl; Nakale's accent had made it into Karl's mouth. It fell out as if it belonged there, all the way.

'Karl, he promised you would be safe. Do you think I just let you fly away?'

Karl nodded. None of that was news. He knew before he called all would make perfect sense. In Godfrey land. Because Godfrey was Godfrey, unless Godfrey was no longer Godfrey. And that would have been a much bigger shock than any story or non-story, any staying or disappearing his father could tell him to do.

'I'm sorry,' Godfrey continued. 'He said you should come. That he would look out for you.'

His voice was all anger. It sounded like it was trying to make it through the teeth.

'Come back now.'

'That's what he wants me to. That's why I'm calling.'

'I'll pick you up. Be good to have you back here. I'm scared shitless, you know. It was supposed to be two weeks. Not two months!'

'It's not two months—'

'Almost Karl, almost. I'm worried. All the time.' He laughed. 'I ain't as tough as all of you.'

Karl laughed too. 'I'm not forgiving you like this, you know. It ain't that easy. Anyways, I'm not done here. Not yet. School's already out for the summer. There isn't really any rush, is there? And I think you owe me.'

The Internet shop owner called the boy away and he jumped up, eyes still fixed on Karl's, leaving the spot on the wall. Karl's eyes followed him. He reminded him of the boy he had been and not been. The softness in the face. The dangly limbs. The intense look, dreamy eyes. Listening to the world, even when one couldn't understand it. Absorbing, learning.

'How about two more weeks? I'm here now ain't I, probably only time I'm ever gonna come here. Might as well.'

By the sound of Godfrey's breathing Karl could tell that he wasn't too pleased. But it wasn't his choice. And he did owe him. Owed him big time.

'Er, I don't want to be funny or anything but how about that emergency fund you always talk about? I think I need a little grant.'

The boy was now helping to stock the fridge with soft drink bottles from a red plastic crate. The talking was less agitated and quiet now; things were slotting into place again.

'I think it's time to call it a day, Karl. Plan another trip, another time —'

'Just need to stay a bit longer. Call it intuition.' He laughed again. 'So you can send that money?'

'Where do you think the money for your flight and everything else came from?'

'Come on, G. Do your fundraising magic or whatever you do. Two more weeks, I promise.'

Karl stepped out of that stuffy cubicle. Dried sweat *hello!* It was so crammed in the thing his nostrils had snorted the sawdust off the plyboards.

'What is your name?' he asked the boy. The words were slow again, melodic, heavy.

'Emmanuel.'

'Emmanuel, I'm Karl.' And the eyes drilled into his again, wide open. Brain working overtime.

'I'm from London. Do you know where London is?'

'UK,' the boy answered without hesitation. A bit of *duh, like, everyone and their granny knows that*. Karl chuckled.

'You are very strong.'

The boy, who might've been ten but looked younger because he was so slender, so small, lit up when Karl slipped him a couple of notes. His head did a three-sixty-degree quick rotation, wary of catching madam's watchful eye. When the coast seemed clear – madam stood on the dusty footpath, chatting to a passer-by – he slid the money into his front pocket. Karl smiled. Emmanuel looked away, shy, struggling to control a grin.

'Thank you sah.'

Karl pretended he was tipping his hat and turned around.

'You are very welcome.' And towards the entrance he shouted, 'Please, madam. I want to pay.'

* * *

The bus driver announced they wouldn't be going any further.

'Diversion. Either get off here or go all the way to Dalston.'

Abu drew attention as he marched from the end of the bus to the front. The driver hadn't even bothered to open at the back. Sure no one with a bit of a brain would get off here. Not now. People looked. He put on his best London massive swag, drawing disapproving looks from the law-abiding citizens from both sides of the bus. All were watching Abu. Most shook their heads. One friendly looking social-worker type tried to stop him.

'Come on mate, you don't want to get mixed up in that.'

Abu grabbed the railing. He was angry with the country but it didn't boil the same way other things did. His neighbourhood. The wannabes who thought they could make his and Karl's life shit as if they weren't as left out from the regeneration. As if there was some shiny future dangling in front of them they could reach for. As if they were not all going to be left behind, pushed out eventually, out of the area, out of opportunities. He was proper vex with Karl. With adults around him. They were worse than the shit he could get in the world at large. They were supposed to have his back. Care. Not dump him in some box where he could hold still, meaning suffocate, until someone remembered that he too had things going

on. Thoughts. Needs. Loyalty was circular. It never ended.
It wasn't supposed to get unauthorised holidays.

Granny lady a couple of seats in front added her five pence
to the social worker's wisdom.

'You people are a disgrace.'

He had heard that so many times it made him laugh.
Sometimes it was said out loud, like here. Most of the time
it was the stare. You. People. A threat. *Hateful looks are a
given if you walk around like me*, Abu thought. *You need to
try a lot harder if you want to get my attention.*

Social-worker type could see his moment slip through fast.

'No need for negative generalisations like that, Mrs. You
people? That is completely uncalled for.'

He should meet up with Godfrey, Abu thought.

'Call me a racist all you want but I'm talking about those
out on the streets.'

Abu watched her mouth open. So many creases around
the lips it was extra skin mini-waves. *Where else were they
supposed to be? Did she ever think about that? It was called
demand and supply,* as far as he was concerned. *Or in other
words: exceeding expectations. You get what you ask for.*

'You don't even know where I'm going or what I'm doing.'

'Are you getting off or what? I'm off otherwise.'

He could see the bus driver looking at him in the mirror.
Social-worker type reached out his hand.

'Come on mate—'

'Whatever. Ain't like you pay my rent, innit.'

His knees popped outward as he bounced down the stairs.
Own that shit, he thought. *You just jealous you ain't got no
youth left in you.*

Off the bus, on to the street. The bus drove off, people
staring, granny looking like she wanted to swear. Social-
worker type looked sad. The streets ahead were deserted.
Voices sounding from nearby but Abu couldn't see anyone.
The street abandoned, like for real. He moved on and now
there were noises like scratching and glass breaking. Around
a bend the first person appeared, and all that hush was over.
Abu couldn't be sure, boy or girl, not that he cared.

Other people followed. Scattered figures hopped towards
the other end of the street without any worry or hurry.
Without any sort of pressure whatsoever. When Abu entered
Mare Street he saw a couple of youths lift a bin out of its

black plastic casing. The top had burned out, the plastic still sweltering, stinking like hell. The two young men were now hurling the metal container from inside the bin, their faces reddened and sweaty. It landed a couple of metres away from Abu, who was looking around for a familiar face.

'Oi, watch it, if you don't want to get hurt. The streets are safe but not safe, dyouknowatimean?'

It was one with the low-hanging tracksuit bottoms. A pair of washed-out navy briefs with a grey elastic band showed his round bum cheeks, the bottoms lingering at the lower end of his backside.

'You just coming? Feel free. Very free. The police can't do shit now, you get me.'

Abu nodded and walked on slowly. He had no business getting involved with them, and no interest. One of his new mates had said something about trainers. About shops that were open *cuz we ain't got nofink from the bloody credit crunch, innit.* Did Abu care about that sort of shit? Not so much. It was just like with Karl, with his people; you gave your all but you were put on hold. On a loop. No one was actually going to answer. So lately he had been forming his own opinions.

'They do say it's a recession now, not just a credit crunch. And a bad one at that.'

But of course no one had really cared for his all of a sudden deep analysis.

He stared at the people running, like a diversity ad gone wrong. Most were young, or almost young. Not all though. Young, old, all types of cultures and shades of skin. Even some posh people in-between. It didn't get more inclusive than this, did it?

A man with hair that had stopped growing in the front carted a boxed flat-screen TV on a shopping trolley. There were more boxes, smaller ones. It looked like a collection of electrical gadgets, the TV sticking out well into the air, the printing announcing its sixty-inch HD beauty. He grinned when he made it past Abu, the little wheels clattering as it dragged along the tar.

'Yu'aright?'

Abu nodded. He lifted his hood over his head and tucked his chin under the collar, undecided. What was he supposed to do? Where to go?

A woman with a sleeveless top and a tight bun that left a razor-sharp fringe covering her eyebrows was chatting on her phone, her arms full with bags of clothing, the mobile tucked between shoulder and ear.

'Might as well innit. Not gonna happen again any time soon.'

She was pulling a holdall behind her, the long handle tied around her hand. Once she passed, Abu could see the shoes and boots, and an expensive looking hair dryer.

His trousers started to buzz. Probably his new mates. He couldn't move. There was more smoke. Crashing noises, glass splintering around him. Behind him, a few older-looking men, well older to Abu, had kicked in a betting shop. The back and forth of people on a mission. A unified mission. *What I get is mine. For all the crap, all the bull, for all that we don't and can't have.*

He could hear Karl's voice, some opinion about how all had gone too far, banks-wise, if Karl still cared to talk about things with him. He heard his own. Talking to Nalini about the slavery trail.

A smile appeared on his face. He lowered the collar so he could breathe better. Nalini. He could see if he could catch her later outside the estate, hanging out with her crew. Now with school break on it was hard to find a minute alone with her. She was either helping her mother, minding her younger siblings, or with her friends. They no longer had an urgent project, a unifying mission of their own. He remembered telling his new mates about Mary Prince when he strolled home from the university library. They cracked up when his words had stumbled over each other in disbelief about how close up slavery was. Right under their noses, or feet, to be precise. He didn't know why he had bothered to share it. They caught him off-guard. It was a Karl thing, the making connections. He'd have got it. They walked on that day, laughing because he was useless to them in that state. *Yeah whatever. If you want to impress a girl, cool, but spare us the details.*

Shuffling feet came closer. Abu turned.

'Here you are. We're on the other side. Someone just turned a car over, about to light it. You're just in time. One big fucking bonfire.'

One of his new posse. He'd probably watched Abu deep in thoughts again. He was losing his reputation. All brainy and thoughtful. Like a bit too much.

'Hi. Cool man.'

He was looking for words. Abu the man himself, lost for what to say. Shit, what next? They already had an uncomfortable bond that he would prefer to erase. But it seemed that nowadays no one gave him any options.

'I'm starving, mate. Might catch up with you in a minute. Didn't even realise I haven't had anything since yesterday's lunch. I'm feeling kind of weak man.'

'There's a chicken place right there.'

He pointed to where a group of three was looking in their direction. They were standing in front of an overturned car.

'Don't know man. Feeling faint. Might be better to sit down somewhere, like proper. I'll catch up with you though. Just text me the stats.'

'Who said you can't sit? All you do is get your order and bob's your uncle.'

He pulled on Abu's sleeve. The other three waved for them to come over already. A couple of other passersby stopped. When they arrived at the car he could see the takeaway behind it. The small crowd that the three from the posse had held back *until our mate joins us* greeted them with a round of cheers.

'I told you it was him.'

The large window front was smashed and both pavement and chicken place were covered in glass. Someone had used a fire extinguisher to break the counter. Another person was helping himself to the food behind it, taking his time to choose. The appliances were all turned on and the smell of warm, used oil was filling the air. It must have been a recent conquest, the shop.

'Hurry up, we ain't got all day,' his mate said. He had joined the others. One had a bottle of barbecue lighting fluid in his hands.

'You know what, I'll have something after. Don't want to rush it. Maybe I'll just leave you to it.'

'Why? You here now. Not like we're going to hang around to wait for the cops.'

He covered the front panel of the car with fluid and lit a match. Then he circled around adding more. Someone else distributed more lit matches and it was now lighting up evenly. Abu's eyes widened. He was speechless. Karl would have been all sinking inside the gut. Nothing would have come out of his mate's mouth. All his processing and shit would have been *bam!*, full halt. Forget mind the gap; try mind bloody life.

Abu's knees jerked his trembling legs. Everyone already branded him a coward. No need to stand here, shaking. His pupils widened as if sucking in the whole Hyundai, complete with flames that licked the carcass. How did he get himself into this? They stood quietly, in awe, although you couldn't really bank this under achievements.

Like any bonfire there was the usual staring into the dancing flames, the thoughts wavering along, moving here and there, transfixed. Only it was full daylight. The burning car made a hell of a heat. It cracked and sizzled and attracted more people. One guy stopped and looked at it close, then at the people gathered. He looked in their quiet faces for attention. Said, 'Run everyone. That thing is going to explode.'

Checked that all started moving then he turned quickly into the next side road. Abu had noticed that the man's hands were empty; he wasn't carrying anything. He might have been on his way home from work. He picked up pace.

The tar hit back at his trainers, very *you see now asshole? But I'm still here for you. Run back home if you have any sense.* He could hear his mates breathing next to him.

'Run, run. That thing is not safe.'

Houses, cars, people, the odd tree, the odd shop, the odd bar, the odd bus stop, the odd junction peeled off the sides of his eyes. He could smell his breath, stinking of fear. Why had they put it on fire if they wanted to whimper like children now? It hadn't been his idea. He wanted to leave. He hadn't wanted to be part of any of this. Rep or cred whatever. Trying to be rough. Bad.

Boom! And one single sound splintered into a cascade of others. A shower of noise. The car, gone. Abu was unfit for this sort of running. From Hackney back to King's Cross. Back to Karl, back to his gentle sense-making, his reasoning and *know too damn much to leave him alone like this.*

Abu ran and ran and his sides hurt, his head felt like exploding, his insides were burning. All the while he thought: *Now I get you bruv. When you can't think no more, that's the best.* When there is nothing else to do or understand, you have to run, as fast as possible. As far as possible. Even if it brings you back home.

He made a left into a side street.

'Let's go this way,' he heard a fear-sweating wannabe shout after him. 'I know a shortcut.'

But Abu knew another solution that had nothing to do with fake friendships and crappy choices. Shortcuts? Whatever. He ducked underneath a crappier fence and ran behind the building it surrounded. There was a little pathway leading back the direction he came from but parallel to it, a couple of streets in-between.

He took off his hoodie and shoved it in the nearest rubbish bin. He looked around. He came out in a small residential street. Nothing was going on here. He couldn't even hear the shouting and noise that had been pumping just ten minutes ago. All seemed like a quiet workday. No one outside. Probably an all-young-professionals road. He fell into a slower jog.

Fast he had done. Now he only had to cover some distance.

19

**How to reach another.
Priorities ... Is it
the same as being on time?**

'So what do you think?'

Karl was scratching off a sticker from the plywood wall in the Internet cafe. He seemed to be getting very familiar with the small cubicle that had the phone inside.

'Karl, London is burning, bruv. Do you pay any attention?'

'I told you not to go.'

'Easy for you to speak, Mr. Leggingitallovertheworld. I had no choice, man. They're on my case. I've been trying to tell you that. '

'You have people on your case anyway. What's different?'

Was Karl actually interested? Or was this just a bit of half-hearted *yes I hear you* thrown his way?

'You.'

Karl's eyes followed Emmanuel, who sat on a low stool in front of the Internet cafe, polishing large men's shoes madam had placed in front of him. His bare feet were covered in red dust. His legs ashy again.

'I'm gonna be back much faster than you want me to. Trust.'

'Are you listening or what?'

'What are you on about?'

Emmanuel's brush slowed down every time madam was out of eye contact. Karl smiled. What was the point of overextending yourself? Smart boy.

'I'm trying to talk to you but you ain't got no time for me, bruv.'

'What's the problem?'

'You, man. You are the problem. Everyone is on my case about you. On top I can't even walk down the street without someone pushing into me, giving me shit.'

'Come on, it's not like this is against you or anything.'

Abu was quiet. Karl could hear him chewing his lip, shuffling from one leg to the other.

'Abu?'

'What?'

'What's up?'

'Nothing. Forget it.'

'Did something happen?'

Emmanuel was now showing off to Karl. The shoe was long sparkling but his lids moved up and down, secretively, checking: was Karl looking?

'I miss you man. With or without you I'm getting stick for sticking with you.'

'Tell me.'

'It's nothing.'

'It doesn't sound like it.'

Abu was still heaving, as if he'd run up the stairs, two steps at a time.

'It's just, I don't know. You think I can choose or not. To do the right thing. Sometimes it comes out really bad instead.'

'What the fuck happened, Abu?'

'Someone got hurt.'

'What do you mean, "someone got hurt"? I thought none of you were caught?'

'Before the riots.'

'Can you speak now, geez, how much invitation do you need?'

'They were teasing me. Funny, just at that spot on Leigh Street. They were younger, not the usual bunch.'

'What did they do to you?'

'Nothing. That's the thing. They gave me some lip; I gave some back. But ...'

'What?'

'The woman ...'

'Which woman?'

'From when I visited your mother. She had a friend over. She was really friendly. Talked a lot.'

'Like non-stop, no pause?'

'Major.'

'Must be Pat. She's great but never shuts up. What about her?'

'I don't know why but she saw me and them, she was just coming out of the corner store there and told them to leave me alone. If they didn't stop harassing me she'd call the police. They just thought, what is this old cow doing here? That's what they said. Punched her. Maybe normally that would've been nothing but they must have caught her in funny way, maybe the angle, you get me. She just collapsed and looked at me with big eyes. They clocked that she knew me and made a runner.'

'What did you do?'

'What was I supposed to do?'

'You left her?'

'I didn't leave her. I called an ambulance. She is in intensive care. Can hardly wake up. Ruptured lung. Had her rib broken, pierced the bloody lung.'

'Shit. Fuck. Does my mum know?'

'Course she does. She is doing the whole police thing, already filed a report. Just waiting for her to get well enough. You see, big time fucking shit. I have no choices. I get a call every day. If I don't see them, they'll walk me home. Whatever I'm doing, one of them always finds me. Every fucking day!'

'Did you go to the police?'

'Are you not listening? They are threatening me. Every bloody day. I need you back here.'

Karl didn't know what to say. On John's grainy TV the riots looked unreal. Blown out of proportion. He had only been gone a few weeks. How could there be so much fire? Abu was usually all mouth, no action. Could talk until Karl was sure he had died of an overdose of tonguelitis. Trouble got to him. Just like it followed Karl, it followed Abu, because he trotted behind him, chatting for King's Cross, not watching out where he went, what was in front. He stumbled into stuff. Usually he was able to shrug it all off.

'Karl, are you there? Say something. What am I supposed to do?'

'I don't know. I don't know. Shit.'

'Come back. I need you.'

The here, the where, the how to reach. The right timing that was what usually fucked things up. Wasn't it?

'You have to say everything to the police. It's my mum's friend.'

'I need you here for that. So far I've been stalling. Come back.'

'Shit, shit, shit.' Karl went quiet. Emmanuel looked at him, eyes wide again. He got that word. Karl was thinking.

'Tell Godfrey. He'll take care of it. You know how he is; he probably knows their parents anyway. I'll be back in no time. Not finished here. Difficult to explain but—'

It was quiet on the other side. Too quiet.

'Abu, please. Just hear me out.'

But Abu had already hung up.

The choices, the wrongs or rights. What when where. Priorities.

20

**You don't need to be
a smart-ass to fuck it up.
You need to be smart to see it coming.**

Karl left the cubicle. He should go back. He really should.
Rebecca sounded livid. His phone was blowing up with her
texts. What was he doing anyway? Not like his father cared.
He just needed a little more time. *These* two weeks. And
Godfrey was the one who would have a way in with some of
the local boys. Doing the Godfrey magic. The diffusing. He
entered the compound, then the buka. There would have
to be some serious begging from Karl's side. Making up for
lousy friendship efforts. Abu would understand. This was
the only time Karl had in Nigeria. It wouldn't come again
any time soon.
   Nakale was waiting. Janoma, his cousin, was sitting on the
bench. Her darkness was seamless, uninterrupted. Deep.
Unlike the last time, when they had met in front of her
Auntie's shop, she was smiling at him now.
   'Hello. Something happen? You remember my cousin
Janoma.'
   'Karl,' he mumbled and stretched out his hand. 'I'm sorry
I'm late, I was on the phone. It was important.'
   'Hi.' She jerked her head to the side, shook his hand half-
heartedly. She was obviously not into the shaking but she
kept it for a while. Maybe she was into holding? She looked
at him again, like last time, cocked her head, smiled, then
got lost as if she was thinking about something. She was in
jeans and a T-shirt, some eccentric pop star's face splashed
over front and back. Metallic blue, red and purple on a
washed-out grey. Style.

'How are you doing? I hear it's your first time in good old Naija?'

It was hard to tell her age. She was sure of herself in a way that was all accidental, thoughtful but mostly dreamy eyes.

'It's alright,' he replied, thankful that his mouth opened at all.

'And which parts are alright exactly?' Janoma's eyebrows raised. She was probably at uni already.

'Well, the vibe. I mean.'

'The vibe?' She laughed and let go of his hand. Her lips, man, when they moved, they blew you off the surface of the earth. Almost brown, a deep purple.

'Wow, you mixed kids sure know how to be specific.'

She turned to Nakale and said something. Karl couldn't hear her. She saw him trying to understand them.

'Either by early afternoon or you have to drop me at dad's at six. You know he is not joking about his timekeeping.'

She was so cool, so together, cleaned up good. It made the air burn.

'Karl?'

Nakale interrupted his analysis.

'She can come with us? Only then we have to leave earlier? So that we can drop her home in time?' All as a question.

'Of course, no problem.' He felt on a mission. A gang. Although Janoma hadn't officially joined their twosomeness; he hoped by the end of the day there'd be more to say on that.

Nakale was interviewing one of the elders of the community for an article he was commissioned to write by an overseas news agency. Well, it wasn't quite an article, more like a report. The correspondent would write their own version later, after a very brief visit to the same area, and without that much engagement. They would take all the credit and be like *what atrocities, unimaginable, so much pollution, underdeveloped* and shit.

Nakale had also collected more samples. He had some new ideas and was restructuring his data. Karl asked if he could take notes for him. Two sets of ears were better than one. Maybe he could even write his own something. Something he could take back to London. Maybe he could use it for his own project week.

It was all very much as the last time. Endless roads with bush and palm trees. Karl was used to the views, settlements and villages along the way. The car took them off the highway to a small junction, life bustling along on all four of its corners.

'We're entering Ogoniland, Karl. I will show you where they captured Ken.'

Karl nodded. Who the hoot was Ken?

'Saro-Wiwa,' Janoma, who sat next to him on the back seat, continued. Karl could feel her breathing, or maybe it was just his own breath. Moving in and out in that obvious manner that makes you even more nervous than you already are.

hotness /hɒtnəs/
noun
    1. Intense.

'Like the writer and activist?' She took his hand and pointed to the left. The car slowed down and was rolling along the smaller street they entered.

'Look there. The sign.' Her hand was cool. The aircon was on. Karl's hand was sweaty.

'MOSOP,' Karl read out. At least that part worked; his speaking faculty did its job.

'Movement of the Survival of the Ogoni People. Nakale, explain it. How should he know these things? Not like he was old enough then.'

She leaned close to the window but deep back into her seat so Karl could poke his head forward. His nose touched the window. Her hand was still holding his; their thighs touched and he could feel her breath close to his ear now. Karl looked outside, then at Nakale, then back outside. What was he meant to do? Just stay here? All close up and shit?

Nakale was deep in thought.

'One day the government decided that it had had enough of leaders like Ken, who spoke up and rallied the people against what Shell and all the oil thieves were doing to our beautiful land. So the military convicted them on false charges and hanged them, although human rights groups and governments all over the world were condemning the whole thing. Some witnesses admitted later that they had been bribed by Shell to give false testimony against what we call the Ogoni Nine. Ken and the other activists.' It seemed

like a thought broke off. 'That's it. Nothing else to say.' He
seemed pissed off.

'Ken is Nakale's hero.' Janoma let go of his hand. Karl
moved back to his side of the back seat, armpits all sweaty.

Nakale was still like, absent.

Karl nodded. It took someone to show you what was going
on, sometimes right in front of your eyes. Sometimes it was
further away. There was more shit in life, much bigger shit,
than your own personal problems. That was for sure. Nakale
was showing him that it mattered how you dealt with it. Not
just your own stuff, but the bloody balance of the world.

They drove on and Karl followed the fleeting images
outside of the window until they got to the elder Nakale
was interviewing.

Nakale and the man exchanged greetings and news and he
led them into a cramped bungalow. The man's two younger
daughters watched Karl curiously. Janoma was already sitting
on one of the armchairs, drifting off in her own thoughts, but
once in a while her eyes met Karl's. Nakale and the man sat
on a small sofa. They started in the middle of a sentence, as
if they had left the conversation midway on their last visit.
Karl was struggling with the heat; the stuffy room offered
no reprieve, no air, no movement. He was glad when they
left an hour later. It had been too hot and he had heard
nothing. The only thing he had observed was the heat that
hovered around every thought and every look at Janoma. He
wanted to be back at John's to think of her, but the thought
of parting made him anxious.

21

**How many times can you turn,
without making your way?**

His mother was waiting for him. Abu pulled the key out and
closed the door behind him. She stood there, arms hanging
by her side.

'I didn't do anything.'

Her head was moving the tiniest bit but he didn't know
whether she was nodding or shaking it.

'I swear!'

It was that much stronger this way. The disapproval. The
not talking made you feel bad whether you had done anything
or not. Abu had expected a *didn't I tell you not to leave?*

Like this, quiet and without accusation, her disappointment
stung more. He lowered his head and tried to thin out to
make it past her without having to touch her. The twins were
in bed. His father back at work. It was quiet in the flat. He
couldn't bear sitting in the living room with her. TV on or
not it would make his insides want to crawl out of his throat.

Godfrey had been summoned. *Be a fucking adult.* In those
exact words. Rebecca had screamed down the phone when
he eventually called back the day after she left her first
message. 'Be a fucking adult and tell me exactly what is going
on. Not tomorrow or when you have time or you're out from
an appointment or when you bloody feel like it. Now!' She
had slammed down the phone again but this time she hadn't
thrown it. One lucky escape was enough; she didn't need a
broken mobile on top of everything else. Mama Abu was in
Rebecca's kitchen. Abu's father was babysitting the twins

at home. Godfrey sat in the armchair. Abu on the couch. Rebecca was standing.

'Abu?'

'I'm sorry, I don't … nobody told me …'

Rebecca walked over and put her hand on his shoulder. 'It's not OK to lie. Certainly not like this.'

He nodded, biting his lips. She pushed his shoulder, motioning for him to join his mother in her kitchen. It didn't take a second and Abu was out of the tense air.

'Just you and me.'

Rebecca leaned on the doorframe, arms folded, one leg casually placed over the other. Her hair was pulled back, tied. You could see everything on her face. The question, the contempt, the anger.

'Me and you, Godfrey.'

'I know …' Godfrey started.

Rebecca just raised her eyebrows, mocking him with such intensity Godfrey couldn't continue. She stared at him until he looked down at his hands, shaking his head.

'Rebecca…'

'Try and explain. Try!'

'There is nothing to explain. Not more than I already said. It was a bad idea, a very bad one.'

'You think this was just a bad idea? Godfrey, do you even know where Karl is? Do you have any fucking clue where my son is?'

And they were back to the heavy silence that felt like an embargo. Nothing in, nothing out. Her foot was moving left and right, hitting the skirting board each time it made it to the right.

'I have all the addresses. I spoke to Karl the day before yesterday. Tunde is in touch with me, regularly.'

'Tunde.' She laughed. 'And how long have you known Tunde?'

He was nodding now. He put his hands over his face, lowered them again.

'I know it's out of order, I know. It was supposed to be two weeks. I had my reasons, believe me. The important part is that he is safe. He hasn't disappeared. Nothing has happened to him. He's simply not come back when he was supposed to.'

It took a while for Rebecca to respond. She was busy processing what Godfrey had said. Or maybe she was planning how best to tell him what a fool he had been. Godfrey got up and came closer but she thrust her hand out to stop him.

'This is Karl. Did you think he would come back when you told him? When has he ever done that?'

She was right. He knew it. But how to tell her that it could have been worse? He could have run away without any sort of update. Money or not. Karl would have found a way. How to tell her that he had been scared, more scared of that than anything?

'I'll call Tunde straight away. Make sure that he gets Karl on the next plane.'

'Tunde is a dreamer, Godfrey. It will be very difficult to reason with him. But what happened to Adebanjo? I thought Karl went to be with his father.'

* * *

'I take Karl. We meet dere.'

Mena was preparing for lunch. Nakale had dropped in on his way to uni. Karl had just joined them outside the building. John was there. He was on his way to arrange something. Probably to work, for the father, but he hadn't said. There was no talk of the father. The word and person. Omitted. It was easy, as they had already stopped speaking much about him over the weeks of waiting for him to show up.

The night before, John had asked Karl, 'I should book your flight back?'

He was polite like that. He was supposed to have booked that flight a few days back when the father went all offensive behaviour on Karl. But he hadn't. They hadn't even mentioned it. After returning from the heavy shooter Karl had just asked how he could help. To give something for all the trouble. John had replied, 'Nothing my friend. No need for dat one.'

Karl planned to leave something. Or Nakale could help him get a couple of gifts for their flat.

To the question, he had replied, 'I'm not yet ready to go back to London. Is it OK with you if I stay for a few more days?'

He had left out that both Godfrey and Rebecca were blowing up his phone. He now left it switched off mostly. Checked for messages once in a while.

And John had hugged him.

'Please. You are welcome.'

The others were all discussing something but Karl got lost in the accent until John turned toward him.

'Auntie says there is something tonight. She wants to take you.'

'Something?' Karl was confused.

Nakale shot Mena a look but she just raised her head, shaking it once.

'John, don't worry what it is. A gathering. A party. Whatever you want to call it. It will be special for Karl. Learn about our country.'

John's eyebrows met in the middle. 'She wants to know if you can go.'

This was the weird bit. Who had authority? Would anyone impose a curfew? If so, who? Karl looked at Nakale, who looked at him expectantly. Mena smiled reassuringly and nodded. John had a question on his face. It seemed Karl would be deciding this by himself; better make arrangements before anyone remembered that Karl was supposed to be in someone's care. Meaning: not going out at night. At least not by himself. Without a guardian. But it was difficult to make out who that was these days. Uncle T was only supposed to hand him over and the father had cleared himself of any obligation, of any involvement, of any interest. Since then Uncle T had found it hard to make a decision concerning Karl, especially since he had to always be back in Lagos for most of the week. And he was still knocked sideways, lost, waiting for the answer to 'But what happened, Karl? What?'

'I'll bring him back.' Nakale reassured. 'Not too late.'

John looked uneasy. 'You will be—'

'I will take care of him,' Nakale added and put his arm around Karl.

'I will be dere John. Don't worry yourself,' Mena said. Her first customer was coming up from the road. 'Nakale if you're not back in time I can take him. No problem.' And she winked at Karl and went to serve her first dish of the day.

It was obvious John didn't know what to say. No one had briefed him. What type of care should he impart? Mena came back out and spoke to him quietly. She took his arm and pointed into the air with her other hand. It was like she was outlining something. Then, louder, she said, 'John, dis be your junction. You can go dis way or dat way. But no be you who is going. Let Karl decide. It will be well. Nakale will bring him back.'

John couldn't help himself. 'You need to leave the junction bit. I was just making a point. Once! No need to talk dat one all de time.' But he laughed. And agreed reluctantly. As long as they were making sure Karl got back in one piece. She went back inside the small shop to prepare for the lunchtime rush. Nakale waved as he walked away.

'I will be there by seven.'

When they got off the okada, Karl could hear music and voices. It was low but it rose above the noise of the street. They had driven through a maze of roads and had come out at a small junction. Mena paid the driver and he sped off the congested road they had come from. It was dark but the street was lined with petty traders, their wobbly tables illuminated by small petroleum lamps. The flames flickered, making it all sweet and romantic. It was busy but it was slower than in the daytime. People had time to walk and chat, to stop and enquire. In-between, a few people rushed ahead, or jumped on one of the buses that didn't quite stop here but only slowed down enough for someone to hop on.

'Come, it is here.'

The open sewer had loose wooden planks over it. Karl balanced, taking care that both feet were evenly distributed. It didn't work if you started too far back and had no weight in the front. Gravity. Inevitably the back end would come up. They passed a single-storey house with a few tables scattered in front. People were drinking and eating, and music came from the inside of the house. A couple of guys looked up.

'Long time.' And shouted something else to Mena. She shook her head and laughed and her backside swayed more as she moved on. It was darker behind and they slipped between other houses, walking on a bit of raised concrete next to the open sewage. People were sitting out everywhere they passed, washing clothes, chatting. After a couple of minutes, they arrived at an opening, a yard, and Auntie stepped down from the low cement rise. Two women were in front of the building. Mena exchanged pleasantries and introduced Karl.

'Nakale's friend.'

Karl said hello.

'And my own.' She poked him.

The welcome was warm and one of the women waved towards the back. The front room led to a narrow hallway. It was a weird atmosphere. Not unfriendly, just expectant. There were about ten people there. Most of them looked up when Mena and Karl entered. A split sec of pause before the chatter resumed.

Janoma was already present.

'Welcome.' She hugged Karl. Karl's body got stiff and inside it melted. Her body. Close by. Touchable. He lifted his head a fraction. Was supposed to be a nod. All he could muster.

Mena looked around. An old couch was at the far end. An old calendar on the wall. An even older ceiling fan was doing its rounds, making it clear that it was a chore. A shelf along the whole side of the one wall, books on it and piled in front of it. A table with papers spread out. Half of the group was standing there.

'Nakale no dey?'

'He's delayed,' Janoma answered and pulled Karl towards the couch. A young man in dark suit trousers and a short-sleeved shirt was sitting next to a woman with big glasses in a green dress.

'My friends Lah and Alera. This is Karl. I told you. From London.'

Lah grabbed his hand. Karl's arm felt like it was coming out of his socket. They had obviously already heard about him. Alera was nodding as if she knew something Karl didn't. Lah stopped the shaking.

'Welcome.' Karl's head went red but he managed to reply a supposed to be casual 'What's going on?' They made room for Karl and Janoma. Mena was across the room now, talking to an older guy with a beret.

'Where is the music?'

'What?' Janoma whispered back.

'The music. Don't you have music at parties?'

Janoma leaned to the side to see him better, confused.

'What party? Is this another London-kid thing?'

'Mena said I was going to a party.'

A couple of people waved. They were leaving early. Or perhaps it wasn't even early.

'This is a meeting to finalise a newspaper. We're all waiting for Nakale. She must have just told you because of John.'

'What's wrong with him?'
'Nothing, but since he works for your father who works
for an oil company ...'
He nodded. His throat was itchy. Anyways, he was down with
it, wanted to learn all things Niger Delta, all things Nakale-
related. So whatever it was, it was certainly fine with him.
Only it was hard to sit next to Janoma. He felt like a piece
of wood; Janoma leaning into him, arm leaning on his thigh,
friendly-arguing about something with her friends, always
including Karl but he couldn't hear them properly and didn't
really understand what it was all about. It was loud in the
room. Even louder in his body. In parts he didn't want to
name. Brain foggy, he nodded and smiled his way through
until Janoma left him to drift.
An hour later, Nakale called the guy with the beret. A
truck had turned over at Rumuokoro Junction. There was
absolute gridlock. He wasn't going to make it. The others
started filing out. It would take long enough to get home
on a normal day but now with the main junction even more
congested it would be an absolute nightmare. Alera turned
to Janoma.
'Should we stay? There is going to be too much traffic
anyway.'
Janoma looked at Karl. His shoulder shrugging was instant.
'Sure.'
Mena dragged a chair over.
'We wait small den I take Karl back.'
There was time anyway. John had said not to come back
too late. But it was only eight o'clock.
Alera turned to him. 'Have you been able to follow our
programmes here?'
'Which one?'
Karl didn't add that he found it difficult to follow TV when
he had tried watching at his father's house.
'Alera is a very good singer.' Janoma straightened her blouse.
'She can't wait for the new season of *Nigerian Idol* to start.'
'Oh like *American Idol*? The singing show?' Karl looked
at her.
'She loves it too much,' Lah said.
It seemed true. Alera moved her head to the side and
paused there. Smiled. Content. With herself. Janoma was
watching Karl. He shuffled on the couch.

'We don't actually have it. I mean not any more. The idol one.' He was getting himself into some speaking disaster. 'Something similar. I mean we have something like it. It's called *The X Factor.*'

Yes, Alera had heard about that one. Mena turned towards them.

'No be Charly Boy dis time?'

'Yes, Auntie,' Janoma replied. 'Have you heard of him, Karl? He is going to be one of the judges this year. Charly Boy. Everything he does … people talk about him.'

'Why?' Karl replied.

'He's like the Area Scatter of our time. He used to dress as a woman—'

Dressing as. Karl flinched. You couldn't see it but his insides were on alert now. It wasn't being like. Doing as if. Not for him.

'—then he was a punk—'

'Dat one no be like Area Scatter,' Mena interrupted. She put her hand on Karl's arm. 'Today everything na promotion.'

'But still. Auntie. He kissed a guy; the photo was everywhere.'

Janoma filled Karl in on the previous year's scandal. Charly Boy had kissed another male musician on the mouth during a photo shoot. The press had eaten it up.

'Oh, wow. Must have been something.'

'It was,' Janoma laughed. Karl moved away a little; there was air between them now. His thoughts were muddled again, racing. Like his heart. Mena took his hand and moved his arm up and down, playfully. Absent-mindedly. Apparently.

'But who cares.' Janoma seemed bored with the topic now.

'Exactly, who cares!' Alera addressed Karl again. 'My dream is to be on the show. One day.'

Karl's voice wanted to do a runner through the back door. He managed a 'Good luck' and got up from the couch, Mena's hand dropped. He stretched.

'Me, I'm getting tried.'

Lah agreed. 'It's a long way home. Better go now.'

When they arrived at John's, Mena filled in the missing link.

'Nakale, he want to show you about our place here, the Niger Delta. Dat's why he ask you to come. All de people dere, they do something. Like Nakale, they write small things. They take samples. They try.'

'OK.' He couldn't see more than her silhouette. They were standing in front of her closed shop. 'Hopefully I get to go again.'

'He will take you. No problem.'

'Do you also work for the magazine?'

'Me?' She turned so suddenly she must have been surprised. 'No. Me I just cook. Sometimes I help Nakale. And Nakale ask me if I can take you because he was not free today to bring you.' She brushed something off her arm. 'And I live closer to here. Easier for me to bring you home.' Her face moved to him. 'But no need for John to know, Karl.'

'Would he mind?'

'It no be good for him to know everything. He doesn't know which way he should go. John.' He could feel her eyes on him. 'OK?'

'I think he is solid.' It had burst out. 'I mean he is a good guy John. No?'

'Oh, he is very good. Too good. Don't worry yourself. Just sometimes it's different if you have to be good to too many people.'

Allegiances. Loyalty. Karl used to have that to other people. Now he was stuck with decisions that couldn't be made. Not easily anyway.

He was ready to go up. They day felt long. Mena held on to the hem of his shirt.

'Area Scatter. He was a musician. But long before you born. One day he go away, many months. Then come back. As a woman.'

The crickets were at it and it felt safe. The darkness. The chirping. Mena's soft voice. They stood. You didn't always have to say so much, did you.

* * *

Abu sat on his bed. Clothes covered the floor. His mates had sent a bbm earlier: *come by hackney l8r.* He wasn't up for going. Let them come for him then. Time for him to grow up. Be the man he always pretended to be.

He got up and put the unworn clothes into the wardrobe, piled the dirty ones by the door. The bed was bundled up. He straightened the duvet, flattened out the creases, looked around. Yes, now this was what Karl was always talking about. Tidiness. Not bad, not bad at all.

Karl. He didn't want to think about him. This being 'away', not coming back. Be a good friend but *come on!* There were limits. Forget even Rebecca and Godfrey. Forget that everyone was like way mad because Karl wasn't coming back. There were needs. Abu's needs too.

He lined his trainers and shoes up on the wall, took out a clean shirt, changed and left his door wide open.

'I'm going out, just downstairs. Probably won't be long.'

His mother came out of the living room.

'I don't want you to go.'

'It's just downstairs.'

She hadn't said anything the last time he'd left. When she had made it clear not to. Her eyes had done the talking. He could hear both his parents later, discussing how to handle this. What the best approach was. Enforcing discipline might only send him further away. Might rupture their bond more than it already had. So they had finally realised that he was here too. That things were changing. He needed some attention, some time. He wasn't really trying to take advantage of his parents' new method. The waiting for him to open up. It was just … life was major shit. And you would suffocate if you stayed at home. Abu looked at her eyes. Looked at his trainers. Opened the door. It was hard. So hard to resist the face, the eyes that were pleading. Sad and hopeful. All at the same time. Abu's foot played with the doormat.

'I don't want you to go, Abu.'

She went back inside. She knew her power. The way Abu couldn't resist wanting approval in her eyes. That sudden smile when she realised he was doing what she wanted him to do. When he was doing the right thing. She was in the living room already. The TV was coming on.

'I know,' he replied. 'I'm sorry. I have to.'

He left the door open.

* * *

Karl stepped into the small shop. It was so dark his eyes couldn't make out anything but contours and shapes.

'Close the door please. My aunt has already finished. I don't feel like dealing with any late customers.'

The enclosed space amplified the scratchy sound his red flip-flops produced on the painted cement floor. How much more aware of yourself could you be?

'Really push it; it's a little stuck.'

Janoma switched on a lamp opposite the entrance. It got all cosy.

'Choose any material.' She smiled.

Karl nodded. The fabrics were divided in sections according to main colours. Rows all neat and efficient, using all the space from ceiling to floor.

'You've done your hair,' Karl said.

'If I don't plait it my parents complain. Then my mother wants me to get a weave. I don't want one.'

'I didn't think it was long enough to get it done.'

'Oh they can, as you can see.'

'Mmm,' Karl mumbled. He had nothing to say. He just liked her face. Liked it so much. The tight braids showed rows of scalp all neat and tidy, like the set-up in the shop. Janoma stood out against the backdrop of colour.

'You know, we don't really go to tailors in London.'

She laughed. 'That's what we do: give material as presents. Just choose something. Your mother can use it on top of the bed.'

The skirt Janoma wore was 'figure-hugging', as they said here. Tight from waist to calves, flaring in pleats. The top was sleeveless and tailored. In the UK sense.

She fumbled in her handbag, then turned around again, CD in hand.

'I burned some music for you. Afrobeat, the current pop music. Maybe you'll like the *vibe*.' She laughed and made a step toward Karl.

Karl's body switched on, head burning up.

'Did you bring your laptop? Or do you want me to put it on your MP3?'

'My phone.' The noise that came out of Karl's mouth: a frog's attempt to free itself from serious captivity. He was trying to get his hand to let go of the door handle, trying to leave this looking at her, instead touch the material, the fabric which covered almost all surfaces, and allow it to cool his burning palms. And the burning in his throat. The burning that just wouldn't leave since Janoma had taken his hand a few days ago when they were sitting together in the taxi. The burning that had returned when she leaned on him at Nakale's 'party'.

'What is the problem? You're marrying that door? Try at least to look like you are choosing something.'

Ha ha, he wanted to laugh. *Nothing wrong with a little affection for our functional items, innit,* he wanted to reply. Something funny. Amuse her. Respond. Do anything. At all. He felt unsteady as he stepped into the room.

'You know,' he started.

'What?' Her face was starting to glow. The sweat.

'You know,' he tried to continue.

'I do actually know quite a lot of things. That's why I am studying. So which thing are we talking about?'

He smiled. She had to be that damn smart-arsey, didn't she. 'You are …'

'I am, that is true. Very philosophical. I hope that's not all of it.' It didn't seem like she was still mocking him. More like a question. They were now facing each other.

'I'm not … I mean, you are …'

Fantastic sort of sense-making, bravo Karl, real fucking brilliant.

The what to do and when to place it. The how to undress and how much to leave underneath. The give someone all that could hurt oneself. Or them. And then stand still. Just stand.

'Why are you not doing anything?'

'What do you want me to do?' It wasn't a rhetorical question. Karl was sweating. 'How old are you?'

'Nineteen. Why? How old are you?'

'Seventeen. Eighteen. I mean, my birthday is next week.' She pulled back.

'Eighteen? OK.' She was quiet for a moment. 'So you have done this before?'

'What?'

She laughed. 'If you say "all the time" now I'll know that you are lying.'

Her eyes opened but she couldn't see anything, their foreheads still glued together.

'So what is it?'

Her mouth tasted fresh, it felt clean, in an *all is good here* way. The way her breath travelled from ear to neck to collarbone to lips. The sucking. His head spun. Her hands lowered on to his bum.

'Cute.'

'Thanks.' He stood stiffer than before.

'You know—'

'That one again.'

She moved her head away and looked into his face.

'I'm trans.' Karl paused. 'Transgender. Some say I was born a girl. I don't agree with that, but anyway, it's complicated.'

It was warm. Hot. Too bloody hot.

'And?' She kept looking.

'So?'

'What's your real question?'

'Are you still interested?'

The door opened. Janoma jumped.

'Good evening, Auntie.' She grabbed her blouse, trying to hide behind

Karl's lanky frame. It was a hush hush situation and Karl was amazed how she managed to get the blouse on so fast, superwoman on a mission, not to save the world but her ass.

Luckily, Auntie was not coming to check on her but to show a visitor from out of town a particular cloth. They had been talking about it beforehand, it seemed. They were so engrossed that Auntie only half responded to Janoma as she lowered herself step by step, backwards down the steps, still in conversation.

'You've done well. Not just the import-export business, but also traditional fabric.'

'Yes. The other store is much bigger. We sell everything from dresses to suits, jeans and T-shirts. All ages. I will show you tomorrow. It has expanded a lot since.'

'And you still bring things from America?'

'Yes.' She turned towards Janoma. 'You remember Janoma, the daughter? She is now studying fashion and clothing technology at Uniport. She helps out here. She came top of her class this year.' Her pride brought all action in the small space to a halt. Long enough for Janoma to straighten her clothes and Karl to ask his face to lose the bloody fluster.

'That is good. God is great.'

'Amen,' Auntie concluded.

Janoma greeted the lady. Then she put her hand on Karl's arm and turned his to face the two newcomers. The auntie smiled at Karl and did the usual 'How do you do Mister, isn't it a lovely evening?' in what she thought was the Queen's English and which she had done each and every time she had met him over the past weeks when he and Nakale stopped by.

'Good evening, ma,' Karl replied.

'This is Karl, a friend of Nakale and Janoma's, visiting from London. Britain. He is choosing some fabric to take home. For his mother. He's leaving soon. This is his first time in Nigeria.'

The family friend looked at the aunt. Eyebrow raising, like *alone, here, the two*? But somehow Auntie did not notice. Distracted, she moved on to a big cardboard box in the corner. Inside were the special pieces she hid for special customers, as she explained to her friend. Or for special friends. The friend's eyes were still a little puzzled, disapproving. When she found her words again she asked Karl how he liked their country and how he was dealing with the electricity cuts, the bad roads, the climate, the food. All the particulars she could think about.

Auntie was going through her box. When she first met Karl, the night they dropped Janoma after the visit to the MOSOP office, she took his light brown face into her hand, turned it left and right, and said: 'Ah, so they neva give you full colour? Dey finish de thing before they could drop de right amount eh? Dis one na too much Europe. Ahbeg where de colour from daddy? Where dem dey leave am?'

Everyone laughed, a bit embarrassed for the shy boy, wanting to deflect from the situation as quickly as possible, although Karl had only been able to partially follow.

'No problem. No be your fault eh. Everyone is different. No be so? Your eyes don cover am well well. And your face. Ah! Fine fine yellow boy.'

Karl's heart fluttered like a trapped pigeon. She was much too close for comfort, but somehow he withstood whatever internal test Auntie had thought to put him through. She let go of his face with a solid nod of approval. Yes, this was a good friend for Janoma. Good-looking, shy, well-behaved, and from the United Greats of Britain, as she liked to joke. She was the one who had suggested to Janoma's father that

a piece of material would be more authentic than anything
nice from their much bigger and more fancy-pantsy clothing
store.

Auntie pulled out a heavy, roughly woven fabric. The colours
sparkled. It looked expensive.

'This one.' She showed it to her friend. Janoma's eyes
widened; she looked like she wanted to grab the piece and
run. Karl cleared his throat.

'I better be getting back to John's. They don't like me
coming late and I didn't expect—'

'Have you chosen anything, Karl?' Auntie interrupted.
Janoma rushed into the convo, anxious.

'I'll follow you. I can, yes Auntie?'

Auntie's friend raised her eyebrows again. Auntie was too
distracted to notice, heaving herself back from the floor with
the material in hand.

'I could come back tomorrow.'

Auntie's friend was *ah ah! These children.* But she didn't
use words, just her face. Auntie ran her hands over the
heavy fabric. There was much to feel. She liked it. A lot. No
attention to her friend, whose eyebrows were stretching her
skin. She was waiting for her friend to tell her how special
this special cloth was.

'You will be back in fifteen minutes, you hear? Tell the
driver I don't have time to wait.'

Janoma and Karl slipped out before the friend could move
her lips. They walked a little to the right, where the driver
waited, but stopped before.

'Can you come tomorrow?'

'Of course.'

'Aren't you helping Nakale with something? He will be
upset if you don't.'

'But I want to see you. We need to finish talking.'

'I'll speak to Nakale. You come at four?'

She dropped him at the little stand in front of the building
and waved when he walked up the first steps of the stairs.
Janoma. He wanted to talk to Abu but it was too late to leave
for the phone shop. John had one rule and that was no
travelling in the dark, anywhere. Unless it was with trusted
company. Someone who knew how to navigate PH.

He washed carefully, slowly, remembering everywhere
Janoma's hands had grazed, where her mouth, her lips had

been. He felt grown up, like proper, with a secret he couldn't wait to share.

Mate, u have 2 firgive me. U right i shud be there. I will b. 1 week. give me 1 more week. im in love

22

**The roads we travel on
in the end have to get to
one point or another,
otherwise it would be levitating.**

Nalini was in the yard, at the fenced strip, giving the estate the illusion of outside space. The large bins – the obligatory recycled paper, cans and glasses, plus the general waste one – lined the metal bars. Her usual gang was there too.

Abu checked them from the corner of his eyes. What should he do? Stroll over, talk to her directly, interrupting her friends? Hang about sheepishly hoping she'd get the hint and break away from the cluster?

Her hair looked like she'd recently done something to it, maybe blow-dried; Abu had no clue what went into the creation of Nalini magic but it was new, that much he could tell. Two of the other girls were busy with it, one trying out different clips, pinning bits of it back, although Abu thought it needed no help whatsoever, really, totally unnecessary. The other was stroking the stray strands of hair out of her face. Organic again, a mechanism; they belonged together, functioned well. It was painful. How was he going to get her attention? He needed to talk to her. All was different now.

'OMG Abu. Here, we're here. Come over.'

The one working with the hair clips, Mel, spotted him. Her hands waved, her smile matching her excitement. He looked around, his face giving away his relief and excitement, just for a second, then back to composure.

'So how are you enjoying the summer? Not that there is much of it. The heat the other day was probably all we gonna get this year.'

They all hello-ed and gave their input on the fact that, as usual, there were no long summer holidays simply because there was no long summer, no bloody relying on the sun.

Afsana looked him up and down as if she was checking for something.

'Don't tell me you're also one of those that went to the riots?'

Why did she have to go straight for the jugular, no warm up at all? Abu's armpits started producing. Sweat. Discomfort. He didn't want to talk about the bloody riots. Nalini hadn't said much but hello. The smile.

'Tell me you were not involved,' Afsana repeated.

'Not really my thing.' What business of hers was it anyway?

She wasn't convinced. She wanted to know precise stuff, not a *trying to get out of it* version with shuffling feet, and a face that looked like it needed some help in putting it back together. It was all a bit too much *eyes for a certain someone.*

'The people watching are just as bad, you know.'

'Why?'

Nalini still smiled. So quiet all of sudden. He could have sworn she had been in the middle of a story just before he came over. 'Should I not know what's going on in my city?'

'Some of the things that are going on are really bad.'

'What's so bad? People get hurt all the time. Right here. No one gets offended. You can't make a move without being wrong. I can't even walk along the street without someone following me around because I look like a terrorist in the making. No one gave a shit about that guy in Tottenham. The one the police shot. No one cared. Now they are all upset because someone is burning a bin somewhere.'

He was getting emotional now. He thought of the hurt he had carried away and no one had cried *how unfair.* Where were they? Every day. When he could need backup?

'Abu, it ain't even about that guy, though. People are just, like, stealing stuff, stuff that's not theirs, you get me. Not like these shops are all from rich people.'

'Some of them are.'

'In Hackney?'

Why were the girls always so quick with the details when the whole world was busy with a Croydon carpet shop on fire? But Abu wasn't sure if these people were rich either. What was rich anyway? Was the fact of a shop enough? He knew a schoolmate's relatives who owned a corner shop.

They weren't any better off. But they always had fresh milk
in the back. That's what he thought. At least there was milk.
And cigarettes and snacks. He didn't smoke but it was about
the point of it. That you had shit available.

'The whole bank thing you know, they are stealing from
us, the little man.'

'You don't even work.'

'Come on, like our fathers. OK yours is sick now but
before. My father. All who work all the time, thinking they
get something. And they put a bit in the bank and think that
one day it's gonna be better. Better for us, like their children,
innit. You know the youth programmes we used to do? Some
were bare fun, going away and doing things. Now all the
money, going straight to the bankers. Nothing left for us.
All closed down.' It had looked like he was digging himself
further and further into a hole he wouldn't be able to crawl
out of, but he knew what he knew.

'If you stand at the side, what are you doing to change it?'

'Why do I have to change anything? I didn't make this mess.'

He could see the way she was processing. Her friend had
stopped the hair-playing thing.

'Why are you going then?'

'Did I say I went?'

'So you didn't?'

She had him locked. Probably hadn't meant to. She was
impressed by his speech. All of them were.

A lot of youngsters migrated to the affected areas for a bit
of fieldwork. Most of them came back with new outfits and
new swag. It wasn't all that convincing because it deflated
in no time once they entered their respective gates and
met their parents, all apologetic stories and hiding clothes.
Abu was exhausted. Nalini hadn't said anything. He hadn't
wanted to go but what the fuck was wrong with it? At least
he hadn't done anything.

It was just, it was just … the city out of control because
the country was out of control because the whole banking
thing had gone like, way mad. Because none of them had
much to be good for. So what?

'For the record: I didn't do anything wrong.'

Afsana looked at him. 'I just don't want you to get into
trouble. That's all.'

Her concern was genuine. He didn't know she was that thoughtful. Didn't know the young women noticed him like that. It felt good and he felt the heat inside him cooling.

'Where's Karl? When is he coming back?'

Abu smiled. Nalini looked at him, they both looked away.

'Bit more than a week.'

'Been away long.'

And Nalini added, 'You must really miss him.'

Abu laughed. Blud, he drove him up the wall. His whole sensitive understanding, yet no understanding when Abu needed it. His disappearing. Fastest running reflex in the borough. But homie had a few things going for him. More than a few.

'I do. He drives me crazy but he's my best mate, innit. We belong together.'

And the girls went all *aw bless,* which made him feel all good about their friendship.

'Hey, I'm gonna see you around. Need to go.' He bounced across the street, around the corner and into his own heaven of brick, mortar and a whole load of cement. In front of the door to the building he stopped and pulled out his mobile.

me too man, me too! call me.

When something else needed to not happen. To not be too present. Deflection. For Abu. If only there was the right amount of deflection. This time there wasn't anything Abu could concentrate on.

He arrived at the gate to the estate. Then it happened. It went something like this:

'So you think you're too good for us now?'

'No man, was just chilling.'

'We have an arrangement.'

And this is where Abu felt times were never going to be different if nothing changed right then, right there. Big mouth, like it was said before, trying to prove something. That day, the world wasn't having it. His world, unfortunately, cared less than a gourmet chef for school dinners.

'I have no arrangement at all, you get me.'

He went out. Just out. Quiet, no sound, like Karl, ages before. Only there was no one to witness it.

* * *

The blouse was coral and low-cut in front. It went well with
the dark jeans Janoma wore. She was sitting outside the
shop on the same sort of low wooden stool Karl saw his little
friend Emmanuel sit on, outside the Internet cafe.

Abu hadn't replied to his latest text. *tried 2 call u. wher u
at? update! ;-)))) details!* ☺

Nalini had really got to him. Abu saying he was in love?
What were they talking about now that the whole project-
week, slavery-trail thing was over? Abu was a big mouth
but he only ever had real convos with Karl, really. Karl was
mad sometimes because Abu didn't even try. Had left them
each time any of the young women in their year came over
to them. Karl was the one who ended up getting close. But
Abu hadn't changed anything about it and kept fading away
as soon as he could. What were the odds? Both of them in
love, first time. Karl was pleased. His flip-flops slowly picked
up dust.

'Hey.'

'Hi.' Heart in overdrive. He wore black trousers, fitted, not
loose like usual. A red, chequered shirt and thin black braces.
Square sunglasses with a thick plastic frame. Red as well.

Janoma picked up the book that fell next to the little stool.

'Thought you were lost.' She turned around. 'Are you
attached to the road outside, or are you coming in already?'
The cheekiness returned to her smile.

'I'm just like, sensitive. I attach to things.' Karl was glad.
His brain still produced decent responses.

'A lot of things it seems.'

They reached the inside of the little shop. The space familiar
and as clean and tidy as the day before. He closed the door
behind him.

'Don't worry,' he said. 'It's a little stuck, I know.'

Her laughter reminded him of the way her mouth had tasted.
Fresh. She turned around and came back up the three stairs.

'This time I think we better lock it.' And without missing
a beat she added: 'I love the outfit.'

And pulled him into the room.

Their mouths found each other easily this time. Karl was
still shy but not so scared any more. She hadn't pushed him
anywhere.

'So, did you know or not?'

'I didn't. How? I've only known you for a few days.'

'But you didn't seem surprised.'

She laughed again. It was a different laugh. Thoughtful. Slow. 'I like you. I have a quick mouth, I know, but I was just waiting for you to do something. You were driving me crazy! I wasn't surprised, I was relieved, relieved that this was ... is going somewhere.'

Now he was laughing. 'You want me that bad—'

'Ha! Mister I've done stuff.'

'I have.'

'And what exactly does that mean? Tell me everything about doing stuff.' She looked at him, hand on her hip. 'Please.'

He laughed again, not even embarrassed. She was playing and it felt good. 'Don't torture me. You've won. I'm an apprenticeship still waiting to happen. I'm in your hands.'

She looked at the floor, then at him again. Her voice was quiet. 'No Karl, I'm in yours.'

'Then we are in the same boat.'

The hands went everywhere. The lips, the mouth. Their clothes piled around them. Their naked skin touched the cement. It helped. It helped cool the heat that rose from the skin. It was strange to have his body all exposed. To show everything. Stranger even to have hers like that, close up. She was so soft it tickled him each time her skin touched his body. Especially when her hands travelled down his arms or up his legs, worst at the back, up the spine. The hairs stood, but it felt good.

Her hand took his and guided it until he was inside her. Moved it, so that he could feel what felt best to her.

Janoma opened, leaning her back against the wall of the shack and reached with her hand between Karl's legs. Karl knelt, his hand deeper, his face between her thighs now until her stickiness spread past his lips, all over his chin, and she moaned, trying to hide the sounds from the outside world. The heat seemed trapped inside their bodies, spreading and trying to push out. Pushed and pushed until her legs clamped his face and she moved her head. Opened her eyes to look at him. He was panting. When he leaned back her hand slid out between his legs.

'Not bad, your stuff.' Janoma's breath was still rhythmic, trying to quieten down.

'Yours neither.' And both giggled, rolling on to the patches of clothing that protected them from the bare concrete. Karl stroked her hair along the lines of the even rows. It smelled of shampoo, hair oil and sweat. She leaned on her forearm and looked at him. Her voice was closer than before, different. There was a them-ness about it.

'You're buzzing.'

'I know,' he replied. 'What you do to me—'

'No, I mean your phone.'

The moments that are not savoured in full because they stop sooner than they unfold. Then the phone keeps ringing. You know how it is.

23

**If we could see everything,
we would be beside ourselves.**

Abu had gone out like tail lights in fog. The real beauty of a knockout is that you drop without doing too much damage. If you're unconscious before you hit the pavement, the fall might not hurt much, your body all floppy and receptive, embracing the hard cement. Of course if you had been kicked by a number of opponents, somebodies who really wanted you to feel it when you woke up, well, then the damage would be well ready for when you bloody did wake up, whether you did or not.

* * *

'Karl.'
  'Godfrey, I will call you back. I told you it costs me to take calls, wait till I ...'
  'Where are you?'
  'Chilling with a friend.'
  'I need to talk to you.' Karl could hear him breathe. 'Now.'
  'What happened? Is mum worse again?'
  There was that pause, the slope, the gap. Open, trip, descent.
  'What happened to Abu? Tell me what's going on! Godfrey?'

* * *

These things you know. In your bones you know them. And you'll be falling, falling really deep, head first. You will put on your clothes while Janoma is asking you what to do, how she can help. And you will look at her, the tears running, and she will help you put your clothes on because you're trembling and nothing works that way. She will sit you on the small chair, next to the cardboard box, tell you it's OK, to let it out and to cry while she slides the flip-flops over your feet. Her hands will touch both of your arms, then your face. She will cup it and then she'll say: 'Whatever you need, I'll take care of it.'

'I need to go back,' you will respond, and look into her eyes and between the two there will be this new thing as if you know more about each other than you do.

'As soon as possible.'

She will understand what you mean and take your hand to lead you to the door. She will look back quickly to check the room is as before. Then she'll lock the door and push you towards John's house. She will call her mother to explain, she'll call Nakale. All the while behind you, her hand will hold you up and lead you. She'll have no questions, but will take your cue when you arrive at John's. She'll introduce herself as your words will be racing and colliding against each other, in the way, too much, the thoughts have no time for this now. Once John understands you will go to the bedroom and Janoma will follow you, the door remaining open. You'll grab your bag, where you kept the rest of the money, your passport and your ticket. Both of you will rush back out in no time while John's wife will look so concerned, the baby sleeping on the rug, on top of a baby blanket.

John saying while you are leaving: 'Do you want me to call your father, Karl?'

And you will turn around again with sudden severity and catch yourself before it just spills out of you: 'No way.' You will thank John and feel it too, feel what the man has done for you, what all types of people have done for you recently and then you will be on the stairs again, downwards. When you arrive at the bottom, Nakale will be there, reaching for your arm.

'My friend. Wetin happen?'

'They kicked him and I wasn't there. He is in bad shape, very bad shape, not here, not conscious, hasn't been, hasn't woken up. The second day now. Two days. Abu all quiet. I have to get home, I have to be there. He should be talking.'

'OK, OK,' Nakale will reply. 'It's OK,' he will say and guard you on one side while Janoma will be on the other. They will walk with you, the short distance to the Internet cafe, but before you get there Janoma will be all organised, forward thinking.

'What do you need to do? You want to change your reservation, right? So someone calls the airline. Will you be calling Abu's people, Karl?'

'Yes.'

'I'll call the airline then. Give me your ticket.'

She will have an in-charge-ness that will make your knees softer than they already are because she will hold you in place, you know it. Just by being her. And you'll hand her the bag so she can take it out since she saw where you put it. And you'll be so grateful that people know what to do in emergencies, and if this isn't one then you don't know, you don't know anything any more.

Abu, come back.

You will think about the kicking and the head and the Abu who doesn't talk any more, the Abu who is quiet and breathing heavily, hopefully breathing, who needs to breathe.

I need you.

At the Internet cafe you'll see Emmanuel, who is playing with other boys nearby and who comes running now that he sees you, his friends tagging behind. He will smile and try to show off his new friend and you will have no time but to say: 'Sorry mate, gotta rush.'

And Nakale will translate it for the boy because your British accent will be thin like proper. No weight, nothing for the boy to catch. And Emmanuel will be disappointed but staying close with his friends, watching you and your mini-operation taking over one computer and two phone booths. And while you are speaking to Abu's mum, who will be crying on the other end of the receiver, Janoma will knock and open the thin door.

'Next flight with a free seat is tomorrow evening at seven. Take it?'

And you'll nod, grateful, so grateful that she knows what she's doing.

'There's a charge. Do you have money?'

And you will nod again while covering the receiver with your hand because Mama Abu is still on the other side and

you don't want to interrupt her with these mundane things,
the details of how you are getting back to see her son. All
you want her to know is that you will be seeing her and
her son in like no time whatsoever. And that it is your fault
because it's always about you and the damn running you do,
all the way out of Abu's range of operation so someone else
has come in, a whole load of them, and have fucked this up,
fucked him up.

Abu. Please. I need you.

Janoma, that angel, will mouth almost silently and you will
have to remember that she just asked you a question.

'Cash?'

And you'll nod again.

'I'll send the driver to their office. They'll hold it.'

And she will return to her phone conversation in the next
booth with the airline and when she softly knocks on yours
again a couple of minutes later you'll hand her the money.
The money you have because Uncle T has been sending
your mum money since your birth. Money to help raise the
child. Money that Rebecca refused but could not stop Uncle
T from sending and re-sending. The emergency fund that
Godfrey used to get you here in the first place.

Janoma will count the amount that is needed. Nakale will be
looking for any message from Abu in your inbox. Anything
you didn't open because really you have been preoccupied
and not opened a damn thing, have not engaged properly.
Anything that can give a clue to why now, why so severe, who
the fuck, what the bloody fuck is going on? But there won't
be any so he will be sitting there, waiting, and Emmanuel
will come and speak with him, or more like he will speak to
Emmanuel. While you'll still be on the phone with Mama Abu,
who says nothing, nothing at all but who can't hang up and
you don't want her to because you are here, not there, and
that means you are wrong. Very wrong. You will ask Janoma,
who pops her head in once more, her eyebrows raised, to
email Godfrey. To give him the details of the flight. And
before you can leave your booth the driver will have come
and picked up the money to secure your flight back. And
within half an hour you will have a return journey, no more
information from Abu's mother other than it is critical, and
you will sit for a moment outside the Internet cafe.

24

Presence is when you sit. Properly.

The sun was setting. Nakale, Janoma, Karl, Emmanuel and his little friends sat outside the Internet cafe. All were falling into deep contemplation after the hectic back and forth of airlines, Godfrey, Mama Abu, Karl's mum.

Nakale informed Karl that he would be staying with him tonight. Janoma called her parents to ask what was the latest the driver could pick her up. The young boys watched and discussed feverishly among themselves, the way kids do when they are negotiating the rules of the latest game.

Reddish strips of light were scattering behind the dusty houses. The commotion stopped. Madam had finished her workday and done all the things she usually did when she was about to get ready to leave. Emmanuel's mother worked nearby in a little stall. His mum could see him if she walked a few steps; the stretch of street was not very long. It looked like there was need of sitting and drinking something.

The group outside madam's shop looked lost. A warm Coke would do. Electricity had gone a while back and she had switched off the generator. The fridge sat lopsided on the two narrow wooden planks that held it up. All silent. She didn't owe these customers anything, but she brought out a wooden bench that seated the three barely adults, the boys already sitting on the red ground. The open sewer dropped down a little way to the side, a cement path leading to the entrance of the shop, covering the a greenish-black thickness, complete with empty plastic bottles and colourful paper scraps. Janoma looked at Karl.

'Finished?'

He nodded.

'What are they saying?'

'Some people found him in front of the house.'

He wondered if Nalini knew. Nobody would have told her. He didn't have her number. He needed to let her know.

'They called the ambulance straight away. The hospital is just around the corner.'

He stopped. Time was making itself very present. Two hours, two bloody hours, stretching apart as if there was no tomorrow needing drama.

'He's been out for two days.'

'Is there anything they can do?'

'He needs to wake up.'

The little boys looked at Karl. He handed them his phone. Another heated argument, now about who was to play the game on it. Madam offered her Coke. Karl bought a bottle for each of them. Their eyes widened and their cheeks collapsed from the intense straw-sucking. *Happiness could be such an easy thing*, Karl thought. It was in those moments. They only came by accident: a collection of people, random. A frame: the surrounding and the opportunity to highlight it. Like madam's offer. He smiled. The first since the phone call.

'So, Emmanuel.'

The boy looked up. His pride was shining so bright it could have switched the electricity back on. Janoma laughed.

'You na like dis man?'

Emmanuel stole a glance at his friends, who were all standing mouth open, Coke bottles resting on chins, straws connecting bottles to mouths. There was no drinking; the noise had stopped.

'Coke is your favourite?'

'Yes,' he replied quickly. And to prove it, he sucked even more on the chewed end of the straw.

'And football?'

'Yes,' all of them replied.

'Which team do you like?'

'Man United.'

And Karl laughed at the knot of them that twisted and unwound itself, excitement pulling and releasing their limbs.

'No, Arsenal na be de one.' Emmanuel was adamant.

Karl felt heavy.

'My friend at home. He dey like Arsenal. Like you. He like am too much.'

Emmanuel was still nodding. Eager.

'What about school?'

Madam came out of the stuffy shack and leaned against the metal bars she would soon lock in front of the door.

'Primary first. He's on holiday now. That's why he is here. To help out and stay out of his mother's way. If he is with his mum, he likes to get into trouble. Walk off with his friends here.'

She gave them all a pretend stern look. 'He listens better here.'

Then she turned to Emmanuel. Emmanuel nodded. Prime position, spotlight on him as he moved his head up and down, shaking off any doubts as to his manners and matters of obeying the rules. His eyes were still on Karl. The tension that held Karl's body was leaving. The little time he had left expanded.

'You know how to use computa?' Karl asked him.

And again the feverish replying started, all boys jumping off the ground, showing off to each other when and how and where and how much they had used anybody's laptop, PC, computer, smartphone, until Emmanuel trumped.

'My friend's uncle, dey get tablet we me go play one game for.'

That was settled, then. The adults hid their amusement. It was simple like that, the showing off. The sharing. The Cokes finished. Time was running out. Karl took his phone back.

'I am leaving tomorrow. I will see you next time, Emmanuel.'

He stroked the boy's hair. Emmanuel looked sad. Karl looked even sadder.

They returned to John's place. Nakale needed to collect the bag he'd left at the buka while waiting for Karl and Janoma.

The two had a minute. Like one, only one.

'So no last kisses then.' Janoma no longer teased. It was pretty shit.

'Looks like we might not get a chance.'

There was silence again, the loaded type, the one you don't want to break because it feels sweet, but it also hurts a whole damn lot. Once they broke it, time would move on. Like fast.

'Why don't you come to London when you are off uni?'

It had been on Karl's mind. Despite all the other urgencies, this one was one too. This couldn't be it. Was Janoma thinking any of that?

'I'll try.' Her eyes followed stuff on the ground. They could see Nakale, held back by Mena. She was waving at Karl, concerned look. Karl waved back. The shop was already closed, but she was cleaning. The counter collapsed yesterday for some reason. Her teeth flashed now and Nakale joined in on the joke.

Karl and Janoma were running out of time. Out of their one minute.

'I want to.' She sounded sad. The air between them melted. They couldn't touch. Not here. 'I want to see you again.'

The little stalls that lined the edge where dirt yard met street lit their kerosene lamps. Inside the houses, people were going about their evening business with the evening noises that came with all of that. The crickets were having another party. Their choral chirping making it all a little more intense. Karl. Heat heavy on his skin, on his mind.

'Please try.'

Nakale was saying 'bye' and he started to walk. It was only a few steps.

'Janoma, you won't just forget me? You'll bbm? I can call you?'

This wasn't going to be bloody *it*, right? Whatever the rest would be this was not the last of it. Right?

'I'll call you as soon as you're back in London. Karl ...'

Karl wanted her to rush, say everything, before Nakale joined them and they had to be a group of friends again, without this, this just-them-ness.

'You're awesome. We will stay friends, right?'

And Nakale reached. Karl took her hand and squeezed it as they walked up the stairs. John was expecting them, his wife behind him, baby in arms.

Nakale insisted. Karl like, *can't really fault my life for not bringing me some good peeps*. Just how to handle them?

'Karl, you are my friend. I no dey leave you.'

And John thought it a good idea for Nakale to stay with Karl for the night. Very good, very good indeed. When he saw how Karl stormed out of the house to the Internet cafe, brain and spirit floating outside the current universe, like the oil on the creeks, attached but not belonging there, he thought company would be good. Janoma's lips still lingered. He smiled, walking up the stairs, stomach in knots. Her skin, her arms, her lips, her breath, her eyes.

Uzo was on her way to bed. John asked if they needed anything. They brought a mat and a pillow. A sheet to cover. Nakale went to wash and Karl waited in the dark lounge. It was slightly cooler. Quiet. The evening had not yet turned into night but John excused himself. He would be up early to help.

After Nakale finished, Karl went into the bathroom and scooped water with a plastic bowl from the big container that was still half-full and stood next to the sink. Washed his feet. Took off the rest of his clothes. Stood in the lukewarm air, in the darkness, closed his eyes and tried to keep the rushing away. The head-on collision. Usually Abu would help out when things like that happened. Or Karl would leave wherever he was, hit the asphalt and let it lift him up and off the ground because he needed the air. Air between his body and the world so his body could leave the dirt underneath. The stuff that fit nowhere. Then he would knock at Abu's door.

But Abu was looking for his own way back in and Karl could not leave the house and Janoma. Janoma, who he had not found yet but was already losing. And Nakale. What to do with Nakale?

25

**Home is always
holding hands.
Without touching.**

'Are you sleeping?'

Nakale laughed. 'Wetin you dey do my friend? You dey wash with toothbrush?'

Karl laughed too. 'I'm just so tired, Nakale. I needed a minute.'

'I dey get am my friend.'

'No, it doesn't work like that. I get it or pidgin, not both.'

'Why not?'

Nakale made bloody sense, like usual. Karl was lost in his track. 'Not sure. You're right. I dey get you.'

'You fi teach me proper London pidgin o.'

'For sure. But we don't call it pidgin.' When had he become such an annoying smart-arse? It was dark. There was no electricity. It was beautiful that way. Quiet. The neighbourhood seemed to be rationing their generator fuel. The thick air lay on Karl's feet, pushing him in the ground.

'You want me to light a candle?'

'Yes now. You fi pack your tings.'

'Not really much you know. I can do it in the morning.' Karl lay down on the slim mattress. This was almost a reversal. Usually he was the one in the middle of the room. Abu the one at the wall. He had put on his boxers and another T-shirt. It was hard to lie down. His body wanted to be lifted, feet on the cool ground.

'You dey a'right?' Nakale all worried, turned towards him, leaning on his side.

'Yeah. How's de mat sef? Sorry, it must be so hard. We can swap.'

'Ah ah! Me I have slept too many nights like dis. No be special like for you Europe people.'
'Yeah.'
Karl was tired of jokes, tired of everything. 'Nakale.'
'Wetin my brother?'
'Janoma.'
'You dey like am.'
'She told you?'
'Ah, no need to talk dat one. Everyone can know dat one.'
'You are not going to tell anyone are you?'
'What?'

The whats of life. Which one? Which one should one convey? All or none? Or stick to the graduations?

'Is it my concern that you, my special friend, like my cousin?'
'Me and Janoma ... this afternoon ... anyway I need to tell you something else.'
The gap. It was reaching.
'We be friends, right?'
'Yes now.'
The heat was like a blanket. Thick one. Maybe it wasn't going to be so bad. If you're enveloped like that what could happen? What the eff could bloody happen?
'You know, on my papers—'
'Which papers?'
'I mean my passport.'
'Which kine problem you get for passport?'
'No problem really, well sometimes ...'
'Karl, wetin?'
'It never say Karl. There is no Karl. Not on my passport.'
They were quiet. Nakale rolled on to his back and folded his arms behind his head. His face was turned toward Karl. Karl spread his legs a little because it was still warm but a small breeze had found its way through the window. No need for those thighs to stick together just because of a little sweat.
'Me ... I don't know how to say am.'
'Karl—'
'Yes.'
'For passport him say you be woman. Na be de thing you fi tell me?'

There was an abyss again. Not a gap. Strike, defeat. No middle part. Nakale shuffled on his mat and one arm came away from under his head. Karl was looking for the right words that would stop this suction that was pulling him into the thin mattress through the floor into the bloody atmosphere and who the fuck knew if his body would hold, if it would remain in one piece?

'How do you know?'

'Mena.'

'But how does she know?'

'Maybe she feel am. Ah neva ask her. She say people pretend that we can know everything by looking and saying there is this side and that side. But we can't. It is never like dat. She say to be a friend is to be there and wait for the time. For the time to talk. And then listen.' He sat up. 'When me and you become friends she tell me, make ah better be true friend if ah be any friend at all.'

'She said that?'

'Yes.'

'And?'

'And wetin?'

'What do you think? I mean …'

'Ahbeg, now you say it be problem?'

Karl's breath was shallow. How great darkness could be. No viewing of his emergency-lighting blush.

'She ask if I be your friend make I be real friend. And me I think I be true friend. No be so?'

He lifted his head, looking at Karl. Karl kept staring at the ceiling. There wasn't anything to see in this darkness but still. You didn't have to face your friend head on. Not all the time, anyway. Fuck that.

'Karl, me I dey stay for here. You need some more explanation?'

Janoma came at eight. Karl was still packing. He and Nakale had chatted for a long time and only fallen asleep in the early morning. He was now sitting in the parlour, breakfast in front. The few things Karl had brought were folded and stored in the backpack. Nakale said he might be able to swing something for Karl and Janoma, a minute of alone time, but when Karl was ready to leave the room that had been his for the last week, the bell rang. When he walked

out, backpack on back, the father was just coming through
the apartment door.
  'Good morning.'

26

**Not all surprises
are justified.**

Janoma looked at Karl. Nakale looked at Janoma, then at
Karl. John was at the door and greeted Karl's father as
enthusiastically as last time. Uzo came from the bedroom
with Rose and showed her to Adebanjo.

Janoma tried to catch Karl's eye. Nakale was doing the
same to see whether he could, should, you know – the good
friend stuff. Karl was looking at his flip-flopped toes. What
a difference a day makes. An hour even. Less than that. A
few minutes later and he would have been at the fabric shop.

The father spoke to John, looked at Karl.

Karl just stood. Right where he had come from the tiny
hallway into the lounge.

'First you stay, now you want to leave so suddenly? You
will come with me.'

Not a question.

'I was about to say goodbye to my friends.'

No answer. The father nodded at John, at the others in the
room, then walked out. Karl held Janoma's hand. A quick
squeeze.

'Better to take your things. Your father can drop you.'

'But there is hardly any time. When am I going to say
goodbye?'

John didn't reply. Fathers superseded friendships; they
could make any decision they wanted. Especially when the
kid in front wasn't your own.

'Send me a message.'

'I will wait in the buka.' Nakale would have to be the most
uncomplicated friend on earth.

'Me too.' Janoma.

Adebanjo took him back to the bungalow. His bungalow. The one in which he told Karl how he wasn't needed here. Only with more harshness. Why was Uncle T in Lagos when Karl needed him? Lately he had got all Godfrey on him when they spoke.

'Give him time, Karl. Whatever it is. He is still in shock. I'll take care of it.'

Karl couldn't pull a *whatever* on Uncle T. He was too nice.

'I brought you here because I want to talk to you.'

Obviously.

Karl didn't want to run out of time just for some half-arsed attempt at bonding. A last meal at the buka, with everyone. Half of the people who mattered already waiting there. For him.

The father seated him on that same couch where Karl had sat the first day of his visit to the city, wondering if he might be engaged in some action thriller intercity search for the father he had never met. His father was well. It was, like, so clear it hurt. No need to get all entangled in things that wouldn't make a difference.

'I have been thinking …'

Karl knew enough about politeness. His eyes looked caring, his mind switched off.

'… and understanding.'

He was thinking of Janoma. How much time they would have? How soon he could get out of here?

'People like you …'

Time for the bracing yourself. The *like you* address was never a start to anything good. Followed usually by a version of: *you people, you are not normal, but I am going to decide to tolerate you while I'll keep making it obvious that I'm the one who is generous here. Because you are not normal.* It wasn't quite the same as friendship. Like Nakale. It wasn't quite like *I'm not leaving you. I dey stay for here.*

'I mean, I don't understand it but it seems …'

Karl looked at his father curiously. He was leaning forward, wanting something. What made him think he cared?

'I would like for you to tell me more.'

He could tell him that he was seventeen. That it meant he could start on testosterone if he wanted to. That he would. Soon. But you can't open a door that has two polished blocks instead of handles. Your hands will keep slipping off.

'What about your wife?' Time to get some bloody answers. Things he was curious about, not the father's version of some weak-arse explanation. 'How come she doesn't live here with you?'

'She lives in Lagos. I just work here.'

'You travel back and forth?'

'Yes.'

'How many children do you have?'

'Four.'

'Four?'

'Sixteen, twelve, eight, and six.'

'OK.' What else? He needed to get it all in there before the father continued on his anthropological investigations.

'Have you told her about me? Your wife.'

'Yes, she is the one—'

Karl interrupted; his surprise Q&A would soon be finished. He had to hurry. 'How comes Uncle T doesn't know then?'

There was a short, annoyed silence. The father turned around quickly. Until now he had looked at the floor in front of his shoes. Now his narrowed eyes scrutinised this person in front of him. Karl shrugged internally. *You know what? Can't be bothered at all mate.*

'Who knows what Tunde knows? He is a dreamer. If he does he probably doesn't care. He has his own way of looking at life.'

The father got all authoritative again, composure restored.

'I have done some research and my wife has supported me with it. She wants to meet you. I have arranged a flight to Lagos at the end of the week.'

Karl didn't say anything. He copied the father's posture, leaning forward, staring at the floor in front of him, hands clasped. Then he looked up, head tilted. *Haha. Yes, that easy. I wish.*

'How did you know I was still in Port Harcourt?'

'Tunde told me.'

It took Karl a minute to compose the answer in the clearest way. Polite.

'Thanks for the offer. Appreciate it.' *Not.* 'Unfortunately, I have to go home. Immediately. I am leaving tonight.'

'Yes, John said your friend is sick. OK, no problem, let's change the ticket and we go to Lagos today. Then you can go

home at the end of the week. I will call my driver immediately.
We can go by the—'
  'I'm sorry. I will have to leave today.'
  'My son, one day will not make a difference.'

If it was that easy, you would take the bait. You would hang,
wouldn't you? Sit the whole thing out. See what's on the
bloody horizon. That's the thing. At any junction something
can happen. Something unexpected, big. But it's only when
you turn into one of the roads, and get around the corner,
that you can get a good view of whether you care for that
oh hello surprise thing or not. Often you fall for that effing
bait, dangling in front of you like *wow, this is some amazing
opportunity*. But sometimes you know, just know, that from
zero to two hundred in no time is unhealthy. To say the least.

'I'm sorry.' Karl paused. 'He needs me. And his family does.'
  'They just accept you?'
  'I'm not going to lie. It took a bit for the parents just to
understand. Once they got it they didn't have a problem
with me staying at Abu's all the time. They never rejected
me in the first place.'
  He didn't feel like there was any need for this convo to
continue hijacking the bit of time left. There was a shortage.
He had places to be, people to see.
  'Maybe I'll come back some time.'
  'I think it would be better if you finish the things you have
started now.'
  'He is critical. He could die, you get me. He could die any
minute.'
  'I didn't know that. I'm sorry.' He paused then added, 'Karl.'
  As if things were different. As if saying 'Karl' now, without
some major contortion, was enough. Karl rose to his feet.
  'Can you drop me at John's house, please?'

27

In and out ...
(fill in the gaps).

If not for Abu's long, frantic breaths, nothing moving except his chest, up and down, but often enough to make sure his body was on track with its oxygen supply, it would have almost been impossible to know he was still there.

Karl? Like, distraught. Proper. Sitting there next to the bed, all tanned from days of life somewhere else, the Nigeria of the West Africa, of the bloody other side of the world.

Nothing was funny. Nothing.

The hospital, the long corridors of hush hush rush, the overfilled rooms. Karl tried to avoid it, at all cost, even when his mother had her stints there. Now it seemed worse, lonelier, more sterile, even less hopeful than it usually was.

First, of course, that vital thing for liveliness was nowhere to be found: Abu's consciousness. Then, let's face it, the babbling, the never-shut-up-when-needed that was missing, made not only the room but also the halls vibrate in silence. Abu's mother in the corridor. The twins running around further down, in the waiting area. Abu's mother, a handkerchief between her hands, folding it, refolding it, unfolding it, neatly putting it in squares and sideways and over the top each fucking way, this and the other, looking at her hands, head down, trying to keep herself in. Keeping herself from just leaking out into the bloody hallway so that she wouldn't be swept up by the cleaner and disappear in the huge, transparent plastic bags that they tied around the metal ring with a plastic lid that opened when they pedalled on the bottom. If she didn't make it, who would be there when Abu came back? If she lost it? Abu's father had tired eyes. His arms were around Karl's shoulders.

'It's good you are back,' he said when Karl walked into the hospital room.

Godfrey had been at the arrival gate, a big bear-like hug and an *if you do that again* look that had a hard time competing with the relief of seeing Karl back in one piece. Godfrey and his good kids *I knew you'd be back here in one piece and look at you* pride that Karl thought was out of place. He hadn't heard when Abu called him. Had not been there. Hadn't returned. Not been a good friend. None of the things he was sure Abu would have done. But then Abu's life was different, always was, always had been. It was shit, really shit. Godfrey had seen Karl's face. All tensed and taut, all *I've been away, I've grown up, see it in the way I look now, independent,* head-on gaze, straight into Godfrey's eyes. No head tilting or shyly avoiding contact, nothing but an *I need to do some stuff. Ain't no point stopping me now.*

And in the car, an angry mother, a very angry Rebecca, waiting for them to come out of the airport. Waiting only because she didn't want to lose it in public. Nigeria? What were they thinking?

There was no stopping Karl. That boy. You could tell he had a new stubbornness. It was troubling.

Abu had been lying there for a little more than three days. Movements yes, pain response, yes, pupils dilating when shone with light, yes, yes. Words? None. Waking, any type of wakeful state in the common sense? Nope.

Karl ran his hands over the brown skin. Abu's arm was floppy but warm. The skin cold but warm underneath. There was life, that much was clear. A sturdy step on the floor behind him got Karl's attention; he could feel Godfrey inching closer.

'As expected, she's very upset.'

'Hmm.'

There are replies that are pointless and everyone knows it, so why bother.

'You've heard what she said, right?'

'Hmm.'

'It could all be fine. No internal injuries, so that is good.'

'How's a head injury better, Godfrey? It's the bloody brain, you get me? The fucking brain!'

'But nothing has happened so far. A little bruising. Most likely he'll wake up and everything will be fine.'

'If he wakes—'

'*When* he wakes up.'

'How are you so sure? How can you be so bloody sure when nobody knows these things?'

'I just know, Karl.' He placed his big-bear big-brother hand on his shoulder, not smiling. That would have been too much, considering, despite his never-ending, happy-ending optimism.

'I just have a feeling. Can't tell you why or how. Just know. Just like I knew I could let you go to Nigeria—'

'You didn't just let me go. I went. I made a point. Wasn't your choice.'

'I could have prevented it. You're not eighteen yet. That visa would have not happened if I didn't have some—'

'Legal guardianship on me, I know.'

'Karl, I've always had your back. You can't say I haven't trusted you. You can't say that. I shouldn't have let you go, that's the point. If anything had happened … your mother … she's pretty mad with me.'

'That's why I said she didn't need to know.'

'She's your mother, Karl. How long did you want me to keep it from her? It was supposed to be two weeks. You ran away. Officially. This time I'm not covering, for none of it. You ran away. Not to Nigeria, but *in* Nigeria. That's how I see it.'

'Suit yourself, if that's how you want to spin it.'

'It's how it is.'

Karl wrapped his fingers around Abu's wrists and used his other hand to check for the few hairs that his friend seemed to have been nurturing since his absence. A lot of things seemed to have changed in those few weeks. Karl started laughing.

'It's not really all that funny, Karl. I am pissed off with you. I'm just too relieved that you are back.'

The giggling went all proper belly laugh. Karl got up to place his whole hand on Abu's cheek.

'That's not why I'm laughing man. Look, he's growing a beard, or not really.'

'And that's funny? It's what happens. Hormones, you might have heard about it some time back when you were still attending an educational institution.'

'Come on, Godfrey. It's funny. Three hairs, but I can just hear Abu's voice, saying, "Well the ladies like a Brad Pitt stubble. A little five o'clock shadow goes a long way."'

And the laughing continued, and Karl pulled Abu's hand closer, no longer holding it between his fingers but just hand in hand. Godfrey's lips now jumping too, his head coming closer to have a little look. He slapped Karl on the shoulder.

'You know how to play a man when he's down.'

'You the one who said you know he'll be fine.'

'When I said talk to him, I meant nice things like "Come back, we need you."'

'I did all of that. The whole flight. Now I got to talk to Abu the way we talk. Otherwise what's the point? He ain't gonna come back to hear some bloody bullshit just cause we're all shitting our pants. You know him.'

He put Abu's arm back under the blanket and straightened the white cover so it looked smooth and tidy. He placed Abu's head smack bang in the middle of the pillow. He would have got a fit if he had known Karl was getting carried away like that. Karl couldn't stop; it burst out again. The laughter shook and rattled and went tsunami, face all wet from the tears. Godfrey banged him in the ribs.

'Hey!'

'His mother … Can you get a grip on yourself?'

And there she was. The small woman who had never needed anything from Karl before. Her shoulders were hanging low, the twins on each side of her, their faces concentrating, zooming in on their brother in the bed.

'Come here,' Godfrey said, and extended both his hands. The twins each grabbed one and stood close to the bed, their little necks craning to see Abu's face. Abu's mother behind them, hiding almost, everything still shut close so that nothing would be able to ooze out. Her face tugged at Karl's insides and the laughter that he hadn't been able to control slipped away into the bleak no-nonsense-ness of the hospital room. His tears dried as hers started to fall again.

'It is the fourth day.'

Karl's birthday came. London was doing a half-arsed late-summer thing. The news was full of catching those who participated in the riots. Every other smart person was busy giving their deep thoughts on the whole situation that had been well fucked up. Whether it was just opportunism, or if it had meant more and showed the state of the country. The state of hopelessness. The way the youth would erupt, the black youth. Or all of them even. Karl was trying to catch up, get a proper opinion on the whole thing.

Nalini and Afsana caught Karl as he was leaving the estate. He wanted to get to the hospital early. They had a birthday card. Nalini hugged Karl. 'Are you doing anything for your birthday? I mean, like, later?'

'Not feeling it.'

'I understand.'

Afsana hugged him too. 'He will be better, you know.'

Nalini put her arm under Karl's. 'His chances are, like, excellent. Like really, really good. It will turn out all fine. Trust me! For real, Karl.'

Karl nodded and looked at her. Her hair was in a knot on top of her head. She wasn't wearing much make-up. Her face was all open, waiting for Karl to let her go on. Talk. Either about Abu, or just chat some shit and make this a birthday. At least. There was a new *we've shared something*. More than they knew how to handle properly. Or at least Karl didn't know how to handle it. Nalini seemed confident. And not in a Godfrey's optimism way but in a *these are the facts of life, you know* way. That you get scared. Scared shitless. And then around the corner … you don't know, you just don't know. Either way, take it a day at a time. Survive that one day. Then look again. See where you find yourself. What the facts of that day are.

'He'll be chatting off your ear in no time.'

'Thanks.'

She laughed. 'Not that I would know. Or at least I didn't used to.'

And Afsana had her own to share. 'And how he speaks to you now. We're all, like, *how did that happen?* Nalini, Nalini … no one knew Abu had it in him. Chirpsing the ladies like that.'

Nalini pushed her off the sidewalk. Afsana's eyes went all wide, telling Karl *yeah whatever, someone is so not upset at all.*

'It's scary, but he ain't dead, you know. Just remember that.'

Karl nodded. 'Thanks.' He started twitching from one foot to the other.

'Yu'aright?' Nalini seemed to have a new detective-type emotional ultra-vision thing going on. She put her hand on his arm. It started to drizzle.

'Yeah. Thanks Nalini.' And Karl nodded some more. 'For the card you know. I need to be off though.'

And he turned around as Nalini replied, 'Let me know if we can do anything,' and 'Happy birthday, despite everything, you know ...' But Karl raised his hand briefly, then turned around with wide paces. He made a left, ran down the road, then right over the traffic light past the Inland Revenue building and started to see the houses dropping away at the corners of his eyes.

28

**How to say those things
that sound better felt.**

Abu didn't wake up that day. The first day of Karl's eighteen years of age.

Karl sat on the bench that faced into the little park. London felt weird. His body was strange in these parts he knew so well, these roads he paced more than a few nights. The grass was supple and green. It certainly wasn't dusty. Some of these roads had some well underprivileged parts, as Godfrey would have described it. But nothing like the Shell lights. He got up and kicked a can of beer towards the bin on the right. Miracle there even was a bloody bin.

When he entered the little phone and Internet shop, nothing like the one in Port Harcourt but just as crammed, it started to rain.

'Hey, it's me.'

'Karl.' Janoma laughed. 'How's Abu?'

'Same. Not good.'

'And you? What's up?'

Karl grinned. The *what to do with this bloody world* disappeared.

'I called you, like, twelve million times yesterday. What happened? You're fed up with me already? Have you been doing stuff?' Janoma laughed. Not really worried at all. He had called her now.

'Lost my phone. I had it the day before yesterday. Might have left it in the hospital.'

'Did you ask lost and found?' Her voice was so close it was confusing.

'No. Should do. Smart-arse. I didn't even think of that.'

'Well that's what I'm here for.'

'No, that's not what you're here for. But it helps. A lot. At least someone has their senses together.'

'That bad?'

'Worse.'

'What do they say?'

'To wait. He's got good chances. Blah blah. Whatever.'

'And what else?'

'I miss you.'

'Me too. Like crazy.'

There was that pause. Burning. It spread in the tummy like Marmite. Only you didn't love or hate it, you did both. Straight away. Because it was left hanging.

longing /ˈlɒŋɪŋ/
noun
     1. A yearning, craving, ache.
adjective
     1. Having desire.

desire /dɪˈzaɪə/
noun
    1. Strong sexual feeling or appetite.
    2. Like hunger, like greed: urgent.

'So?'

'So what?'

'What are we going to do?'

'I don't know Karl, I don't know. I need to see you again.'

'You do.'

She laughed. 'Not sure about yourself at all.'

'That's a no-brainer cause that's what you're here for. To be with me.'

Strike. Matched. Defeated.

'You've been doing stuff.'

'What? What do you mean?'

'You've grown yourself new confidence.'

'Janoma.'

'Yes?'

'Can you come? Please.'

29

Turn, turn, turn.
And then pick up the pieces.

'So why are we all here?' The counsellor was an older woman, her hair white, loose on her shoulders. Karl always thought it looked a little thin but even thinner today. Godfrey was optimism display to the max.

'I think we need to all just check in with each other properly.'

Rebecca looked at him. For real? Now you want to check in? She turned away. Karl sat in the middle, couldn't move without taking sides.

'When was the last time you did? I mean, like this, the three of you,' the counsellor continued. Godfrey wasn't usually part of the package deal. Not in her office.

Rebecca looked at Godfrey. Karl looked ahead. Counsellor looked at all of them, rotating.

'A while back. We used to ...' He looked at Rebecca. Pleading.

Rebecca opened the door. Metaphorically speaking. Briefly.

'I'm angry. Very. It's not just about how dangerous and irresponsible this all was. Not just that you lied but that both of you thought I wouldn't understand. And that I'm no longer part of it. Of anything that has to do with you, Karl.'

Karl turned to her. 'It's not even like that.'

'Everyone knew. Except me. I call you and you pretend you are somewhere in the countryside. The English countryside.'

They were all silent. There was nothing to say. But the white-haired woman thought differently.

'And why is that, you think? Rebecca, do you want to start?'

'Actually, I don't. I would like to hear from Godfrey. I would like to know what made this OK.' She leaned towards him. 'How did this work in your mind? I did *not* give up guardianship. I invited you in to *support* us.'

Godfrey's body folded, smaller now.

'I know. It just sort of ran away … sort of all went its own way, you know. It made sense, although it didn't, if you know what I mean … I don't even know how to explain it.'

'Try.'

The counsellor still rotated her friendly face. Karl still looked ahead. This wasn't about Godfrey. Not really. He was just getting it because he should have known better.

'I would've gone anyway, Mum. I would've. I needed to see my father, Nigeria. See something other than this bloody city.'

'You won't be able to get rid of me—'

'How could I want to get rid of you? Never. But you kept that from me. My whole life! I wanted to be myself. Karl. Without the bloody street telling me otherwise.'

30

**The coming and going.
If only you could decipher
the logic.**

Karl sat with his mother, watching *Newsnight*, talking about the state of things. The riots he missed, the school time he missed. The stuff they talked about in therapy. How they became estranged; reliant on the little network to support Karl. The guardianship from Godfrey. How she wanted it revoked, if this was how they went about things behind her back. The everything she missed because they did not have a tight relationship any more. Not her words, of course not. She said 'no meaningful relationship' and 'not trusting any more'. Everyone knowing him better than she did. It wasn't alright like this, to run away and not tell her the truth. Not even if he was eighteen. Not even if she was sometimes very ill. But she understood 'being your own person', and the world trying to tell you otherwise. The small world that you sometimes couldn't escape unless you left. She had done that. A long time ago. Not much older than Karl. She had been feisty and sure of herself and not known what she was doing at all. They fell silent then, left it there. You couldn't say it all in one go.

It got darker in their living room, but they didn't put on the light. Karl sat on the couch with her, and when *Newsnight* finished, she turned the TV off. Karl just looked out the window for a very long time. Didn't say a thing. Until she broke the damn silence.

'He will be fine, you know.'

'I hope so.'

When Karl slept later, he dreamt his mother was running after him in a water park, the fountains spraying both of them and their laughter so loud and wild it woke him up. The first rays of light were creeping through the blinds. He left a note. *Out for a run. Found my phone. I'll be back for breakfast.*

It was still quiet outside, houses all dreamy and inattentive. Instead of sprinting around street corners, he walked until he arrived at the hospital. It was too early for visiting hours but he knew a way of sneaking in to the chair by Abu's bed.

When Abu opened his eyes, Karl's face was slumped over. Abu all clueless. What the heck was going on? And why was Karl all droopy-shoulders, about to hit the floor with a big sliding-off-that-chair move that was not cute at all? Abu wanted to laugh but it was difficult to remember how to do that. Instead, his mouth moved, the lips remembering the way they used to work that whole area, a mind of its own, tongue adding the rest.

'You're back.'

And he fell. Karl. Banged his elbow on the linoleum. Awake in an instant. Then remembered where he was, that he wasn't supposed to be here yet, that he needed to be quiet, that they could tell him to leave. But before he made it up off the floor something sent him straight back.

'When did you come back?'

31

Who waits
for whom
and at which corner?

'Nurse.' Karl jumped up from the floor and landed next to Abu, hugging him, laughing, crying, then careful, then scared.

'Nurse!'

A tired, round lady came in. Her uniform was immaculate, if you wanted to use such a heavy word. Some ironed shit right there. Her eyes looked sleepy, overworked. Karl had seen her around a lot. Her eyes looked at him – *what?* – then at Abu, then back.

'He's ... look! He's awake. His eyes ...'

The dragging feet almost leaped forward and in one coordinated swoosh the nurse took Abu's arm into her hands, felt his pulse, asked him if he knew where he was, placed the cold end of the stethoscope on Abu's thin hospital gown. She listened to something Karl couldn't hear, then shuffled out to get the consultant on duty. Abu's eyes closed again, face scrunched as if in pain, head tilted to the side.

'That light man, you can kill someone with that.'

'Of course,' Karl replied. 'I can fix that, just a sec bruv, won't be a second.' And hurried to the switch by the door. Then it was gone. The light and the spark that had ignited Abu out of Nirvana. By the time the doc came he was out again: nothing at all, nothing bloody at all.

'He was awake. I spoke to him—'

'He was, he seemed to respond well and understood that he was in here. Of course he didn't know why,' the nurse reported to the doctor.

And it started again: the testing and looking at Abu closely. Karl shushed out of the room but returned as soon as the

doctor let him, like a lover on the rebound. There was nowhere
else to go. He had to stay. The doctor apologised but said it
was a good sign nevertheless. That there was more hope;
he had been waiting for some improvement.

'All developments are promising at this point. Be patient.
Your friend is fighting.'

And Karl took his position by the bed again, impatiently
settling in.

but where wd I stay?
  mine of course where else
  & ur mother?
  ill speak 2 her
  *before I get there, pls! don't want 2 turn up & left standing
in that british rain of urs :-þ*
  haha. u wont
  check
  ok

u still there?
  I am
  i miss you
  miss u 2. will ur father let u come ???
  He will have to say yes. It's good for my studies
  Will he?
  Yes.
  Maybe he'll think ur running away
  says mr. running just to get a life
  it's different
  how?
  have nowhere to be still

'What's wrong with this place? Some sort of light torture?'

And something fell again. Karl was dropping the phone.
He looked up and reached for Abu.

'Can you like make up your mind? Stay this time, bruv.'

Abu looked at him, puzzled.

'Please.'

Abu's eyes focused. He turned towards Karl, less pain in
his face, more real action in his movement.

'When did you come back?'

'I'm sorry man. I'm sorry.'

And tears fell. The guilt that made Karl's chest an abandoned warehouse. Heavy and empty at the same time.

In the end, Abu remained on the conscious side of reality.

32

How loud
is a vacuum?

Abu quiet. This was definitely new. Like so effing quiet you would not believe it. It made Karl uncomfortable. He felt like shifting on his chair, shifting while standing, when walking, or when on the mattress in Abu's room. He couldn't find a still point, nothing to hold on to because Abu gave nothing back. No reassurance, nothing but the stillness that penetrated inside Karl's chest, cold and unforgiving.

After days of coma induced by a minor head injury, because his brain hit the front then the back of his skull, when they had shown him how to worship the ground, he woke up, most of himself intact. His brain had flopped forward and backwards, like the way the wannabes slammed them in the fence that time, and the bruising caused him to be out, seven days straight. No bleeding, no nothing. *A lucky, oh so lucky boy* the doctor had said. Nothing but some mood irregularities, some attention problems, which wasn't so damn new; memory might need some recap but nothing that could not and would not be dealt with. No need to worry.

He saw the special therapist every day while still in hospital once he woke. Now he was home with his mood irregularities and Karl missed the chatting that had never been quiet and irritable but straight out of the tap in one long gush.

Not like Abu had ever been the one with the best organisational skills. Now he had exercises for that, to make sure he regained them, but after another week it was clear there wouldn't be much of a lasting problem. *As long as he could lose the bloody moodiness*, Karl thought. He rolled over in bed, feeling guilty. Things were back to normal, if you could call an almost-death normal, if you could call running away to the other end of the world normal, but at least he was back to his floor position, lying awake now to make sure Abu was still breathing. As long as that happened, he knew it would be fine.

Karl was now talking non-stop, whenever he didn't feel the responsibility pressing on his chest, making his vision dark with stars popping out in front of his face, air making itself rare. When he had enough breath he was chatting for King's Cross, Nigeria and the fucking universe. Yakking for Abu, trying to make up for things he should've/could've/would've done, for things he wished he could do now, like take away the pain that was dropping on his friend's face like there was no tomorrow. The way he retreated now, his eyes there but all the rest gone someplace else, processing, Karl hoped, but he wasn't sure. It didn't seem like Abu had really come back.

'Your birthday soon. Wanna go go-karting? Heard someone talk about it this morning. Sounds like major fun. I think Nalini would be up for it.'

Karl was talking into the dark. No telling if Abu was still up, but since they had nowhere to be the next morning he thought he'd try.

'Headache. Sounds like headache to me. You do know that I just got my head kicked in?'

Karl could feel Abu staring, not at him, but at the bloody ceiling. The way he talked it was clear that he wasn't interested in having a real convo. Not about go-karting or anything else. Nothing at all. Again.

'Of course, stupid me. Sorry man. What do you want to do?'

'Don't matter. Nothing is fine with me.' Abu pulled the blanket up to his chin and sighed his *whatever* way, the one he acquired out of nowhere. 'Nothing to celebrate,' he continued.

'That's not true. I know this is some heavy shit, but Nalini. You're in love and stuff. She's, like, crazy about you. You're not even *talking* to her.'

Abu was quiet. Karl was sorry. All that talking meant he wasn't waiting it out any more, wasn't paying attention to when Abu wanted to bring things up himself.

'Just give him some time,' the doctor had said.

Karl wanted Abu to help. Do that chatty-chatty business and tell him *easy bruv, no problem whatsoever, listen to me. This is how you do it.* This would be how Janoma would come and stay, and his mother would be fine with it, and her parents as well. He couldn't take any more extended therapy across continents to cover the next set of disappointed adults. Chances were if he didn't play this right, Janoma would be lost. For real.

'You could transfer.'
'It's not that easy. Do you think they are going to take me in London, coming from a Nigerian university? You have no idea! And I'm not dropping out. I've told you, I'm doing stuff. Going places. You can't ask me to change my life because we met for ten minutes.'
'More like three weeks.'
'My point.'
'Well, you're coming here now, so we can see if—'
'I won't drop out!'
'Nobody asked you to drop out!'
'Good. Then we're both clear.'
Karl sighed. 'We are. I just meant if there was a way … you know.'
'I said what I had to say. Understood?'
'Yes ma'am.'
'Very funny. Take me seriously.'
'I am. Sorry.'

* * *

But Abu had nothing to say, nothing to add, no *what was that all about*, no analysing; he just wanted to rest, be left alone, talk minimum and stare at the twins. They got all 'caring siblings' on him and were the only ones who could deal with his silence. Needed nothing from Abu but to sit somewhere close to him and look at him from time to time. Azizah would hold her hand in front of his mouth if he got too quiet, nod at Aazad, whose face would return to whatever he was doing before they stopped mid-action to look at each other, then their older brother. They had noticed how he had left the building. Mentally. Totally unavailable.

And no effort ever to tell Karl off or how he could get back to their friendship. If he'd changed forever, or if this was a phase. And all the things that happened to Karl. And to Abu. Here. And the other friendship that Karl hadn't yet told Abu about. The good friend in another city, in another set of rules, in another country, which really meant another world. The one who had thrown him in the cold water to say two things: *grow up!* and *here, here is my friendship. I need to prove nothing. I just do.'*

Karl wanted to tell Abu. Ask whether he would come, wanted to come to this bloody Nigeria, the literal bloodiness of it, the part where rain poured sour with residue of gas. Where a long chimney could extend far into the sky and spit flames like no man's business. Wanted to show him the pictures on his phone. The articles Nakale had given him. What to do with that info? What to do with all of it?

He called Nakale. Not when he was over at Janoma's house but at an appointment time made by text. Relationships needed reliance. There was no need to mix things up; he had learned that much. Everyone should have their own equal share, their own bit of prime-time. Nakale had all sorts of questions. He had already emailed Karl. Could he help out now? Help get some of the details?

There was a case in The Hague. There was also a recent oil spill in the mighty US of A. That one was, of course, much more pressing, because it was about American lives. Nakale didn't get why his type of data never made any headlines like that. Karl didn't know what to say. This beyond-King's Cross was a new way of looking at things. Godfrey said it was a sun thing: the we-revolve-around-it. The sun being the effing centre of attention. So no one cared for lives that came from places that were so far away in their orbit because everyone was so busy being close to the main action. To the main player.

In the end it was the only place that really mattered. Karl didn't have the heart to tell Nakale what Godfrey was on about. And that he thought he was right. But eventually he had to ask him how to spin the Janoma thing. There was no one else to go to. Would her parents let her stay with him?

But Nakale asked about Abu first and the tears wanted to fall again but it all just went dry in Karl's throat and eyes.

'Physically, he's all fine. Miracle really.'

'And what does he say?'
'Nothing. Nothing at all.'

Nalini spent her time meeting Abu outside in the little bit of green arranged to break up the tall rectangles of concrete that sat between the posh bits of the area.

'Karl, he's fine, I think. I don't think he's mad at you. He's just quiet, doesn't say much to me either. It's only been two weeks. Give him time.'

Then Godfrey.

'So. Can we recap the whole thing now that we've made some progress? Please?'

'Again?'

'I'm talking as in how to go forward.'

'What do you mean?'

'He called.'

'Who?'

'Your father.'

It was annoying. Those bloody commentaries.

33

Time is a conundrum.
You're forever chasing its tail.

'What does he want?'
 'I think he just wants to know you. Call him.'
 'Godfrey, I'm not all that bothered. I've had enough bonding problems lately. Gonna stick to what I know.'
 'And what is that? What about Abu? All seems to be different. And that girl—'
 'Woman! Young *woman*, please. And that is *exactly* what I'm talking about. Things are different. And my priorities are fucking intact. You have no idea. The father isn't one of them.'
 Godfrey turned quiet. He sat on Karl's bed. Karl looked at him. Godfrey looked at his shoes. The afternoon was fading quickly. The right and wrong things. The eighteen years of age. The getting used to not having to be the meddler. Of adulthood. Independence. The knowing your place. Which sometimes was stepping back. Like, way back.
 'Understood.'

Karl called Uncle T. They chatted like they used to. Catching up on Abu and Rebecca. On London. But then he went all *Game Over, come clean already.*
 'Karl, you still haven't told me what happened with your father. He has been trying to call you. You have to speak to him.'
 'Yes, Uncle. I will call him back. I have been busy.'
 When he called John, he filled him in on all the latest developments. Rose was crawling now. Karl promised to call again soon.

He had things to do. Nakale was devising the details of the master plan. Janoma was to follow Uncle T on his next business trip to Italy. Gain first-hand experience in buying. You had to do buying when you did fashion. You did. Surely the parents would understand that. See how indispensable such an experience was. Italy. Fashion capital! But also, she could buy some things for the shop. Uncle T had already mentioned he needed an assistant. He was so busy these days Karl didn't think it would take a minute to convince him. Janoma was a model student after all. Shopkeeper. Only Italy wasn't London. How to get her there?

'I have an aunt in London. I dey try eh.'

Karl could almost see Nakale's ear pressed into the phone in the crammed booth. Maybe Emmanuel was hanging about, trying not to cause any trouble. It was shit being so far away.

'My friend wetin you go do with Janoma?'

'What do you mean?'

Nakale sounded puzzled. His voice didn't drop, it stayed level, as if it had nowhere to go.

'Wetin you wan do? She will return to Nigeria after small time.'

Everyone and their bloody planning. He couldn't escape it. If they could just, like, leave him to it for a minute. Could a brother not get a bloody minute?

'I just want to see her.' Pause. 'I thought she really wanted to see me, too.'

Nakale's laugh sounded resigned. 'My bruv. No dey worry yourself. She dey do. Only this going to London ... De whole thing, na be harder like dis.'

Karl sighed. 'It's already hard.'

'Hey.'

Abu was lying on his bed, perfectly groomed.

'Hey. Are you going out to see Nalini? Was just coming for my headphones. I left them here.'

'No, just lying here.'

'Can I sit?'

'Why so formal, man?'

'Why so formal? Cause you ain't speaking to me.'

'I ain't what?'

'You're not speaking to me. Abu—'

'I'm speaking to no one, in case you haven't noticed. Pay some attention, mate. I thought you had my back.'

Karl smiled. Something was giving. He could feel it.

'I do.'

'Then give me a fucking break.'

And Karl went for his headphones, which had slid under Abu's bed. Dust was stuck to the padded parts. He brushed it off.

'Hey, want to stay at mine to mix things up? Mum and me changed the rooms around. I got the bigger one, am out of the cupboard.'

'What? How did that happen?' Abu sat up, automatically smoothing his trousers. The beige stuck out against the navy-patterned duvet cover.

'Side effect. All the talking we've been doing.' Karl stood in the middle of the room.

'No way. She really just changed it?'

'Yes. I didn't really want it at first. Why, you know? Mum needs her space too. But I'm trying to get that woman to come here. The one I met in Nigeria. I told you. Janoma.'

'And your mum swapped rooms with you so you two could have space to fool around? Wow, my man, my man, you have got things—'

'No, she doesn't know yet. I still have to ask her. But you have to be prepared.' He laughed.

'Does that mean you'll no longer be here?'

'Depends on you.'

'Just 'cause I nearly died doesn't mean you have to act like *I* left *you*.'

'Not bitter at all then.' He didn't laugh. There was nothing to laugh about.

'Sit down already, skinny arse.'

He sat next to Abu. 'It's called "keeping trim".'

'It's called "being knocked out and your friend not being there for you".'

Karl hugged him from the side. One arm behind Abu's shoulders, the other in the front, but to reach properly his body would have to come off the bed. He hovered, wanting to step to the side, but Abu's knees were in the way. It was a bit pathetic. To get to a proper hug he would have to almost climb on Abu. Wasn't quite what he had in mind.

'OK, not working the way I thought it would.'

Abu burst out laughing so hard he had to cough.

'You are a mess, you know.'

'Just didn't think sideways hugging would be such hard work.'

And they screamed. Mama Abu knocked on the door.

'Everything fine?'

She saw them next to each other, laughing, hitting their legs, boxing the sides of each other. Smiled and closed the door gently.

'Sorry?' A question.

'I'm on it. Give me some time. But when your woman is here and you ain't bringing her …'

'No way. I'm dying to see what you say. She's cool and … beautiful.' He looked at Abu. 'And she has a quicker mouth than you. You two will leave me behind.'

'Still catching up, heard the doctor. But I'd get your dreamy self any time. You're slow sometimes you know. Smart, but slow.'

'I just need my time.'

'Sometimes others need yours too, bruv.'

'I said sorry.'

'Not quite the same as listening to what I have to say, innit?'

Abu put his arm around Karl's shoulder.

'Simples. You just do the arm. No need to go for the whole body invasion. See? No problem whatsoever. You're slow man. Like I just said.'

Karl smiled. 'So Nalini …'

'Man, we need to talk.'

'That's what I'm *saying*. Mum is waiting, though. I promised to cook dinner with her. Fancy coming, or what exactly did you dress up like that for anyway? Haven't seen you make an effort since—'

'Maybe I was waiting for you.'

He jumped off the bed and raked in the bottom of the wardrobe for matching trainers. He found an old pair, behind a few boxes, baby blue, like the crisp shirt he was wearing. Black ash stains were smeared over one side. Some memories. The shock that rings after, long after the brain stops hitting the skull.

'Karl, it's not the hospital.'

'About Pat, mum's friend?'

'I didn't …'

'What do you mean? You made your statement. You told them who it was. You did, right? It's my mum's friend!'

'I know.' Abu pulled out the trainers. They were the right colour for the combination. He looked at the top, thinking. 'I sort of told the police. Not all.'

Karl went all major pissed off.

'Calm down. Not yet. My memory you know, they're all giving me space anyway.' He loosened the laces. Those cases …'

'What cases?'

'You know, the riot thing. They are going to go down on that hard.'

It was a question. One with a full stop, with a certainty.

'What you mean 'on that'?'

'Where you been? The rioters. People. Anyone they can get. De yout dem, anyone the slightest bit involved, man. Do you pay any attention?'

'And you were?'

'Did you read my texts or what? They are going to try to pin something on me.'

And Abu told him about running and the smell of fire in his nostrils, the explosions that didn't just make good TV, that wasn't just some abstract reality of some other part of the city but that had burned right in front of him. Had sent a flying piece of burning foam that was probably from the seat on to his trainers. And how now it rubbed a whole lot of wannabees the wrong way.

'That's how it all started.'

'You were there when they burned a car. So what?'

'What do I know? All I remember was that I was too good for them. You know me; given the wrong bit of opportunity, I just let out a rant. A long one.'

'And …?'

'How slow are you? They kicked out my tail lights.'

'Have you heard from them since?'

Abu chucked him his phone. It landed on the bed. 'Just go through.'

He sat the trainers on the floor. 'I was wearing the blue hoodie with these. I hope it done me good service.'

'What?'

Karl was still fumbling with Abu's phone.

'CCTV. From my face making news. You forgot how to get to the bloody text? Give it to me blud, you're killing me.' He walked over and opened the first message.

'You know they still use smoke signals there.'

'Thought so. At least if it ever kicks off again here you can let me know where you are. Probably not where the action is.'

'Very funny. So what am I looking for?'

'Just go through it, you'll see. It's pretty entertaining.'

Karl started to read.

'Ignore Nalini's messages, OK.'

'Why spoil all the fun for me, I was looking forward—'

'Just do it Karl. Start from the back, work yourself to today.'

Wakey wakey.

Karl looked up at Abu. 'Is this when—'

'Second day of coma. Of course I didn't read it then.'

'Who from?'

'Unknown number.'

'I see that, but you have no idea?'

'Not sure exactly. Probably one of the guys responsible for Pat. Think they're clever … Trying to pin the whole car thing on me. Police could probably find out who it is in no time. Isn't there like GPS on these or something? They know I won't go.'

'But why not, Abu? I still don't get it. They almost killed you.'

'Your answer right there.'

The texts came daily. They weren't threatening, not in so many words.

Don't worry bruv wont say anything to anyone just coz u blew up a car. Cctv prob didn't get you at all

Then there were details of things he had apparently taken. Places he was and how it was nice to catch up, even if the sender didn't quite agree with vandalism just because everyone else was doing it. Or with stealing. Details of the clothes he was wearing. How he covered up but the photos would probably still be enough to identify him.

There were fifty-four messages. Three a day. Morning, lunch and dinner. Always the same time. Somebody had a lot of time and free texts to hate Abu.

'You have to report them. It's just going to go on forever.'

'I won't. Go to the newer one. Last week onwards.'

Wow, gr8 girlfriend. Cute! Sure, i'll keep an eye on her, no probs mate. That's what i'm here for. My pleasure.

'You know they're just bluffing, right? Sounds too much like a TV show.'

'Not going to the police, Karl. Let's go and cook with your mother.'

Karl handed him the phone. His friend had decided to get rid of the three and a half hairs that had not made any stubble at all. His haircut was fresh, scissor sharp and recently gelled. He didn't look at Karl when he took the phone and put it in his trouser pocket. Everything was neat. The outfit, the hair, the room. Only thing that was stalling this whole show of neatness was the way out.

Karl's mother had started cooking by the time they finally made it to the small flat.

'I thought you had forgotten me, Karl. Abu, so lovely to see you. How are you?'

'Thanks, Rebecca. Very good actually.'

He still felt even shyer than usual around her, although since she had motioned for him to leave her and Godfrey to talk alone, she had not shown any sign of anger towards him. Godfrey was responsible, as far as she was concerned, for dragging both Abu and his mother into the whole thing. Knowing full well that they were close. That they would have to lie. It was Godfrey and her who were still working on their relationship. On a more honest new base, as Rebecca said.

'Glad to hear,' she replied and smiled. 'Things are hopefully getting back to a better place now. For all of us.' And she looked at them, not wanting a reply.

Karl showed Abu his new room. It wasn't all sorted out yet, just a couple of boxes of his stuff there and the beds exchanged. His mother had moved into the tiny single because she was using the rest of the flat more anyway. And Godfrey was going to help.

'What do you think?'

'What do I think? Your mother's ace.'

Karl beamed and looked around the room. The window faced the street; he liked it that way. His single bed left enough space to walk around if Abu wanted to stay. Or Janoma, if Karl's mother let her. She might. There were no pregnancies to fear; he had prepared this argument for when the *you are too young for this sort of commitment* would come.

He didn't need to move his wardrobe, there was a closet in here that was more than enough. The rectangle room would keep feeling airy, big; somewhere where he could stay. Without the walls closing in. Space for those thoughts. Friends. Rebecca's tough year had finally turned good patch. The doctors were hopeful it would remain that way for a while. She'd rearranged the whole flat and thrown out things they didn't need. Made room for their new lives, she said.

Abu sat on the bed. His phone vibrated. 'Like clockwork, I told you.'

The message on the display was another sorry excuse for a threat.

'If you don't go to the police what are you going to do with it, with them?'

Abu shrugged. 'All your stuff is in those two small boxes?'

'Some of it is in the closet.'

'So my birthday is tomorrow.'

'I know.' Karl looked at his friend's clean-shaven face.

'What should I do?'

'Whatever you want.'

'I mean about Nalini.'

They were back in business, all the way. Rebecca was calling from the kitchen.

'That's your mum. Seems like dinner time.'

'You staying here tonight, for a change?'

The phone was still in Abu's hand, the message in the dark now that the display light had gone off to preserve battery. 'Let me just check with my mum.'

But it didn't sound like he called his mother at all when someone answered the phone on the other end.

'OK, I'm getting bored of it. You want to get me, do it already. You want to tell the police something I ain't done so you can feel better about what you have, I have one word for you. Four letters: CCTV. Good luck mate!'

Bam.

Hung up, dusted this off his experience board.

He turned to Karl, who stood at the door. It started raining outside. Abu shrugged again.

'Eighteen tomorrow blud. You're right. Done with that shit.'

Karl held up his flat palm. Abu walked over, high-fived him. It all came together; you just had to apply yourself. Like one of his teachers didn't get tired of saying.

After dinner, they laid out a few blankets and extra cushions
on the floor. The beige carpet was soft and made up for the
mattress that wasn't there, that hadn't been bought yet.
Karl pushed Abu on to the bed and chucked him some new
sheets to lay out.

'Do you think I'd let a half-dead man sleep on the floor?
Besides, I'm used to it.'

And he told him about John's flat and the thin mattress
that had reminded him so much of Abu's place. Only that
there hadn't been anyone to talk, like, proper talk to. Until
Nakale. But that was different too. A learning, a big-brother
situation, a getting-to-know-each-other and being at ease, but
it wasn't the same as knowing each other your whole life.

And Abu talked about Nalini and the slavery trail. How he
wanted to impress her but didn't even know why. How he
never used college to impress anyone, and Karl said: 'Because
you get bored as soon as the "assignment" is involved.'

'Innit. But then it wasn't just for *her*. I wanted to know. It
wasn't an assignment; it's real, you know.'

Morning came. They finally fell asleep, heads on crossed
arms, both on their stomachs, turned toward each other. The
milky sunrise lifted the room into a bright orange before it
settled on that nondescript white that hung low over the city
on too many occasions.

Karl woke first and snuck out of the room. There was no way
they weren't going to celebrate today. For the both of them.

Abu was born this day, eighteen bloody years ago, and
they were tight as ever.

34

**Sometimes
you just have
to lean in.**

She was standing at the entrance to his building, back to
the gate.
'How long have you been here?'
Nalini picked up her bag from the floor, shy all of a sudden.
'Since nine. I thought you lot were up early.'
Abu was confused. 'You're waiting for me?' It was already
after ten. He was coming back from Karl's to let his family
congratulate him on his big day, then he would catch up
with Mr. Transformed, who had said he needed some time
to work out the details of Abu's birthday programme. Nalini
here, now?
'I've been waiting anyway.'
Her expression changed and they were facing each other.
Now it was Abu who felt there was nowhere to look, nothing
to do. Nalini nodded. With purpose. Today they were going
to speak.
'Should we go somewhere? I mean, I need to go up soon,
my mum will be disappointed, it's my birthday and—'
'I know that it's your birthday.'
Abu's thoughts seemed to make a U-turn and for a split
sec there was nothing. Then he pulled her by the hand
back from the small street to Euston Road. They crossed
and walked towards the British Library, then past it where
it was quieter. No one they knew would be here. Not this
early. He was rushing, but with steady steps, not hectic, just
determined. There was a green bit behind a small street and
Abu motioned to the bench. When they sat there was nothing

else to do but look at each other. And away. At each other.
Away. They hadn't said a word since they'd left.

'Do you, I mean, can I ask you out?'

'Out where?'

'I mean, I don't know.' Abu's eyes were pleading. *Help us out here.*

She leaned her head on his shoulder. 'Everybody thought I'm so strong, I knew how to handle it. Brave, you know. That I was doing exactly the right thing.'

'What are you talking about?'

'You. I'm talking about you.' When her head lifted he could see the tears. 'And nothing. You did nothing.'

'What do you mean?' He had put his arm around her shoulder.

'Nothing but breathe.'

He pulled her in and she gave in to his arms. When his hand touched her cheek it moved further, to her ear, to her neck. His face followed until he was close to her face.

'And now I'm back. I can talk a whole lot, you know. Soon you'll wish I'd just shut up and just breathe. Trust me.' He was whispering in her ear.

'Never,' she replied. Louder than him. 'But don't just talk. Not all the time, anyway.'

He leaned in, his head tilting so he could smell her neck. The skin there. He had to put his mouth on it. His tongue moved upwards, found her lips. She kissed him. Back. Nalini. His head was spinning.

35

**Full circle is sometimes
like derailed. You have to
start from scratch.**

He started calling. Karl's father. At the most annoying times.
Uncle T had given him Karl's number when he never made
that promised call. Whatever happened in that one hour
after Adebanjo finally reappeared, surely it couldn't be so
bad that it kept father and son apart? Uncle T didn't think
so. Couldn't imagine it. And now Adebanjo flung himself
all the way into project reuniting with and getting to know
Karl. After the event. After when he should have been there.
At the airport for starters. Then in his own house in Port
Harcourt. Around. For Karl. Instead of pretending he had
disappeared. It was difficult to be excited when Karl knew
the only reason he had been MIA was to avoid him. It made
it harder even to have any faith into this being more than a
random thing. Adebanjo was just feeling guilty for having
wasted everyone's time, as far as Karl was concerned.

Karl booked a table at the pizza place in the Brunswick
centre for Abu's birthday. A whole table just for them, Nalini
and Afsana, the families. Reserved and everything.

'Did it in case,' Karl said. There was no 'in case' really; it
just made it all proper dining.

'Table for ten? Abu, right? Please come with me. It's right
there. And a happy birthday to you.'

Abu was pleased, all smiles. Then to triumph the whole
thing the waiter added: 'Sir.'

Eighteen promised to be big. Bigger than anything before.
As for the party: they could always plan a proper one another
time. Or go to the movies or stuff.

Godfrey stopped by and Rebecca and Abu's parents, twins in tow. Just for a minute, to share a soft drink and give some presents. Let the youngsters do their thing. They could always celebrate another time, now that Abu was back. Karl was back.

Then Karl's father called. Annoyed the hell out of him, which got his mother alert now, wondering what put Karl on edge like that when he was all smiles and giddiness just a second before. So far Karl avoided telling her the details. The counsellor had said, 'A step at a time'.

Karl left the restaurant and stood in the plaza surrounded by shops, flats above, hanging over the whole thing, fanning out so that the lowest were the most in, the highest further back, so everyone got some light. All of it was supposed to be some good inner city space, and just a few years earlier, had been nothing at all. You know how it is: nothing but some ugly architecture, almost abandoned, but now all poshed up. There was even a water feature that usually had no water, but when it did, and if the sun was also out … you can imagine. London can be like that sometimes: convincing. Telling you that nothing at all was wrong with this place, that in fact it was proper beautiful.

Karl sat on the concrete edge of the waterless water feature. He could still see the others inside. Abu shining from his eyes, the same way his clothes stood out. Every other minute glancing at Nalini who was all chatterbox again, head thrown back when laughing, her hair falling down her back. Abu was watching her every move from the corner of his eye.

'I don't think you have to do anything man. Just keep talking to her.' He had told his best friend the night before. 'I'm not sure why, but you seem to be doing this thing right, very right. Just be yourself. For some very strange reason she's crazy 'bout you.'

Abu had thrown the pillow. 'It's called being irresistible.'

Karl had no idea. How right he was doing things with Nalini. They hadn't had time to speak.

Nalini brought a present. A belt that was not from some brand but that would still stick out and more importantly, match Abu's shirts. She was making a point about the riots, about the things that were taken. How people had loaded up on branded clothes. They talked about it the other day, Nalini all intense. 'I don't care about the big shops, I get that, but Abu don't tell me that it was just about some big chain. It wasn't! Some neighbourhoods were proper mashed up. It could be one of us, you know, I mean some of the shop owners. Your older brother or something, trying to make it.'

But Abu had done some thinking too. 'Yes, true. But still.'

'Still what?'

'Things are wrong, Nalini. People were just showing how wrong. You don't always get to go to the boss, innit. You don't even get close to where the real shit is sometimes. You just get angry when you are angry, wherever that is. But that doesn't mean Tottenham wasn't real. Some people were really about that Duggan guy.'

Nalini had been quiet. 'OK, fine. I see your point. When you put it all together.'

'It's too many things to say it was about this and that because it was too many people, you get me.'

You didn't need no bloody riot to have some nice things. That was Nalini's point. Abu agreed. But maybe you needed a riot to show how fucked up the country was. How pissed off people were about it. Even if there were some who didn't even care about that, but just cared about themselves. You could find those anywhere. Abu felt all mushy when he put the belt back into its box.

There was another side to all of it. The small picture that was so big it hurt sometimes. It was so huge you couldn't see all of it; the showing up, the being there for your inner circle. The making that happen.

loyalty /ˈlɔɪəlti/
noun
      1. The quality of being loyal.
      2. Massive feeling, all intense and proper real.
      3. Holding up your people. The right ones.
      4. Being there for them as in reliance (they can rely on you).
      5. Reliance as in bond, as in trust, as in depending on you
      6. As in: I got you.

Adebanjo was going on about how he wished to have a conversation, a really proper one. Revisit what they hadn't been able to finish when Karl rushed off. Karl mmm'ed his way through. Not today. No way. And he thought of how he had not rushed off at all but had been there much longer than was good for his relations here. Too bad life couldn't wait for everybody to sort out their stuff. How it was always when it was too late that the penny dropped.

Luckily he, Abu and Godfrey, his mother and all had other chances. He wasn't so sure about the man on the other end of the line. One thing was for sure: he loved the sound of his own voice. Loved the way the authority dropped in it, heavy, like it just laid down the earth itself. He seemed like a guy who told, not asked.

Abu, still at the table inside, was raising his shoulder, and giving him his *what the eff?* look. Karl shrugged and promised the stranger on the phone he would call back the following day. It had been seventeen years without a father. A few weeks of his existence and Karl decided this chapter was better closed.

He slid the mobile in his pocket and walked back into the restaurant, sat beside Abu, handed him the smart shirt and sparkly bracelet he'd bought, with a little help from Godfrey and Rebecca. The thin leather band held pretend-diamond sparkle blobs, small and round. The adults, the older ones, left, taking the twins with them. They all trailed down the stairs, past the old-fashioned cinema, down to the street that led back to their flats.

The youngsters stayed, chatting, totally old skool; although the gadgets were displayed all over the table, the grinning and sharing was like, face-to-face, until it was time to call it a night.

Abu received a few more texts. More threatening, more specific in what and how they would, could, and wanted to do him in. He kept them all. CCTV, GPS, all that sort of stuff could tell the location. It could tell the same story the texts were trying to deflect. There was no need to overreact. You just had to wait and see. Karl was still trying to get him to call the police.

'If you know they can't get you 'cause you got stuff on them, why not get it over and done with?'

Why not? Because Abu turned eighteen a few days ago. 'New and improved version, innit. Not taking threats any

more. That was before. Now there is standing my ground.
Wear them out. Let them come.'

Karl figured he always stood his ground and said so. That
he was usually talking too much while doing so.

'That's what I'm saying. Gonna be different now. Anyone
coming to threaten me, I'll give a piece of my mind. I'll do
it when the time is right, innit. No rush.'

Godfrey was trying hard to get back into Karl's good books.

'I was wrong. I know it. It wasn't just outing you, I swear.
It was about your safety.'

Karl was like *I swear? You got to be kidding me* and not
convinced. That sort of intel, personal one, was never
disclosed, unless there was explicit permission. Godfrey
didn't have that and couldn't get out of it now, after the
event. He could have asked; he could have just discussed it
with Karl. There had been no need for a clandestine affair.
Godfrey countered, 'But you wanted to keep the whole thing a
secret,' and lost Karl again. Nothing but side-eye in response.

He started pressing Karl to deal with it already. 'Call your
father. First you blackmail me to let you go and now you
can't have one conversation with him?'

Karl following Abu's lead. No need to show any fear if you
got none.

'Not calling, simple as that. As soon as I have something to
say, I will. Until then, I'll handle my own things. And while
we're at it, don't ever chat my business to anyone again
without asking.'

He and Abu had fallen back into twin mode like sales after
Christmas: straight away.

'Do you have some time, mum?'

'What is it, Karl?'

'I want to talk to you about Nigeria. Why I went, I mean,
why I really went.'

'Good,' she replied. And meant it. 'Good that you are finally
ready.'

Karl came in from a morning jog. He now called it that.
Running was for avoiders. 'To let you know which one is
which.'

Abu laughed. Who cared, like really? As long as you arrived
somewhere you wanted to be, right? And if not? Well at least
you got out of the house, fresh air and everything.

'Just going to jump into the shower.'
The water washed away the sweat that pooled on his back,
at the neck and much lower, where his shorts started. He
turned the tap to cool and held his face up. The pressure
was strong enough to make his face tingle. He could feel
the drops pushing out of the showerhead, collecting on his
skin, sliding down the rest of his body.

What to say today? About fathers and mothers. About how
life was. All the things they left out and hoped either of them
would manage, without explanations.

His father had called four times. Each time Karl came up
with excuses. The last one was no credit. Then he tried a
trick he heard someone tell another person on the bus once.
They both worked for a telephone marketing company but
the second person had just started. The one who was there
longer gave her friend some sound advice: 'When they get
too rude, and I tell you they will, just put some paper over the
receiver and crumple it. Ask in your best voice, "Connection?
Hello? Are you still there?" Then you hang up. No need to
take shit you're not getting paid for.'

Abu and Karl had laughed about it, dying to try it out the
next opportunity they got but they never did. It worked with
his father, he hoped. He didn't feel like having to explain
what the strange noises were. And why he now even hung up,
after seeking him out and making all that effort. Everyone
needed time to process. Now Karl did. Something like that,
if his father cared at all for such on-point conversation.

He soaped his body from top to bottom, carefully leaning
against the tiled wall, raising one foot to spread the toes
and wash. Couldn't hurt to give it an extra scrub. Abu and
his new wisdom gave his own advice right back. 'Just be
Karl.' The soap ran through the outlet in the enamel and he
turned the water off.

His mother waited in the living room. It was a little more
cramped since they had re-arranged the flat. Godfrey was
still due to come through with his promise of painting their
'what do you call it – crib?' He needed a language upgrade,
urgently. It was too much trying to fit in.

'Some juice?'
'Thanks.'
He sat on the armchair facing the coffee table and the
three-seater that was so small that Karl kept wondering if

it had meant three-in-one, rather than for three people: you in the middle, bag on the left, phone on the right, full. They were opposite each other, Rebecca and Karl.

'I guess there are many things we haven't talked about.'

'I know you're trying your best. I ain't complaining.'

'No, let me finish. Nobody knew how badly or how quickly I would become ill. I didn't, my parents didn't. You tumble into it and react in the heat of the moment. You don't always make the right decisions.'

She was looking for the words, the ones she had tried to keep from Karl for all his life.

'I wanted to protect you.'

Wasn't it always about that? Protecting someone you loved because if you didn't you might see the pain in their eyes and that could break your heart, like proper.

'And now?'

'What do you mean, Karl?'

'How come you're telling me now?'

'You found out more than you should by yourself.'

'More than ... I think—'

'Karl, I just mean, I should have been the one to tell you. I let you go all the way to Nigeria.'

'You didn't know.'

She was quiet. The evenness in the air smelled fishy. Like when you've been made a fool.

'You knew all along.'

'What are you talking about, Karl?'

'Nigeria. You just said you let me go. So, you knew. Godfrey probably told you and you both thought I needed this so I can gain independence and find my own way.'

'Not at all.'

'Then what?'

Karl stretched his feet, flexing his toes. The tan lines were still visible, showing clearly where the flip-flops had been, where the sun had warmed his feet.

'I meant in the scheme of things, Karl. It had to come to you going off because I didn't tell you the things you needed to know.'

She got his attention.

'The things you deserve to know.'

'He didn't even know I existed!'

It burst out. *Just be yourself, whatever that means, whatever that would be.* Rebecca looked at him, carefully examining his face.

'He keeps calling. First he wanted nothing to do with me, when I wasn't the daughter he was now expecting. Now he can't stop wanting to "get to know me and learn more". Whatever. 'Cause his wife has a little more sense and made him come back to see me. But I'm not interested any more. I just want my peace back.'

'Well, you went to seek him out. It also means something to him.'

'Why didn't you tell him you were pregnant? Why didn't you tell me anything about him?'

The questions. The answers. The sense that sometimes eludes them. The forgiveness one must ask for.

'I thought it would be easier. You were unplanned. A lucky accident. The best part of my short relationship with him.'

'What's so awful about him that you couldn't tell him, or me?'

'Nothing.'

She looked down at the worn carpet, then out the window. There wasn't anything to see there. Nothing to latch on to.

'It's complicated.'

'You're not a Facebook status!'

He vowed that he would be calm, would not let feelings run away. Just find out how it had all happened. He had been surprised that she hadn't been more outraged at his disappearance. The therapy sessions, yes, but they seemed to 'break through' in no time.

'Why don't you tell me about meeting him?'

Then what?

'I already did. I arrived, he saw me after some disappearing act, then didn't like the look of my gender and told me to eff off in other, more carefully chosen words. That's it.'

He deserved to make his own decisions, to ask the questions he now knew his mother had been lying about. There wasn't anything his father had done to match that. He didn't matter.

'And now?'

'Mum, I don't think it's fair. Why?'

'Karl, sometimes you are young and stupid and—'

'For starters, you never told me about Nigeria. That you went there.'

'It was one short visit.'

'It wasn't short! You volunteered for *months*. And the only way I know is because Uncle T told me. You never even thought it was important for me to know.'

Her eyes were tired, weary. Not as pain-filled as usual, when she was losing her energy. It felt like Karl was the parent, the one asking questions while the teenager avoided eye contact, answers, anything that made real sense. Her foot scraped along the carpet, tracing its tiny patterns with her toes. Her skin glowed.

Karl was impatient.

'How come we don't speak about this?'

They both knew it. Stress triggered relapses. Karl had taken that on. Like proper. As in way over the top. She would break, he thought, so he ran longer and faster until the choking stopped and he could breathe again. But he no longer ran, he no longer left things behind to shut them out. He stayed now. In therapy they talked about the network. The 'who called the shots, made decisions', Karl-wise. They had talked about that Godfrey had taken liberties. Rebecca was still the mum, whether she had a depression from time to time or not. That depression didn't mean she couldn't be there for Karl. It had never meant that.

'Nobody ever asks what I want. Not properly. Not even you.'

'I ask all the time.'

'Mum.' Karl was calm again. 'Really?'

It was quiet. You couldn't say everything in one go but it still had to come out. Sometime.

'There was nowhere to breathe here for me. Yes, all of you are very understanding. Abu is like the best. Ever. Like ever ever. His family ... I would die for them. They have done so much. The lot. Godfrey ... But where am I? Where am I in all of this, really?'

'What do you mean?'

'There is no wholeness. Nowhere I really am. With all of you I am the problem that needs to be taken care of, that needs to be protected. On the streets, I am the freak. I was not here. I didn't exist.'

His mother's mouth was open but her eyes were looking into nothingness. Not at him, not at anything in particular. She was ready to avoid this, deflect from the words that made a lot of sense.

'You don't really have the space for all that's going on in
my life. Or maybe I think you don't. I run so I don't have
to scream, so I don't say things that will upset anyone. So
I don't say: I want to know. What it's like to be me. What
it's like to be a young man. Without the baggage, without
a helping hand that makes sure I land soft because surely
someone will trip me up. I want to know those things. What
it's like to not take care of you—'
'I never asked you to—'
'I know that. But I do it anyway. How do you think it is to
see your mother in pain? Like all the time. How do you go
and say *Hey, I think it's time we move on up and bring in a
bit more normality into the mix. Not just support groups and
support people and support whatever. Just a young person who
is going to be a man. Let us find out who that is.* Not, *he was
always so sensitive but he's making it anyway.*'
'We can do that—'
'We will do that! I need it. I don't need you or anyone to
protect me from things by keeping them away. All I need is
to know that you are with me. That I can trust you. That I
can talk to you and get an answer when I need to.'
Her eyes were starting to focus again. Karl was catching
up with his breath. It had been calm, or at least calm-ish, his
outburst. Still, that was a whole lot of getting it out.
'You were always smart.'
'But?'
'No but. It's just that you're even clearer now.'
'I stayed in Nigeria, I stayed longer because I was being
myself. I wasn't a problem. I could see who I was, from the
outside. Because other people saw me for who I was, not
how hard I had fought to get there.'
The how to say everything and find the right words, the
right sentiments.
'I think I understand.' She stopped. Her chest was moving
up and down quick now. 'You don't deserve to see how I
struggle sometimes. Just to be free of the heaviness that
consumes me in those times. Not often, but when it gets
that bad I'm knocked out. I didn't know how to keep that
from you.'
The flat was breathing now too, they could hear the fridge
humming in the kitchen.
'Don't keep it.'

She looked up.

'Don't pretend it's not there. It doesn't make it any better. Or easier. Not for me.'

Karl's pocket lit up. The sound made them both jumpy. 'Just my phone.' He looked at Rebecca. Her body had relaxed, her shoulders were easing down. Karl's eyes brightened.

'A friend of yours?'

'What?'

Janoma texted that Nakale's aunt had agreed. She might even be OK with Janoma spending some time with her 'study mate'.

'Perfect.' Karl looked up. 'What did you say?'

'Oh, you just seem so happy. Is this a friend of yours?'

He looked at his mother.

'You seem to have grown estranged,' the therapist had said. There had been major sobs at that point, as you can imagine. 'Maybe you just have to restart from zero?'

Those lovely insightful declarations. Where were they now? At a hundred? A hundred and five? At sixteen? That was the problem with categories: how to fill them.

'My girlfriend, mum. I met somebody in Nigeria. She is coming to London for a visit. With Uncle T. She studies textiles and fashion so she can help him out.'

It was out, in one go.

'OK, wow, that's a lot.'

His mother's bafflement matched his excitement. Both were well beyond hundred and twenty.

'Where would she stay?'

'In my room? She has an aunt here so she'll probably be there most of the time. But if she lets her, can she stay here?'

The phone buzzed again. *call me asap. Developments* ... Abu.

'Yes?' He looked at his mother. He needed to make phone calls.

'This is all a bit quick. How old is she?'

'Nineteen.'

'We'll talk about it more but in principle it is OK. I want to speak to her parents though, and her aunt when she's here.'

The kiss landed on her face as the arms wrapped around her neck.

'You're the best.'

Her smile was weak, like in, totally caught off-guard. Karl's fingers were typing replies already. He was walking to the hallway.

'Karl, I didn't know what to do. Your father, he just changed so quickly. Tunde had warned me.' It wasn't a happy soul-bearing; it was laboured. Every word had to be forced out. 'I had much more in common with him. Tunde. We ended up spending much more time together.'

Karl nearly fell over as he changed direction. He had almost made it out of the room but life didn't always wait until you were safe on the other side.

'Not like that.'

There was cement in the air. It wanted to crush you. But Karl pushed back.

'Tunde wanted but I said no. Chose your father but he seemed to forget about me the minute I left. I didn't think he would stick around for you. I didn't want him to disappear on you. He was supposed to come for me in London. I called and called, never got a hold of him. He let Tunde make excuses. Finally he confessed that your father had moved on. Straight away. Met his wife. Her family were well off; they had opportunities for him. I don't know if it was that, or if it was just one of those things. We were young.' She laughed. 'Everyone wants opportunities. I had none. I was a working class girl. Ran away from my family to some country in West Africa they had never heard of. And I had taken it all so serious.'

The sun was hitting through the closed window, warming the room up.

'I just fell pregnant. Totally unexpected. I was embarrassed, Karl. That your father wasn't reliable. That I had fallen for it. That Tunde had been right.'

she hadn't seen in years or ever met in the first place. O
her second day, she could finally get away for a couple o
hours but Rebecca demanded to be kept in the loop. 'I wil
give you time but I want to meet her first. Not last again.'

They had spent the rest of the short afternoon in Karl's
room before she had to rush back.

'I liked your texts yesterday evening.'

'Which part?' Karl could smell her body. It made his nose
flare the slightest, his eyes unfocused. He put his head on
her shoulder.

'The part where you said I was even more beautiful than
you remembered. That you missed me. That you couldn't
believe how lucky you are, we are, and I'm here.'

She took his head into her hands, looked at him.

'Pretty much all of it then.' His lips were curling upward.
She laughed and pulled his face closer. Took his upper lip
between hers. Played with it travelling from one corner of
his mouth to the other and back on the bottom lip. When
she extended her tongue, Karl felt the dizziness.

'Mum is out.'

At his, she sat on top of him. He reached inside her jeans,
underneath the underwear and entered. She pulled her top
over her head before she leaned in, moving into his hand.
His free arm wrapping around her naked torso, he took her
nipple inside his mouth, rolled it between his lips. Sucked.
Released. Bit. Released. Looked at her as she moved on top
of him.

'There is more here.'

he how to do it. The more of it. The futures that have to
e made otherwise they disappear before they have been.
ow do you do it? How?

36

We could all come running and speak about the world.

Karl was so proud he was no longer touching the ground
with his feet. Abu was busy walking in a funny way, to get
glimpses of Nalini and to show Janoma that they were like,
totally in control. They owned the streets, practically. He knew
Janoma knew better but he couldn't help himself. A visitor
from Nigeria? He would polish the pavement if he could. You
had to show proper hospitality; this wasn't a *happens all the
time* thing. Karl hadn't said very much since they had all
met up with Nalini, Afsana and a couple of the other young
women who had been around that time when Abu went all
deep on the economy and the riots. Then Mark had texted
– he must have heard somewhere – and Kyle and him had
joined too. They had taken her to Giraffe at the Brunswick.
World Kitchen. It seemed appropriate. Had taken over the
restaurant and driven the waiter up the wall with their changes
to the menu. Abu had organised it this time because Karl
had become useless. Couldn't talk properly, couldn't think
properly and certainly couldn't organise shit. All he could
do was smile at her, hold her hand, and nod along when she
spoke. Abu knew they were speaking when it was just the
two of them but with others Karl seemed to find it hard to
keep his cool. Janoma.

She had brought Abu music. 'I'm so excited to meet you.
The Abu!' She had hugged him. Abu thought Karl must have
had a hand in that but Karl said it was all her. She had done
the same when he was in Nigeria. 'Education,' she called it.
'You know we have the tightest beats. You don't even have
any idea yet.'

They left the restaurant and turned into Judd Street. Nalini and Afsana had taken Janoma in the middle and were telling her about the neighbourhood.

'It's famous really for the Bloomsbury Group. A bunch of writers and whatnot. But then there is this other history. People who were involved in enslaving others lived here.'

Behind them, Kyle was telling Abu a joke. Karl was staring ahead. Mel and Tammy, the other two young women, were trailing behind with Mark.

Tell her about Mary Prince, Nalini.' Afsana turned around to smile at Kyle.

'She wrote a book about her experiences of being a slave. *The History of Mary Prince*. A West Indian slave. They had brought her from Antigua. It was the first book about a black woman in the UK. Can you imagine? All she went through and then she wrote a book when nobody wrote books!'

The fire in Nalini was obvious. Janoma nodded. They had stopped at the traffic light across from the new fancy hotel.

'Powerful!'

'You also write? Karl told me you're part of a magazine or newspaper.' Nalini pointed down the road. 'You see there is the train station we told you about earlier. The Eurostar goes to Paris and stuff.'

Janoma followed her hand with her eyes. Karl and the others had caught up and they were all crowded around the traffic light post.

'I just go along to some of their bigger meetings. My friends write for the paper. I'm useless at writing. All I can do has to do with the sewing machine and the drawing board.'

Afsana touched Janoma's jacket. It was navy, tight fitting with strips of African cloth sewn on. They fanned out from one point on the lower back. 'Did you make this?'

'Yes.'

'Wow.'

Janoma smiled. 'You just need a bit of patience.'

'And inspiration!'

'I'm sure you could come up with something. Once you sit down.'

The light turned and they crossed. Janoma turned back to Nalini. 'And I guess no one is talking about this Mary Prince?'

'Not so many, no.'

'I know this from home. Everyone likes to talk about t[h] or, in fact, make money from it. No one wants to talk [a] the devastation.'

'Here too. Not oil, of course. But some of these stree[t] proper poor. People, I mean. But if you look at it fro[m] outside, how does it look to you?'

'Yeah, I understand. Especially here.' They had st[opped] again. The construction here took over half the stre[et] the whole facade of the train station. They looked [at] the hotel that had recently reopened and towered ab[ove] whole block. 'Very … what is the word …'

'Posh.' Afsana put her arm through Janoma's. 'Po[sh] let me just say it: a bit over the top.'

Karl held on to Abu's sleeve and the two whispered. [They] looked at them. Karl jerked his head back.

'Hey, I want to show Janoma something before sh[e'll] be back at her aunt's. We'll catch up with you later.'

Abu led the group away after Janoma promised [to be] with Nalini and Afsana again. Like very soon. As [soon as] possible. Karl pulled Janoma into the smaller street [and] He pointed at a bench ahead and they sat.

'Me and you.' Janoma was grinning.

'Finally.' He ran his hands over her back and played [with her] neck. His lips followed and his tongue played with[...]

'I couldn't even speak with everyone around.'

'I noticed! I come all the way and all you do is wal[k] like your legs are made of wood. Without a joint for [...]

He laughed. She put her arms around him and p[ulled him] closer.

'I like your people.'

'Thank you.'

'Thank *you*! This was a real welcome party. And [I never] had one.'

He had been at the airport three days before. W[ith flowers] and everything. Her auntie was picking her up but [he could] not go. Auntie came with a cousin and her two [...] Karl managed to hide the flowers in a plastic ba[g...] too early to lose Auntie's support by way of susp[icion...] hitched a ride. Unfortunately, he had to sit in th[e front,] secret hand-holding. They had dropped him [off] back in town and all he had managed was a hu[g. Days] after, Janoma had to do the family rounds. Mee[ting]

37

**The next level
needs not new players`
but a change of scenery.**

She didn't reply but her breathing got louder and more rhythmic. She flung her arm around his neck when she came and held on to it.

'What are you talking about?' She was still catching her breath.

Karl held her with both arms.

'What are we going to do?'

His hand was playing with her breasts. He kissed the space between them.

'The time is already running out.'

There had been possibilities before she arrived. Now the days were speeding by. This would be over before he knew it.

She rolled on to her back next to him. Her knees up, she pulled her feet close to her bum. 'I think this is when you have the cigarette in the movies.'

He pinched her.

'What?'

'I'm trying to talk to you!'

'And I'm trying to have a moment.' Her head was turned up and he could see her smiling. He stretched out beside her, blowing through pursed lips.

'I hate cigarette butts inside the house.'

She nodded.

'Karl.'

'What?'

'Come to Lagos.'

'To do what?'

She was leaning on her arm now. Her face. It was as exciting as the first time he had seen her in front of her auntie's fabric shop. Her eyes made his insides ache. The way she smiled with them. At him. She started playing with his shirt. Opened it and pulled his T-shirt up a bit. Kissed the skin underneath.

'Uncle T has offered me a job once I finish my diploma. Very small, but I could add some of my designs, he says. If it works, then more. If not I can still work for him on his imported lines.'

He turned to her. 'That's fucking brilliant! Why didn't you say anything?' He grabbed her and pulled her on top of him, rolling from side to side.

'Because. I want you to come too.'

38

**Everything runs according
to how you have set the bar.**

Abu slid down the street, light-footed, Karl bouncing behind, grin his on face, shoulders relaxed, dreamy eyes focused. The pair of them like a cut-out from an urban youth-wear magazine. The shades, the textures, the different pieces that came together. All proper. You couldn't complain. This was style. Except Karl noticed Abu's trainer now, something black smeared over one side. Funny he hadn't seen it all these days. How not, like whoa, what was going on? Right? Janoma, all was Janoma now. His attention all over the place.
    'I like her. She's perfect for you.'
    'Told you.'
    Karl was grinning.
    'Your mum's cool with her?'
    'Loves her. You said I can please people's parents? You should see Janoma. We should open a centre together, give workshops on how to wrap parents around your finger.'
    The sun was finally setting. Abu had met Karl back at King's Cross station after Karl dropped Janoma off in East London. It got quiet as soon as they entered Argyle Street.
    'Just her aunt. We only have a week and she doesn't want her to stay at mine.'
    Abu waved it off. 'Take what you get for now. Then make your plans.'
    'Yeah.'
    Abu looked at him. 'You have some plan don't you? You didn't go through all of this to never see her again?'
    Karl pointed at the black smear on Abu's trainer but Abu shrugged like he couldn't care. Did proper mean he had to throw away a pair? Of course not. It just meant that some

shit had burned into the side of one of his trainers. He took
it as a trophy, a reminder. Big mouth didn't mean wrong
crowd. Not for him. He wasn't that stupid.

'There might be a plan.'

Abu was all over the place still, walking the same, taking
over the pavement walk as earlier. Happy. His main man and
the whole crew. It didn't get much better than this, did it?

'I'm listening.'

'It would involve me leaving again.' Karl avoided Abu's
eyes. 'Like longer.'

Abu's head was moving but he didn't turn to Karl.

'Yeah.'

'Yeah what?'

'I figured this much.'

They stopped in front of the school gate.

'I mean it's like new and I don't even know how and
everything, let alone what my mum will say or Godfrey. Of
course Godfrey doesn't have much to say and actually my
mum ... I'm eighteen innit, but also how would it work and
stuff, so really at this point—'

Abu slapped him. Not in the face but on the hand. Took his
other hand and placed it on Karl's mouth. Started laughing.

'Do you ever shut up?'

Karl surprised, shocked for a sec, then realised his mouth
was running and running and he was standing still. Long
enough to figure shit out.

'I'll come visit.' And Abu started walking again. 'A lot.'

Karl, giddy again, followed him, imitating Abu's bowlegged
strut.

The wannabes appeared out of nowhere – trademark anyone?
– right at the bottom of the street. This wasn't their usual
route but they cowboy-style positioned themselves in the
middle of the pavement, nodding with cocky smiles. Abu
started laughing.

'What's this supposed to be? A threat?'

Karl, all caught up with what plans could be made, not
paying attention until one kicked his shin.

'You want to go down, like you used to? *Carla.*'

They had to make their minds up. Was this a question? Was
this for effect? Karl all busy with *what the heck next*. Didn't
even notice the way they tried to tower over them. A whole
group of them.

'But we're not here for you, sweetheart. We're here for your friend. Your boyfriend right, you can tell us, we don't mind. We're all for gay rights, you know.'

They were five this time. Karl didn't know the other two. The threesome was familiar. Predictable shit like this was boring, so last season. He had other things on his mind. Abu was still laughing. 'You really need to start getting your facts straight.'

Karl kicked the shoe that was in front of him back, looked at Abu like not today, so not in the mood. Abu laughed more and more, mouth open, head thrown back. Abu was ready for standing his ground, was defo not getting his arse kicked. Not by some wanna be someone grand.

He put his arm around Karl's shoulder, whispered, 'Just follow my lead, I'm making a point here,' pulled him close, planted his lips on Karl's, all gentle, all meaning, held on there, soft lips on soft lips, Karl's face in his hands. He could feel the plumpness pushing back at his. His legs slightly apart as if he was imitating some movie star. Held his lips on Karl's. Just held them there, steady on his feet, relaxed, taking his time. Then he let go, looked into Karl's eyes, way deep. Looked and looked and waited, Karl's face still in his hands. Karl a tad confused, but smiling. Their friendship, it was even more than just tight. It was being yourself. All the fucking way.

Then Abu started talking again, out loud for the shitheads around them but really for Karl: 'I love you.'

Looked and looked and smiled and raised his voice.

'I love you, man.'

He stuck two fingers up in the air, took Karl's hand and walked away. Simple. Hand in hand. Teamwork. He didn't look back when he started speaking again. 'Come after me if you want. It's getting boring now, innit. Seem to be losing your magic; you almost doubled in size. You're five now?'

It didn't matter where. It mattered how. How to be in life. And then it came flowing back, right back to the source. Of course not always exactly the same way.

Karl was laughing too. Abu was smooth, you could say what you wanted.

'If I was you guys, I would take it a bit easy.' He stopped Abu in his strides, pulling at his hand, turned only his head around. 'Almost-dead woman? Not very funny, not at all. If not for this one here' – and he raised Abu's hand, still holding it – 'I'd be blabbering whatever I know, and as you know that's everything there is to know, as far as Abu is concerned.'

'That wasn't us.'

They were coming after them. Two of them more nervous than the others now. Caught off guard, there were things to hide and other things that had got out of hand.

'It was just supposed to be a scare. Those guys, they're out of control. Next generation, you get me. Still have a point to prove. Wasn't us at all. Nothing to do—'

'Why are you telling us? You want some fucking redemption?'

Abu was surprised. Karl had pulled him back, turned around completely. Calm as fuck. No running, no disappearing in his eyes, no nothing, just straight on focus.

'If I was you I would shut up and leave it. It ain't going to be your words against Abu's. It's hers against yours. And you broke her bloody rib. Punctured lung. Serious shit. But your choice of course, your choice ...'

You look at it from this way and it is nothing. You look at it from that way and it is still nothing. You look at it with closed eyes, shut everything out, listening, really seeing, seeing what is there from the inside, and it is everything. You can call it karma, you can call it heavenly intervention – whatever floats your boat. Truth is, you can't see everything; you can't bloody take in a whole junction in one go. Not possible. Half of the time you get it wrong, see only the upcoming traffic. And still you'd act as if you've invented the effing wheel.

What's knowing? Same as seeing. Overrated. Unreliable. If you ask me. That's why they tell the story about the two friends. The friends who had never quarrelled.

You can't know everything by looking at it. Impossible. You cannot know what the other sees.

When the time comes, you can ask.
That's all.
And listen.

Esu, do not undo me,
Do not falsify the words of my mouth,
Do not misguide the movements of my feet,
You who translates yesterday's words,
Into novel utterances,
Do not undo me,
I bear you sacrifice.

– Yoruba prayer

Acknowledgements

There are many people to thank, too many to name here, but I will say thank you for the numerous acts of kindness and help, handing me from one Nigerian journalist to another and then to activists in the Delta, answering awkward questions or otherwise passing on relevant information.

A special mention is due to Ashai Nicholas for their suggestions and critical comments on an earlier draft of the novel, to Shaun Levin for his solid *writerly* friendship, and Pamela Lawino for talking things through and her belief in my work.

I would like to thank Tessa McWatt for her mentorship and feedback during the PhD, when the novel was still called *Fishing for Naija*.

To the whole Cassava Republic team and their collective brilliance. And Bibi Bakare-Yusuf and Jeremy Weate for an incisive editorial eye, helping to elevate this to its new format.

I am grateful for the generous opportunities to develop and write some parts of the novel at various residencies: Hedgebrook, Djerassi and Künstlerdorf Schöppingen.

My deepest gratitude goes to Natalie Popoola for her unwavering support and faith in me. And to Tamu, who slept next door while I finished this other baby.